The Good Italian

STEPHEN BURKE

HODDER

First published in Great Britain in 2014 by Hodder & Stoughton
An Hachette UK company

First published in paperback in 2015

1

Copyright © Stephen Burke 2014

A CIP catalogue record for this title is available from the British Library

ISBN 978 1 848 54917 3

Printed and bound by Clays Ltd, St Ives plc

Hodder & Stoughton policy is to use papers that are natural, renewable and recyclable products
and made from wood grown in sustainable forests. The logging and manufacturing processes are
expected to conform to the environmental regulations of the country of origin.

Hodder & Stoughton Ltd
338 Euston Road
London NW1 3BH

www.hodder.co.uk

For Jane

Lightning struck a dead tree fifty yards to her left. The stark flash illuminated the downpour in front of her and the barren plain beyond. Away to her right, the long line of steel railway tracks was reflected briefly. Using it as a compass, she adjusted her direction in parallel, before everything went dark again. The lightning could strike her, she thought, finding the shortest route to the ground through her body. Perhaps she had earned this.

Aatifa did not stop, keeping up her rapid pace. She listened: only the rain, nothing else, apart from her own footsteps on the stony surface. Her breathing too, loud and laboured; pushing herself on. Were they already after her? The storm would wash away her tracks but it would also mask any sound of pursuit. At least the angry sky would keep the wild animals lodged in their hiding places.

A thunder clap reverberated deep inside her and before it faded, another blinding flash, nearer this time and behind her. In that split second of light, she saw the palms of her hands. The blood was still there, mixed with rain now and running down her fingers. His blood.

She bent down and grabbed a clump of dirt, rubbing it between her hands until they hurt. Then cupping them in front of her, she caught a pool of raindrops and washed the gravel off.

The Italian's life was valuable to them, and they would seek to exact a price from her for it. But she wanted to live. She had reason to.

Chapter 1

ENZO PEELED HIMSELF off his damp bed and took a salt tablet with water to rehydrate. The cool of the floor felt good beneath his feet.

Warm, unheated water trickled out of the shower and he began to scrub himself methodically. If he didn't do it at least twice a day, the earthy aroma of his own body would follow him around like a lingering shadow. Apart from a deep tan from the neck up, Eritrea had not changed his appearance. He was still an average-looking man of forty, slimly built, with a body that had never been fit.

As he dried himself, the majestic voice of Caruso wafted up from the gramophone in the living room. Each time the tenor reached the peak of a crescendo, he sang along with him.

Standing now in front of his wardrobe mirror, he adjusted his tie until it was flawless. Then he pushed open his bedroom's tall wooden shutters, letting in a blast of East African light. As his eyes adjusted to the glare, he took in the view once more. Sprawled out below him were the city's Ottoman-built rooftops and beyond them, stretching all the way to the horizon, was the reason for his presence here. Massawa had the biggest and deepest port in the whole of the Red Sea and he was its harbour master.

The Colonial Office's advertisement for the Massawa post had appeared a month after he had broken up with Silvia, on the brink of their marriage. It had been a mutual decision, no great fuss. Instead of being depressed, he found their separation a release, giving him the energy to seek a brand-new start. 'That witch is making him throw his life away,' his mother had cried.

In the distance he heard the muezzin calling the local Muslims to prayer from the Sheikh Hanafi Mosque. Beyond that he could see the elaborate spire of the Orthodox Christian cathedral peeking above the rooftops. The early Italian colonists had brought a gaggle of missionaries with them but Christianity had beaten them to it, having already taken root here a thousand years before. It had come via Syria and Byzantium, an ancient interaction that had left its traces in the refined features of the Eritreans themselves. On his arrival in 1930, five years ago, that had been the first surprise.

Outside, his Italian neighbours were kissing goodbye on their doorstep. Enzo nodded politely, and he and the husband walked in parallel down their garden paths, before parting ways on the street. The wife, Eva, was one of those pale, skinny, northern women who didn't eat enough and were always complaining about some imaginary ailment or other. There weren't many Italian women out here, so Enzo took pity on her and would occasionally chat to her over the garden fence.

As he walked along the unpaved, dirt streets, the city came to bustling life around him. Massawa's market could never be called elegant but it had its own charms nonetheless. All around him the local stall-holders were busy setting up fruit and vegetable displays under rickety makeshift canopies. There were baskets of freshly picked tangerines and sacks laden with black cumin, cardamom, coriander and Indian long peppers.

Other people were on their own way to work too. Nine out of ten were Eritrean, most in traditional African clothes but a few, the ambitious ones no doubt, wore suits.

The other ten per cent were Italian men. The Italian community here was so small that most of them knew each other well and some kissed cheeks and stopped to chat. No one paid Enzo any attention as he walked on, not even the Italians.

The closest he came to contact with another living being was an unhappy, one-humped camel that almost knocked him over in a narrow alley. Enzo stumbled backward to avoid being trampled and one side of his suit received a heavy coating of dust from a wall. The young herder apologised profusely but Enzo assured him he was fine. He brushed himself down and continued on, twisting his arm up to look at the grazed elbow. There was no avoiding it: he would definitely need new suits.

Enzo rounded one last corner and there in front of him was the Red Sea. He scanned the bay quickly but he was, as usual, disappointed. Apart from some Arab dhow fishing boats, there was only one medium-sized Italian ship at anchor. The noisiest sound in the port came from the pelicans, fighting over scraps of food being thrown overboard by the merchant ship's captain. Enzo saw the man turn towards him and he hurried into the harbour office.

Inside the main room his staff, a mix of Italians and Eritreans, were already at work. As the sun rotated around the building each side would spend several hours with its shutters closed to prevent the interior from turning into an oven and baking its occupants. With the clerks sweating and chain-smoking in semi-darkness, it resembled an opium den more than a functioning government office.

Daniel, Enzo's young Eritrean assistant, spotted his arrival and hurriedly picked up some papers from his desk. Tall and good-looking, he had prominent cheekbones and wore thin-framed spectacles over his bright, blue eyes. Daniel wore his tie all day too, though he had grown up in this heat.

'Good morning, sir.'

'It is not good, Daniel,' Enzo replied. 'We have the biggest and best port on the whole of the Red Sea and yet no one uses us. Do you know why?'

'No, sir, I don't.'

'Neither do I, neither do I,' he sighed.

Enzo opened his office door as Daniel held out a document in front of him. After inspecting it quickly, he signed it and handed it back. Then he closed the door, leaving his assistant to speak into the wood: 'Thank you, sir.'

Enzo had taken the highly unusual step of promoting Daniel as his assistant at the end of his first three weeks in charge, simply because he was the only person who seemed to know what he was talking about. And he could do it in several languages too. It was remarkable for someone who had not attended school. Imagine what he could have become with an Italian education, Enzo thought.

His office was made of wooden window frames on two sides, carved as an afterthought out of the larger open-plan room. The walls did not reach the ceiling, so he could not escape the noises from the main office and only the metal Venetian blinds hanging on the glass stopped him from being permanently on view.

Sitting down at his desk, he adjusted his collection of ink stamps until it was just the way he liked it and then proceeded to open the morning mail. He was in the middle of reading and sorting each letter when his rhythm was broken by the sound of someone shouting. He opened one of the blinds an inch with two fingers and peered out. The merchant ship's captain with his blotched red face, and wild, unkempt beard, was standing in the middle of the main office, holding a crate of something in his hands.

'Can't you see what you are doing to me?' he bellowed. 'Look at this stuff!'

Daniel tried to put his hands out to stop him, but was too late. The captain upended the crate of oozing, noxiously rotten fruit all over the floor.

'Now, it's all yours. You can have the stinking lot, you bunch of whores.'

Enzo closed the blinds quickly as Daniel entered. 'Tell him I'm out, would you?'

'I know you're in here, boy,' the captain shouted over the wall. 'You've stopped me from sailing for a bloody week, you son of a bitch! Who's going to pay for my cargo? You'd better or else you're going to see my fist!'

Enzo felt the blood drain from his face.

Daniel returned bravely to the fray. 'When all your paper-work is in order, then you will be allowed to sail. The regulations . . .'

Enzo peered out again in time to see his assistant being winded by a hard shove in the chest.

'You know what you can do with your regulations, sonny,' the captain spat. 'Where is that little weasel? I'll wring his scrawny neck . . .'

Enzo looked around for somewhere to hide. The only option was under his leather-topped mahogany desk which would have been too undignified. New voices joined the argument outside as the port police arrived. He opened his door, and watched them haul the struggling captain out. Punches flew from both sides and the police gave a few extra in retribution for previous encounters. Relieved, Enzo returned to his desk.

'They've arrested him again,' said Daniel, sticking his head round the door.

'Some people just have to learn, Daniel. Follow the rules: happiness; don't follow the rules: misery.'

Enzo chose a stamp from his array, blew the copper base clean, inked it, and then firmly slapped it down on the page in front of him: APPROVED.

Under Enzo's guidance, the harbour office was now running so efficiently that they could deal with the limited amount of work they had in a very short space of time. By mid-afternoon his staff were usually doodling on the headed stationery or, worse, asleep. The only other distractions available were the two Italian women he employed who were the object of much chatting up by the male staff, even though they were both engaged and neither was likely to come near the awards end of any beauty pageant. One of their husbands-to-be, a Fiat car mechanic, would sometimes arrive unannounced and stand in the doorway, keeping tabs on his betrothed and, more importantly, her male co-workers. No words ever passed between the happy couple, but for the few moments the jealous mechanic was around, the entire male staff suddenly became very busy workers indeed.

Enzo himself did not seem to come under suspicion which made him slightly depressed. He was a single man after all, still almost in his prime. Why should he not be a suspect?

Since today was no busier than usual, there was nothing else for it but to count down the hours by sneaking out a novel from his top drawer. Sea adventures were his favourite, cut-throat pirates and stormy seas, damsels in need of rescue and cannon battles sending sailors down to the murky depths.

It had never been like this in Genoa. There, ships were coming and going all day long from every corner of the globe; most of the time he never even saw the vessels he was entering into his logs. He longed for Massawa to have such busy times.

The sun was fading as he walked home and the market stalls were almost all gone. Swallows darted over his head flying between their clay nests under the rooftops while skinny dogs helped themselves to the leftovers from the day's trading. The salty smell of the sea on the evening breeze brought some relief to the narrow streets and he enjoyed the cool currents on the back of his neck. The city was at its most beautiful at this time, the red sunset bathing the arched coral stonework. It wore its history on its sleeve: Turks, Egyptians and now Italians had all left their mark.

When his first two-year spell had come to an end and he had decided to stay on, the decision had been an easy one. There was nothing to go back to in Italy. His sister Maria had promised to visit him but she never had, though she did write regularly enough. His mother was much too old and frail now to manage the six-day voyage. When she had hugged him goodbye at Genoa's quayside, she had tearfully predicted that she would never see him again.

'Of course you will,' he had assured her. After all, he wasn't going to America.

He lingered outside a gift shop, attracted by a cage containing a large parrot that was completely grey except for a flamboyant set of bright red tail feathers. The Eritrean shopkeeper hurried out of his doorway.

'For you, sir, only fifty lire.'

Enzo smiled and walked on.

'Forty, a special price for you, sir, just forty – that is a real bargain.'

Enzo sat down outside a bar under an archway, at a circular wrought-iron table as far away from the other customers as he could manage. Opposite him a group of Eritrean men, young and old, chatted and played dominoes. Some puffed away on hookah pipes. They spoke a mix of Tigrinya and Arabic, neither of which he understood. Tigrinya meant the speaker was likely to be Christian; an Arabic speaker was more than likely Muslim.

He ordered a glass of dry white wine and drank it quietly on his own. Since the day of his arrival he had never once felt threatened among these people and he just took it for granted now. He guessed that they caused no trouble because they could see that Italy had brought only benefits. He drained his glass, paid his bill and in rudimentary Italian the bar owner wished him a good evening.

At home, he put on Caruso once more and then sat and ate a little bread and cheese. Soon he began to regret his listening choice. 'The Elixir of Love' had put him in a melancholy mood, so he stood and turned it off.

He shaved before retiring so that he would not be in a rush in the morning. Then he lay naked and sweating on his Italian sheets on his Italian bed. He left the shutters open to let in the night-time breeze, for all the good it did. The thermometer was still hitting thirty-five degrees.

His mind drifted to thoughts of home and he wondered how Silvia was back in Genoa and if she had finally married. He pictured her with a baby and a husband, and he gave the husband a face, not his own, but the Fiat mechanic's from Massawa.

Chapter 2

THE PIERCING SOUND of the telephone ringing woke him from an uncomfortable sleep. He was one of only a handful of people in Massawa to have one at home. The wooden telegraph poles planted at regular intervals up the street came to an abrupt halt outside his house. It was supposed to be for work emergencies but there had never been one of those. Only one person ever called him. Rising slowly, he walked down into the hall, naked, feeling in dire need of a shower.

'You've forgotten, haven't you?' said Salvatore at the other end of the crackling line.

'No, I haven't,' Enzo lied. 'I'm coming.'

'Get the morning train. We'll have lunch too.'

'I can't, I have to work.' He looked towards the hall door and was shocked to see that it was pitch dark outside. 'It's still night-time!'

'It's five thirty but I knew you'd be up.'

'I wasn't,' he said, rubbing the sleep from his eyes, 'and why are you?'

'Party at the chief of police's house. Just in. All right, eight o'clock then and don't be late,' ordered Salvatore and hung up without saying goodbye.

Enzo cursed and hauled himself back up the stairs. His head had only just resettled on the pillow when he opened his eyes again and frowned. What in God's name could he get for a present?

By half past six, his long shadow was stretching out in front of him as he walked through the empty market and the silent alleys, past the wedding-cake façade of the Bank of Italy. He was standing on the quay long before the ship's funnels were visible against the rising sun.

Today's visitor was *Queen Eleonora*, the fortnightly supply ship sailing out of Naples. He walked along the dock as she was being unloaded, inspecting each newly arrived wooden crate as it was hoisted by rope up and out of *Eleonora*'s hold. Daniel was already on deck supervising that operation. Behind him, Eritrean dockers piled the smaller sacks directly on to donkey carts, delivering them to warehouse storage, except for perishable goods which were bound for the ice house.

A dozen passengers disembarked down the gangplank, all men. Of these, a couple were soldiers and the rest looked like farmers. Enzo pointed them in the direction of his office. He recorded the names of every Italian who arrived here by sea and that was nearly the entire colony since few made the journey by land, and only a handful ever came by air.

A larger group of nearly thirty Italian men, dressed in suits but with their jackets off, waited on the quay to depart. They chatted and smoked among themselves and looked with disdain at the new arrivals.

Opening a well-worn, leather notebook, Enzo began to write.

Goods IN . . . 10 tonnes of dried pasta . . . 1 tonne of assorted biscuits . . .

20,000 bottles of red wine ... 10,000 of white ... 1 motor car.

He looked up enviously as one of the new model Fiat 1500s was gently winched off the ship. Even the happy departees had stopped their chattering to turn and watch. It was no doubt destined for a judge or one of the factory owners. Certainly not for him on his government salary which was even less now after Mussolini's belt-tightening pay cuts. As the car's wheels touched down softly, the Italian dockers and passengers applauded. The Eritrean workers looked bemused: there was no one inside.

The Italian dockers gathered around it, gawking in the windows at the pristine upholstery and the new state-of-the-art features. Enzo clapped his hands to get them back to work just as a middle-aged Italian with slicked-back hair sauntered up the dock. He was accompanied by a strikingly elegant Eritrean woman. Enzo recognised him as the owner of a local leather factory, one of the few who were making money here from the cheap labour on offer.

'A beauty, isn't she?' said the man, admiring his new automobile.

'Yes,' agreed Enzo, 'it is.'

He held up the release papers for him to sign and as he did so he noticed the plain gold band on the man's wedding finger. There was a wife back home somewhere who either didn't know about this other woman or pretended not to while her husband stockpiled cash into their bank account.

The woman, dressed in a frilly white blouse and grey pencil skirt, smiled at the Eritrean dockers but they all looked away quickly.

Once the pair had driven off, Enzo walked on down the quay and sighed at a much smaller pile of crates.

Goods OUT, he wrote, *2 tonnes of coffee beans . . . 1 tonne of cotton and . . .*

He looked behind them for the next crate but instead found a forlorn-looking old man sitting on a pile of battered luggage. The old man glanced at him and they recognised each other, even though they hadn't crossed paths much since they had landed here on the same ship. He had boarded at Messina in Sicily, dressed then, as now, in peasant farmer attire. The old man looked away again, evidently not in the mood for conversation.

They had spoken briefly, while anchored at the Great Bitter Lake on the Suez Canal, about their reasons for coming to Eritrea.

'To get away from bastard Italian tax collectors,' the old man had said.

Back then, he had been optimistic about the parcel of land he could afford and the plans he had for it, but looking at the motley array of suitcases things had obviously not panned out well.

'Signor Pasini, isn't it? Taking a trip?'

The old man didn't look up. 'I'm going home. I've wasted five years of my life here.' Then he caught Enzo's eye to make sure that his bitterness registered. 'The colony is a failure, you know. This is not Italy.'

Annoyed, Enzo turned and pointed to the national colours flying on a pole above his office.

'That's not what the flag says.'

Pasini dismissed him with a wave of his hand and started to collect his belongings. Enzo made to help but the old man grunted that he didn't need any. It was quite a juggling trick to get all his luggage in the air at the same time but he managed it. Enzo pictured him on a Sicilian hillside somewhere with a lamb over his shoulders and several under each arm. He watched as Pasini struggled up the gangplank, his suitcases noisily bashing against each other. Halfway up the old man stopped and turned.

'You should leave too,' he said, 'while you still can.'

Enzo replied with as much conviction as he could muster. 'We are building something here, Signor Pasini, however slowly.'

Pasini gave him a pitying look and continued up the gangplank.

The bright flower of colonial optimism had withered away long ago and in the last decades the politicians back home had seen Eritrea only as a bottomless money pit. There was prestige, of course, in having colonies like the great European powers. But prestige alone did not employ the thousands of jobless in Italy's south or enrich the political caste. Belgium had found rubber in the Congo and it had made them rich. Britain had mined gold and diamonds in the Cape and that had made them rich too. Eritrea had none of these and consistently had the wrong colour on its balance sheet.

He stood on the quay, watching until *Queen Eleonora* was just a smoking dot on the misty blue horizon. The ship had taken away more passengers than she had brought and a smaller cargo than she had unloaded. He wondered how long it would be before that same vessel would carry him away too.

By mid-afternoon he was on the Massawa to Asmara train, with the large caged parrot perched on his lap. His bright idea was already a cause of regret as nothing would stop the bird from squawking. The other passengers had found it funny for the first few minutes but by the time an hour had passed they appeared ready to throttle him and his feathered companion. Eventually, Enzo resorted to taking off his jacket and wrapping it around the cage, and darkness shut the creature up. He relaxed for a while until the unmistakable odour of fresh bird droppings began to permeate the stale carriage air.

Enzo had boarded the train directly from Massawa's quayside, crossing the causeway that connected the island, on which the old town and port were built, to the mainland; passing the salt pans on the way where the sun dried out pools of sea water. The train had made short time across the rugged, flat countryside outside the city, but slowed down now as it began the long struggle up the mountain to the capital, Asmara. The meandering upward track hewn out of the rocky mountainside was a triumph of Italian engineering, but every trip still pushed the steam engine to its limits. There were sections where Enzo found it best to look in towards the mountain, shielding his eyes from the sheer drop that loomed down the other side. The journey was exhausting, taking several hours, over bridges and through tunnels, picking up pace briefly on straight sections, then dropping to a snail's pace again as the gradient turned skywards. Angling his nose away from the bird, he closed his eyes, hoping to doze.

By the time they were on the final stretch to Asmara, at nearly eight thousand feet, the air had changed completely from the heavy humidity of sea level to a thin and pleasant breeze. Enzo shivered but his jacket was still over the birdcage and he wasn't going to risk retrieving it just yet.

Salvatore had badgered him many times to move up here. How could Enzo stick the thick climate down below? But he had to be where his ships were. He couldn't very well run the port by telephone.

'Why not?' Salvatore had asked.

Stepping out of the train station, there was Asmara in front of him: an Italian mirage in the middle of Africa. Half the buildings were newly built in art deco style. Palm trees lined the wide main street. Popular Italian and American music blared from bars as they overworked their espresso machines inside. Movie posters advertised the latest Italian hits. It even smelled like home, with the heavy aroma of garlic and onions.

'Little Rome' they called it, and with good reason. On the streets, Italians outnumbered the locals and the Eritreans who were out were dressed like Italians. Any traces of the real Africa were well hidden or in European disguise. Enzo could see the attraction; it was as if they hadn't left home at all. Feeling the cool mountain wind through his shirt, he buttoned up his jacket, and wished that he'd brought a light jumper.

On the main street he entered a noisy bar carrying his equally loud present. The place was packed, like a Saturday night in Genoa's old town and Enzo had to elbow his way through the throng. It was dark too with the only light coming from moody red lamps on each of the round, glossy black tables. He spotted Salvatore in a horseshoe-shaped leather booth, looking handsome as always in his full army colonel's uniform. Salvatore jumped up and greeted him warmly, kissing his cheeks three times.

At six feet tall, with his broad chest, jet-black hair, well-trimmed moustache and the roguish twinkle in his big hazel eyes, Salvatore exuded strength and effortless charm. He had been this way ever since they were kids, outgoing enough for both of them, allowing Enzo to relax and be his true introverted self.

He offered up the bird.

'Happy birthday. I didn't know what to bring, so I got you this.'

The bird spread its wings and squawked out louder than the band.

Salvatore was momentarily at a loss. 'This is my present?'

'I can take it back . . .' Enzo suggested. A vision of himself and the bird sharing a return rail carriage flashed before his eyes.

'No! I love it,' said Salvatore, smiling.

He hailed a waiter and the man came over instantly.

'Look after this carefully for me, would you? And don't let Giuseppe cook it.'

'Of course, Colonel,' said the waiter, taking the bird away to the kitchen where it could witness lesser species being plucked and baked.

'You really like it?' asked Enzo.

'I've always wanted one – how did you know?' Salvatore put his long arm around Enzo's shoulder. 'Come on, I'll introduce you.'

At their table were another Italian man and two beautiful Eritreans in their twenties. Both women were dressed in Italian-style, calf-length skirts with short jackets and sported the latest bob cuts with finger waves.

'Everyone, this is my oldest and greatest friend, Enzo.'

'Hi, Enzo,' they all chorused in party mood.

'This is Zula, and Enrico – mind your wallet around that guy – and Sarama.'

Sarama was hanging on to Enrico's arm which meant Zula was with Salvatore. The last time he was in Asmara it had been a different girl and there were quite a few before that.

'Hello,' Enzo said, doing his best to match the mood.

'Enrico works for the railroad,' said Salvatore, as they sat down.

Enrico nodded and shouted over the Eritrean band's passable cover of Benny Goodman's swing, 'How was your trip up?'

'I'm always just grateful when we haven't fallen down the mountain,' replied Enzo.

Enrico looked shocked. 'Oh, that could never happen,' he said. 'It's completely safe, one hundred and ten per cent, believe me.'

Enzo immediately started worrying about the trip back home. Salvatore summoned a waiter again and got instant, respectful attention.

'What will you have?'

'A Moretti, thanks,' said Enzo, since everyone else was drinking beer.

As the waiter scuttled away, Enrico nodded towards the entrance. An important-looking man had just arrived with another Eritrean woman in tow. Their age gap made him at least old enough to be her father and quite likely another generation too. Enrico and Salvatore excused themselves and Enzo watched as his friend greeted the man with his most winning smile.

'Judge Muroni, how are you? You look great, what have you been doing?'

The judge looked pleased to see him too. 'There you are, Colonel, I've been looking for you!'

Not for the first time, Enzo thought that Salvatore was a burst of colour compared to his own shade of grey. He glanced awkwardly at the two girls until Zula mercifully broke the ice.

'Salvatore said you have a very important job, Enzo.'

'Oh, did he? It's not so important. I run the port down in Massawa, that's all.'

He was pleased to see that the girls were impressed.

'That must be very interesting?' said Sarama.

'Sometimes, yes,' he agreed.

The girls waited for him to elaborate but nothing came and he sat there smiling stupidly. He could see that they were rapidly getting bored so he forced himself to make an effort.

'One day, if I keep doing things right, I hope to get to run one of the bigger ports at home, like Naples or Genoa. Massawa might be a good stepping stone.'

The last part was drowned out as Salvatore returned and immediately injected some life into the party.

'Girls, you missed me, I know, I apologise. Allow me to make it up to you. Filippo! We need spumante.'

Everyone smiled, including the waiter.

The bar was another Italian mirage with a dash of Americana. The decor, the music, the atmosphere were all imported but it was the Eritrean women who looked alien here. The truth was the opposite, Enzo knew. They were the ones at home and everything around them was out of place, including the clothes they wore next to their Eritrean skin.

A small table had been placed near the stage especially for the judge and his girlfriend. The judge was talking to her and she was smiling and nodding back, but she didn't look comfortable. Enzo had seen this before back home: wealthy, powerful men seeking the company of younger women. This pretty Eritrean had the same nervous look, hoping that other people were not taking too much notice.

Meanwhile at Salvatore's table the spumante bottles contin-ued to flow one after the other. Enzo nodded and smiled and laughed at the right times, although he hadn't uttered a single word of his own. He drank faster than he should have, knowing that it would loosen his tongue.

Later on, while Enrico and the girls were energetically swing dancing, he and Salvatore sat watching them. The judge's girlfriend was up too, having some youthful fun for a few moments away from the old man.

'Another farmer left today,' said Enzo. 'That's seventy gone already this year.'

'So? Let them go. What do I care about farmers?'

'You'd better start. If they all leave, then there will be no reason for any of us to be here. We need people, money, investment, if the colony is to survive.'

Salvatore slapped the table good-naturedly. 'Serious conversation is banned tonight, it's my birthday.'

Enzo smiled. Salvatore was allergic to serious conversation on any night or day.

He clinked Enzo's glass for the hundredth time that evening. 'Thanks for coming. You are my only friend, you know.'

'You have lots of friends,' Enzo protested.

Salvatore waved his hand dismissively. 'Hah. Not real friends, not like you. You and me go way back, we know each other. They'll never understand,' he said, nodding towards the dance floor. 'Some people, you meet them and they pass through your life, like your ships. The important ones stay, like you and me.'

Enzo nodded. Salvatore was always a sentimental drunk.

'Listen to me, Enzo – are you listening?' Salvatore said, pointing his finger at him.

'I'm listening.'

'You should get yourself one, you should.'

They'd had this conversation many times before, the first on the day of his arrival when he was hardly off the boat.

'No,' said Enzo once again.

'Why not? Everyone's doing it, even the judge over there. They're good-looking, right?'

Enzo looked across at the dance floor. 'They are incredibly beautiful,' he conceded.

'Even a blind man knows that Eritrean women are probably the finest in the world,' said Salvatore. 'And they cook too and clean for pin money – but best of all they don't give you a pain in the ass like Italian women.'

Enzo shook his head and the colonel sighed.

'You remember when we were kids, and we used to steal figs from Capurro's orchard? You were always the good boy who wouldn't come in.'

Enzo nodded. 'I didn't go in because I was scared, but I was always the one to get caught just the same.'

Salvatore grinned. 'That's because you ran like a girl.'

'Thanks for that.'

'Don't mention it. Now listen, as your friend, I am telling you, go into the orchard, it is full of fruit.'

'I don't want complications.'

'Life is complicated,' said Salvatore, throwing up his hands. 'Look, Enzo, Enzo, Enzo – have some fun before you die, please?'

Enzo was saved when the girls returned and pulled the colonel up to dance. They took one look at Enzo and mercifully left him where he was.

He had often wondered what had made them friends as children; not what he saw in Salvatore but what Salvatore had seen in him. He was smarter, it was true, and he would help Salvatore with his school work if he could get him to sit still for long enough, but this wasn't enough to explain a lifelong friendship. Perhaps Salvatore liked the fact that Enzo didn't need to be entertained. Or that he brought stability amid the sea of faces in Salvatore's endlessly revolving world. Maybe he appreciated that Enzo didn't want anything from him, as so many of his other acquaintances seemed to do.

As the evening began to wind down, the young Eritrean singer shouted out, 'Colonel, how about a song?'

The crowd cheered as Salvatore put on a show of reluctance.

'No, I can't, no – don't make me!'

'Oh please, Tore, do,' the girlfriends protested.

He made a big deal of giving in which was followed by more applause. Then he climbed up on stage, and put his arm around the singer's shoulders. Together, they began to croon the old Neapolitan ballad 'Santa Lucia', with the soprano saxophone and the accordion players joining in at the second verse. Salvatore had a strong sweet voice even if he was slightly slurring the words. The men in the audience began to sing along too, emigrants remembering their home. Zula and Sarama smiled but Enzo could see that the resonance of these childhood memories was lost on them. While their attention was fixed on the stage, Enzo studied them, his eyes drawn along the line of their figures despite himself.

It had been five years since he had touched a woman and he had almost forgotten what it felt like. He had never taken a local girlfriend here because it did not seem proper to him. He did not want to be like the old judge, who was having trouble staying awake on the other side of the room.

Salvatore made it all seem perfectly natural. His girlfriends appeared genuinely to enjoy his company and he theirs. Perhaps he was just being a prude like Salvatore said, a stuffed shirt who needed to let go and live a little. But correct behaviour was something he tried to uphold in all parts of his life; it was important.

For several nights, Enzo dreamed of Zula or Sarama. He preferred dreaming of Sarama as she was not his friend's girlfriend but he could not control who came in and out of his dreams. He guessed that Salvatore would only laugh anyway, and call it progress. Once even the judge's girlfriend had appeared. But in his dream she did not looked around, embarrassed, to see who was watching them.

On the fourth night he lay on his back, half awake, watching the electric fan draw windmill shadows on the ceiling. He heard a large owl make a heavy landing on the flat roof above him, rest a moment and take flight again; then some time later the steady clip-clop of a camel, perhaps a stray that had wandered across the causeway into town. He waited, but couldn't let himself go and no dreams came. Though he was sure he was conscious, he found that he had no power to move his limbs. He wondered if death were to come to him now, whether it would be so different.

Gradually, sensation returned to his fingers and toes and he found that he was able to sit up. He took a pencil and paper and wrote a brief note. Then he rolled it up and threw it on the floor. The next five drafts met the same fate. After reading the seventh several times, he decided that it was satisfactory. He put it beside his bed, propped up against the brass figurine night lamp, assuring himself that he would tear this one up in the morning too.

Chapter 3

THE NEXT DAY Enzo was just about to leave when his eye was drawn to something on the floor under the bedroom window. It was one of the rolled-up notes. He turned to look at his bedside table and there sitting on it was the final version. He hesitated, then walked over and slipped the paper into his jacket pocket.

On his way to work, he stepped inside the door of the gift shop. The owner was setting up a display of animal hide shields next to another of oriental fans. He gave Enzo a genuine smile of recognition, and then his face clouded.

'It didn't die, did it? I can replace it without delay if—'

'No, no, it's still alive,' Enzo assured him. 'In fact it was very well received.'

He touched the note in his pocket, the sweat from his hand dampening the paper.

'You have need of another gift?' asked the shopkeeper.

'No,' said Enzo. 'I need a favour actually.'

He pulled out the piece of paper and the man took it from him and scanned it quickly.

'Of course, sir, I will do this for you. It is not a favour, for such a good customer.'

Enzo smiled. He had only ever bought one thing from him

and it would be a year until he would have to choose another present for Salvatore. He resolved that he would definitely buy that one here too.

The gift shop owner ushered him back outside. 'Please, you watch from there.'

Enzo stood in the street as the man placed the note prominently against his front window beside a stuffed warthog.

WANTED: CLEANER/COOK

The day from then on was less eventful. There were no arrivals in the port apart from the comings and goings of the local turbaned fishermen and by lunchtime the office was once again full of workers killing time. Enzo stole a glance at his sea adventure novel in the top drawer but he could not concentrate. He stood up and looked out through the blinds at his staff. Only Daniel was busy; he always somehow managed to find something that needed doing. Finally, to everyone's relief, the working day came to an end.

On his way home, Enzo deliberately walked past the gift shop again. To anyone else his note would have appeared tiny amid the motley collection of goods on offer but to him it seemed to stick out a mile. He might have retrieved it there and then, had the shopkeeper not been inside dealing with an Italian child in search of a toy. The boy's mother noticed him hovering outside and he walked on quickly before the shop owner saw him too.

The following day, as choppy waves lapped gently against the quay outside, Enzo sat with his eyes fixed on the old ship's clock on his office wall. He stamped the papers on his desk absent-mindedly. He had allowed himself to launch a vessel on impulse, and now whatever it was that he had put to sea was about to come home. Opening his door, he called to Daniel, 'Anyone?'

'Not yet, sir,' said Daniel.

'That's good,' Enzo said, frowning.

Daniel walked over to his side.

'I've changed my mind, Daniel,' Enzo said, once no one else could overhear them. 'If anyone comes just send them away. You can tell them I'm not hiring after all.'

Daniel didn't bat an eyelid. 'Of course, sir. I'll look after it.'

Enzo returned to his desk and breathed normally for the first time that day. Half an hour passed during which he forgot about the clock and the note. Then there was a familiar double knock on his door and Daniel entered.

'A few have arrived, sir,' he whispered. 'Should I still tell them to go?'

Daniel had not followed his instructions but Enzo was not annoyed. In fact his pulse rate had suddenly shot up.

'I suppose it would do no harm to see one or two,' he said. 'Give me a minute.'

Daniel nodded and went out.

Enzo quickly smoothed down his hair, pushed his desk nameplate out front and centre, and fixed his tie.

A light, delicate knock came and he wished his heart would stop beating so loudly.

'Come in,' he said, attempting a deep, authoritative voice.

He glanced down at his work, and slowly up again, as if tearing himself away from important matters. Then in walked an Eritrean girl aged no more than twelve. He stood up, flustered.

Daniel came in quickly behind her.

'She doesn't speak Italian, sir. She's here about the employment you advertised?'

'Yes, I see. She's . . . ah . . . younger than I expected.'

The girl spoke a few words in Tigrinya to Daniel.

'She says she works hard.'

'Of course, I have no doubt,' said Enzo.

The girl rummaged in a pocket and handed him a piece of crumpled paper. It was a reference from an Italian nun on convent-headed notepaper.

'Thank you. Very good,' he said, trying to convey that he was impressed. 'Will you tell her that I'll keep her in mind?'

Daniel translated and she turned and looked at Enzo with displeasure. She was obviously smart enough to know a rejection when she heard one. Daniel ushered her out.

The next girl was at most a year older than the first but spoke a little Italian.

'Good morning,' she said politely.

'Good morning,' Enzo said. 'Could you wait here for a moment?'

He found Daniel just outside, pretending that he had not been eavesdropping.

'Are they all like this?' he asked.

'No,' said Daniel, nodding to a long wooden bench near the door.

On it were seated a dozen school-age girls and one old Eritrean lady, dressed entirely in black, who might have been seventy or a hundred, it was hard to tell. A portrait of Mussolini looked down imperiously from above their heads and Enzo found himself trapped for a moment by the Duce's gargoyle-like gaze. He forced himself to look away.

'Right,' he said, without hiding his disappointment from Daniel.

He returned to his office and spent the rest of the afternoon giving each applicant a brief interview out of politeness. It was long and tedious but he felt he deserved this punishment.

When the last one had gone, he sat down and held his head in his hands. This was all Salvatore's fault and his own too for being stupid enough to listen to him. His first instinct, not to complicate his life, had been proven correct again.

A change in the room's atmosphere made him look up. A woman was standing in the doorway, watching him. She was ten years older than Zula and Sarama; mid-thirties maybe and tough, with a face whose lines spoke of hardship. Her gently curled, shoulder-length hair was parted in the middle and hung out thick and wild, as though it were a plant left to grow as it wished. Her clothes were plain and traditional, a beige-coloured dress with a white shawl draped over her shoulders and sandals that had seen better days. The most striking thing about her was her eyes. They seemed almost jet black and he found it hard not to stare into them.

'You want a cleaner who cooks?' she asked briskly, now that she had his attention.

'Yes, I do,' he said, composing himself.

'For how many?'

'Just one,' he said. 'Only me.'

'Wages?' she continued.

'The going rate – I don't know, whatever that is.' Now he was getting irritated. Here they were, already talking details and he hadn't even decided if he wanted to hire her.

'The hours?' she went on, working her way down through an unwritten list.

He stood up and tried to assert some authority. 'Your evenings would be your own. I need the house cleaned, my meals cooked. The job is live-in.'

At this there was an awkward pause.

'You would of course have your own room. It's comfortable, I believe.'

She nodded without comment. They both stood looking at each other across the desk. She hadn't lifted her gaze from him once. He knew that he was supposed to ask the questions now but suddenly he couldn't think of any.

He wished again that he'd torn up the note. That he'd befriended someone else at school instead of Salvatore. That he'd stayed in Genoa and not come here. That he'd married Silvia and lived a normal life. Then he realised from the curious look on this woman's face that all his mixed-up thoughts were visibly playing out across his own.

'One moment,' he said, walking out quickly and making as wide an arc around her as his office allowed.

Outside, he caught Daniel pretending not to eavesdrop again. Enzo leaned against a wall away from the door, where the woman couldn't see him.

'You want me to get rid of her, sir?' whispered Daniel.

'Are there any more?' Enzo asked, although he could see the bench was empty.

'She's the last one. Is everything all right?'

'Yes, thank you. You can go back to work, Daniel, I can handle it from here.'

His assistant looked unsure but he nodded and left him alone.

Enzo shifted slightly along the wall so he could see the woman through the open doorway. She looked completely unnatural standing there in his tidy office, surrounded by files. Or perhaps it was the office that was unnatural and she was the only real thing in it. She was undeniably attractive but there was something about her that made him uncomfortable. Her direct manner for one and that piercing stare full of something he couldn't put his finger on. Those eyes reminded him of the dark surface of a deep well at his grandfather's country house in Liguria. Black because it was so far down in summer that no light penetrated, and even though the water inside was crystal clear, the only thing you could see was the reflection of your own face looking down. He stood there silently, watching her as she picked up his nameplate, glanced at it, and then put it back.

He decided that he would not hire her; it was too great a risk. Tomorrow he would forget all about this business and life would go on as before. Walking back in, he repeated the same exaggerated arc around her and once he was safely berthed back behind his desk, he said, 'Well, if you want the job . . .'

The words were out of his mouth before he could stop them. She seemed as surprised as he was.

'I can start today,' she said.

He was thrown for a moment and noted that she seemed to be able to do that to him at will.

'No, tomorrow is better. At eight? I'll give you the address.'

'If I could get the first week's pay in advance?' she said.

Once again he thought, maybe this was not such a good idea. Could he sack her thirty seconds after he'd hired her?

'I suppose that would be fine,' he said. 'I will have it for you tomorrow. Is that all right?'

He imagined that she was wondering whether he had enough money in his pockets right now. He did, but at least he could take command of this one thing. He was to be her boss after all. Enzo was already the employer of three dozen people, but she would be a new frontier. He had never lived with one of his staff before.

She nodded, then made to leave without a 'goodbye' or a 'see you tomorrow' or even a 'thank you, I won't let you down.'

As she neared the doorway, he asked, 'Your name?'

'Aatifa,' she replied.

A moment later she was gone.

'Did any of them suit, sir?' Daniel asked with a hopeful expression. 'Did you find what you were looking for?'

Enzo thought for a moment and then replied, 'I don't know . . . I hired that last woman.'

'Oh . . . good,' said Daniel, his face clouding as he looked after Aatifa.

There had been a long gap between the 'oh' and the 'good'. Even his assistant was worried now.

That evening Enzo stood in the living room trying to imagine it from a newcomer's perspective. No one ever came to his home apart from Salvatore who arrived once in a blue moon to sleep off another alcohol-soaked night. Sometimes an incapable Italian plumber came to work unsuccessfully on the bad pipes. He was no doubt related to the tailors who came here because they couldn't sell a suit back home; the quality of work was identical.

In his letters to Genoa, he would often remind his sister Maria of her promise to visit him but she hadn't been swayed yet. Lately she had started asking after Salvatore too. They had once been an item in their teenage years though she had swiftly moved on to a more dependable man. Her husband proved to be as solid as a rock. She had loved him and he her, until typhus took him before his time, leaving her to raise two young children on her own. Now she had a gap in her life and was no doubt wondering if her old flame might fill it. Enzo wanted to steer his sister away from this idea, for her own sake, but he could never think of a good way to broach the subject.

He picked up a book from the shelf and an almost invisibly

fine layer of dust stuck to his finger. Rolling up his sleeves, he decided he would have to do the whole house. He did not want Aatifa to think he lived in a pigsty and she would be able to see the level of cleanliness that he expected. After boiling a large pot of water on the gas range, he started mopping the tiled floors. Then he dusted the shelves book by book. He had read every one of them, some twice. Next he tackled the hall, beginning with the marble-topped telephone table and the large cherrywood coat rack. He stood for a moment with his back to the front door, facing into the house. This would be her first view of it tomorrow. He decided that it was missing something and he resolved to fix it in the morning.

When he had finished scrubbing the bathroom from top to bottom, he gave himself a hard look in the mirror. He consoled himself with the fact that he could not really be called ugly. Perhaps a woman who had not set her sights too high might see something in his eyes or in his smile?

In the bedroom, he stood for a long time gazing nervously at his double bed. The mattress had a hollow groove in the middle, a perfect mould of his body, the lonely shape of a bachelor. At the top lay one crumpled pillow. He opened his wardrobe and rooted at the back behind an assortment of blankets. There, he found another pillow exactly like the first except that it looked brand new from lack of use. He placed the pair side by side at the head of the bed, stood back and considered them. Then, losing all courage, he hid the second pillow under the first.

Downstairs, he sat at the kitchen table and opened a new leather-bound notebook, the same as the ones he used for taking notes at the port. With a pencil and a wooden ruler he began meticulously to divide each page into three columns. After several pages, he stopped. He looked down at the empty rows waiting to be filled and wondered if she would be there that long. Maybe she wouldn't even turn up in the morning. He stared into space, conjuring a picture of her in his mind as she had stood in his office. It was not hard to do. Her image was already burned into his memory.

Chapter 4

AT FIRST LIGHT, Enzo hurried to the market, and bought two bunches of purple lavender from one of the traders. Then he returned home and arranged the flowers in a porcelain vase on the hall table, turning each bloom to show its best face to the doorway.

At seven thirty, he stood nervously at an upstairs window, looking up and down the street. There was no one out and about yet, except for the flying insects; a giant black beetle crashed into the window right in front of his face. Below him, Enzo noticed the array of brightly coloured flowers in his neighbours' gardens, unfurled for the morning sun. His own garden was neat and well tended but there were few flowers in bloom. It seemed sad compared to the others.

A movement caught his eye and he saw Aatifa stopping at the top of the street. She was wearing exactly the same clothes as the day before. In her hand was a piece of paper which she was holding up towards the street sign on a gable wall, and he realised she was comparing the arrangement of letters on it with the handwritten address he had given her.

He watched her follow the house numbers painted on the gate pillars until she reached his. She almost spotted him at the upstairs window but he ducked out of sight just in time. As he hurried down the stairs, he heard her opening the small, squeaking iron gate. Before she could reach out and lift up the brass lion knocker, he opened the door.

'Good morning,' said Enzo, trying a pleasant, non-threatening smile.

'Good morning,' she replied, without smiling.

'Please, you're welcome,' he said, beckoning her in.

Had she been an Italian woman he would have offered to take her bag from her, but he was unsure of the correct protocol for this encounter so he said nothing. She looked first at the lavender in the vase and he was pleased that he had gone to the trouble.

Then he began to show her around his modest house.

'The living room. The kitchen – not so big.'

She stared out of the kitchen window. The back yard was an unsightly patch of scrub grass that he had never got around to tackling.

'This way,' said Enzo and she followed him up the stairs.

'The bathroom, the plumbing isn't great,' he said. 'We'll have to share this, is that OK?'

She nodded, apparently surprised that he was asking.

When he opened the unused bedroom that was full of his Genoa life in boxes he was momentarily at a loss. 'This is the storeroom,' he said finally. Then: 'My bedroom.'

She looked round, impressed by the size of it, he could see, and especially by the view over the bay where the early sun was glistening off the turquoise sea. He let her take it in for a few moments before they continued on to the opposite end of the corridor.

'And this is your room.'

It was less than half the size of his, with a narrow single bed, but it had the same view. He was relieved when she put down her bag at last.

'Is it all right for you?' he asked.

She nodded, her eyes drawn out to the sea once more.

Now that the tour was over, he wasn't sure what they should talk about. She followed him back down into the pristine living room.

'You've had a cleaner before,' she said.

'No, never,' he replied, and quickly changed the subject by handing over the money that he had counted out earlier: 'Here is the first week's wages, as you asked.'

She took the notes and put them away in a hidden pocket inside her dress. He waited for her to say thank you, but she didn't seem to think it was called for.

Then he opened the new ledger on the living room table, pressing down the pages neatly. He had already written in separate columns on the first page today's date, the first week in September 1935, and the amount he had just given her. Now he pointed at the third column.

'Sign here, please, a record of payment.'

Taking the pencil from him, she bent over the table. She looked a little embarrassed as he watched her slowly write out her first name only in capital letters. It was better than an X, he supposed. He closed the ledger again and put it away on a shelf.

'What should I do?' she asked.

'Oh,' he said. He hadn't thought that far ahead.

'I'll look around and see?' she suggested.

'That would be good,' he said, relieved, before adding: 'Just, I like things where they are.'

She gave him that look again, obviously still trying to figure him out, then glanced at the kitchen.

'Dinner?'

'Yes, good,' he said. 'You can decide. Anything will do. Surprise me.'

Her face remained unchanged so he counted out some more housekeeping money and put it on the table.

'This should be enough to buy whatever you need. All right then, well, I think that's everything. Have you any questions?' he asked hopefully.

She shook her head.

'Fine,' he said, disappointed. 'Well, I'll go to work then.'

It was odd leaving a complete stranger in his own house as he closed the front door behind him. He knew absolutely nothing about her. She had asked all the questions at the interview, if it could be called that. He hadn't asked about her experience or if she had references, or any of the things he had asked the others. What if she intended to steal everything he owned? What if that's what her half-empty bag was for, to stuff with all his valuables? He thought about what she could carry away easily but he didn't have anything precious. All his worth was in town on deposit in the Bank of Italy. He began to feel guilty for thinking these thoughts.

Then he realised that he had not moved beyond his doorway and that he had been staring at his two neighbours the whole time. He turned away as the wife, Eva, caught him watching her and her husband going through their morning ritual. The affectionate kiss on the cheek, the packed lunch exchanged. A meal perhaps lovingly made by her in the knowledge of what he liked best and that would keep him going for the day. This was not his life and probably never would be. He nodded politely and walked on.

*

The hours passed even more slowly than usual in the harbour office. Enzo had completed all the work he had to do in less than two hours that morning and his sea adventure novel no longer held the same pleasure for him; his own life had become more interesting.

The telephone sat invitingly on his desk in front of him but he decided not to tell Salvatore about his new housekeeper just yet. In his personal work notebook, under today's date, he wrote in large letters: 'Aatifa – first day' and beside that '?'.

As the clock struck 7 p.m., his staff made their usual stampede for the door. Daniel waited patiently in the main office for him to come out so he could lock up. Inside, Enzo sat at his desk, suddenly reluctant to go home. He thought about telling his assistant to go as he had to work late but Daniel would know this was a lie. Then another thought occurred to him. Aatifa would have made dinner and it would be impolite for him to come home late. There was nothing else for it, he would have to leave. They walked down the stairs together in silence and Daniel locked up.

'Goodnight, sir.'

'Yes,' Enzo replied, distracted.

He walked home at a snail's pace, the setting sun beating him to its own destination as it melted down into the mountains. On his street, in the half light of dusk, he hesitated a few feet from his front gate. No going back, he thought, you live here. He braced himself and went in.

His first reaction was the odd sensation that came from the presence of another human being in his sanctuary. The second was relief that everything was just as he had left it. He saw Aatifa busy in the kitchen and was about to greet her but she immediately turned back to her work. She is right, he thought, people do use too many unnecessary words.

The living room table had been set for one, so he sat down and waited. A few moments later she started to bring in the food, first a basket of freshly cut bread which she placed in the middle of the table. On her next trip she brought out a glass jug of water with slices of lemon floating on top.

When he was sure that she couldn't see him, he watched her, her body, her hair, her hands, her eyes, her clothes, her toes protruding from her sandals. He could smell his own bathroom soap on her but it was different, nicer somehow. Whenever she turned in his direction he broke his stare quickly, but she never actually looked at him. He could see that his house was strange to her, as though she were still getting used to the space. She would walk from one position to the next but would arrive half a step short or end up too close and then have to adjust slightly. He had noticed that people in traditional dress, with robes to their ankles, moved along like shifting sands, gliding across the floor. It was a more elegant movement than that allowed by the European man's gangly trousered leg or the women's pencil skirts.

Finally, she brought out a pasta dish and placed it directly in front of him. Then she hovered uncomfortably until he picked up his fork. She left him to eat alone, going back to her chair in the kitchen, which she had positioned just out of his sight.

Enzo looked at the food for a moment. It seemed normal enough to him so he took a small mouthful. It was simple and tasty, lightly salted aubergine with a little olive oil. She was a better cook than his mother who had managed to assassinate even the most rudimentary dish. His late father had always been the meal maker in their house, and after his death he and his sister were reminded of his loss, three times a day.

'It's good,' he said loudly.

No reply came back. She didn't return until he had finished.

'You'd like more?' she asked.

He didn't wish to offend but he was already full.

'No, thank you, that was just the right amount,' he said softly.

Seeming not to care either way, she took away his plate.

Enzo sat awkwardly for a few moments, hearing the tap water running into the sink and then he got up and went to the kitchen door. For a second he thought she wasn't going to turn to look at him but eventually she did.

'Right, well, goodnight,' he said, before turning on his heels and walking out.

An hour later, he was still sitting on his bed, fully clothed, when he heard Aatifa's footsteps in the corridor. He saw her shadow move past under his doorway. Then her bedroom door opened and immediately closed.

Standing now at his window, he heard her rusty shutters being pushed open. This was followed by silence, and he guessed that she had gone to bed. He looked out at the rooftops and the clear starry sky. The night's rising moon was the same shape as the crescent on top of the mosque. A bright movement caught his eye and he looked down and saw a scrawny white kitten on a rooftop across the street. The animal had not seen him yet but the quiet was broken when he heard Aatifa calling the creature. The kitten turned sharply and froze, locking eyes with him. Then the kitten's head turned a little more to the left as he spotted Aatifa. Enzo imagined her sitting on her window sill, ten yards away from him, staring out. She called the kitten again but the animal continued on his way.

When all was quiet once more, Enzo began to undress. He

had forgotten to shave and would have quite a layer of stubble in the morning. It would have to do because he felt unable to leave his room now. He had already transferred his dressing gown from the bathroom to his bedroom, knowing that his days of walking around the house naked were no more. This was his own private space but it no longer felt that way. He considered dismissing her in the morning, but on what grounds?

Aatifa got up before him, leaving her bedroom door open to allow the fresh morning air to flow down the corridor. In the kitchen, she began to prepare coffee the local way. First, she roasted the green coffee beans in a frying pan on the stove. The small room began to fill with smoke, so she opened the back door to clear it. A few moments later she noticed a tiny white head and a pair of opal eyes appearing at ground level. The kitten from last night had arrived, no doubt attracted by the smell of the beans. Aatifa smiled and coaxed him in with a little meat. He didn't need to be asked twice. When he had finished eating, he sat down on the floor and watched her.

Aatifa placed the roasted coffee beans in a bowl. Then she knelt on the floor and furiously ground them with a thick wooden stick until they had become as fine a powder as she could manage. The kitten rose and approached with his tail in the air to see if he would be allowed to eat this too. Aatifa pushed him away firmly with her hand. Then she poured the ground coffee into a long-necked clay pot, filled it with water and sat it on the stove to boil. She expected the Italian would come down soon, once the aroma reached his room.

Sure enough, she heard movement upstairs, so she encouraged the kitten out of the back door. He refused to oblige so she rudely shoved him out with her foot.

The Italian entered the living room, dressed in a suit, and she gestured towards the steaming cup of coffee on the dining table. He sat and she waited.

'Something to eat?' she asked.

'No, just this, thank you,' he said with a smile, so she left him to it.

She enjoyed her own coffee, sitting on her chair in the kitchen. The Italians could never make it like this, no matter how hard they tried.

A few moments later, she saw him crossing the living room and then heard the front door closing. It was a relief to be alone. There was a persistent scratching noise from outside and she opened the back door. The kitten crept in warily, watching her feet the whole time in case he got another kick.

'You think this is your home now, do you?'

By way of answer, the kitten sat on the floor in the same spot.

Aatifa went back into the living room and walked along beside the books. She could not read any of the titles but she pulled out a few encyclopedias, and looked at the pictures in one about the Roman Empire. Then she noticed the gramophone unit against the opposite wall and, standing upright underneath it, a neat pile of records. She sat on the floor with her legs crossed and flicked through them. On the cover of many there was a photo of the same smiling man, dressed in an expensive-looking black suit. She put these back and picked out one with a robust-looking woman on the cover. You have never been short of food, she thought. Carefully she placed the record on the gramophone, and wound up the motor by hand, the way she had seen in a café. Then she set the needle on it. A few crackles came out of the inbuilt speaker and a male voice said, 'Luisa Tetrazzini performs "Addio del Passato" from *La*

Traviata.' After a pause, the woman began singing in that odd, high-pitched style the Italians liked.

She left it playing and went upstairs to run herself a bath. Passing the overloaded storeroom, she decided her new employer was a hoarder of objects. Did he not know he couldn't take it with him when he died? Her own cloth bag contained almost everything she possessed in the world. She owned little not because she was poor – which she was – but because she did not care to accumulate things. Some people were determined to miss what was important, she thought, grabbing their way through life like fools. Her own aims were fully connected to the precious breathing things that were part of her and nothing else mattered.

The warm water came gushing out of the tap into the free-standing, cast-iron bath; then it began to splutter and stop. She took off one of her sandals and firmly whacked the pipe, free-ing the air lock and sending the water tumbling out in full flow again. She thought about closing the door but then she wouldn't be able to hear the music. She was pretty sure that she would not see the Italian again until the evening, so she undressed and climbed in. A bath was a rare pleasure for her but she looked one last time at the open door, listening. When there was no other sound except Tetrazzini, she lay back and relaxed, letting her head sink completely underwater for a few seconds, before surfacing again and enjoying the sensation of the drops drying on her face.

She closed her eyes, soaking until the record finished down-stairs and the water had turned cold. Then she climbed out and dried herself with her own small towel, starting at the top with her hair, which had been temporarily knocked flat by the wet-ness. When she had dried her feet, she used the same towel to dry her wet footprints off the floor. After that she left the bathroom, taking the damp towel and every other trace of her presence with her.

Once she had dressed, she collected her now empty bag. Downstairs in the living room she randomly pulled one of the encyclopedias from the bookshelf and stuffed it inside. The kitten watched her leave without budging from the section of floor he had laid claim to.

The Italian woman next door was tending the yellow roses in her front garden when Aatifa came out of the house. She looked at her suspiciously at first but this changed to surprise when she saw that Aatifa had her own key. She still didn't acknowledge her and Aatifa ignored her in return. Pleasantries and chit-chat were for others to waste their time on.

She crossed through the market, but then headed away from the port, passing through narrow back streets where Eritrean men were delivering gas bottles and other supplies to the various local and Italian businesses. Then she was in a residential street full of large villas, bigger than Enzo's house. These gardens overflowed with red and white bougainvillea and the sound of bees at work filled the air, but she paid no attention to any of it. As she continued on, the buildings became more and more run-down. Some were just broken ruins left by the big earthquake in 1921. Aatifa had not been here to witness it but she had heard all about it.

Finally she left the city behind altogether and walked across the causeway to the mainland. She didn't stop until she had reached the area where the poor Eritrean families lived. Here, scattered around a flat plain, were hundreds of huts made from mud and stone with straw roofs. Smoke from dozens of cooking fires hung low above them, and down the centre of each street was an open sewer attracting every fly for miles. Italians would call it a slum and few had ever visited it but this had been the way of life here long before they had come.

There were no street signs but Aatifa knew her way through the unplanned maze. She walked past the hut that had been her home until yesterday but was completely empty now. A few cooking utensils lay on the ground outside where she had left them to make it appear that the hut was still occupied. A sandy-coloured gecko was busy investigating the inside of one of them.

Money never came without work, she thought. It must be an easy life to be rich. If she had been wealthy she would not have needed to become a housekeeper for this Italian. That had never been part of her dreams but she did not have the luxury of choice. It would have been better too if this new job had come without the live-in part but it did, so that was that. She would wait a while, until she felt the work was secure, and then she would try to get some money for the hut.

A few streets further on, she arrived outside another larger hut. Iggi was standing in front of it smoking a rolled-up cigarette. Barefoot, in an open white shirt and sarong, his tightly cropped hair looked almost shaven and his face wore its usual cynical scowl. He acknowledged her coolly. They had not liked each other from the beginning and she did not expect that to change. He made way for her as she bent her head to go in, then threw away his cigarette end and followed her. Inside the dirt-floored, sparsely furnished room was Iggi's wife, Madihah, and almost hidden in shadow and wrapped in a thin black shawl, an eight-year-old girl, Azzezza. Aatifa smiled when she saw the girl looking up at her and she took Enzo's encyclopedia from her bag and handed it to her. Azzezza's eyes lit up, grabbing hold of it with outstretched arms.

'It's just to borrow, OK?' said Aatifa in Tigrinya.

Azzezza nodded earnestly, as she opened the book with great care. It gave Aatifa pleasure to see that she understood the meaning of the printed words.

Iggi and Madihah waited expectantly behind her. She took out her first week's wages from inside her dress and held it out to them, but no one moved, leaving her, hand outstretched, as though she were a beggar. They would do this to me, Aatifa thought, punish me for helping.

'You want me to keep it, is that it?' she asked loudly.

Neither one replied so she put the money on the table. Madihah picked it up without a word of thanks and went to hide it in the small back room. Aatifa stared angrily at Iggi but he just walked silently outside. She turned to Azzezza who was already engrossed in the encyclopedia and oblivious to the adult goings-on. At least she was pleased, and that was all that counted.

Madihah returned and stood in the doorway, arms folded. There was less tension in the air now that Iggi had gone but still Aatifa decided to leave before she said something she would regret. She had done so many times before and would probably do it again, but not today. Bending down, she kissed Azzezza on the forehead and she let her kiss her cheek in return. She didn't bother talking to the other two again.

Aatifa paid a brief visit to her old hut for appearance's sake and then made her way back to the market. There, she looked around and wondered what she would give the Italian that evening. It had been a long time since she had had to think about feeding anyone else but his meals would need daily planning, she realised, and this irritated her. She had better things to think about. It would not bother her to eat the same food day in and day out but no doubt he would be expecting variety.

She decided she would pick five meals and repeat this every five days. These would have to change with the season depending on what produce was available. So in four days' time she would do aubergine with pasta again and for today she decided to buy a fish. She loved fish herself and she began to think of the upside of cooking for him. She would get to eat some as well and even the kitten would benefit too; he could have the carcass. A large silver and grey sea bass caught her attention. Its owner, a turbaned fisherman, had only one eye and was getting so old now that his days of going out at night in a boat would probably soon be over. The price she paid him was a little too much but it was the Italian's money. He wasn't aware that he was doing a good deed, but she thought he might receive the luck that came from it anyway.

The smell of the cooking fish made the kitten whimper. He paced the kitchen floor in figures of eight around her feet, almost tripping her up several times.

'Be patient, little one; if you are then you will get some,' she said. The smell was making her own mouth water too.

When the Italian arrived home, they didn't speak but Aatifa sensed that he was watching her closely. She put his plate on the table in front of him, with three-quarters of the fleshy, succulent fish. Then, just as she was about to leave she saw that he was struggling to say something.

'You can eat here, if you like,' he said.

He almost sang the first word as it came out and he followed it with a strange throat-clearing noise. Aatifa looked from him to the table, then went to the kitchen and returned with a plate of food for herself.

There were three chairs available to her, two on either side of him or the one directly opposite and furthest away; she had already chosen that one. The portion of fish she had reserved for herself was much less than she had given to him, and he looked at her plate awkwardly.

She waited for him to start and he saw this and dipped his fork into the juicy fish. Then she ate slowly, so that she would not finish minutes before he did. When he was done, she stopped too, and took both plates away.

After he had retired early once again, Aatifa brought the fish head and tail into her bedroom where she had hidden the kitten. He gratefully devoured the whole lot, licking his paws afterwards. Then he curled up beside her legs on the bed, purring, with his tail patting gently against her calf.

Chapter 5

WHEN ENZO ARRIVED for work the next day, he found Salvatore in his office, on a rare visit down the mountain for army business. A personal delivery had been waiting for him in Massawa since the last supply boat. He smiled as he ripped the brown paper wrapping off the large lumpy package, revealing a brand-new set of golf clubs that he had bought from a mail order catalogue.

'What are you going to do with those?' said Enzo. 'We don't have any golf courses.'

Salvatore ignored the question, too engrossed with the novelty of the different-shaped club heads. 'So how's things?' he asked.

Enzo decided to downplay his news.

'I hired a housekeeper.'

There was a moment of stunned silence before Salvatore broke into the broadest smile. 'I don't believe it! What is she like? When can I meet her? How is it? You remembered how to do it?'

'We don't sleep together,' Enzo replied, almost apologetically. 'She has her own room.'

Salvatore looked at him as though he had just said the most peculiar thing. 'What do you mean you don't sleep together?' he asked.

'Sshh, not here,' said Enzo, closing his office door quickly, for all the good that would do.

Salvatore threw the bag of golf clubs over his shoulder and brushed past him. 'Follow me,' he ordered.

He marched out past Enzo's staff who all greeted him enthusiastically, particularly the two engaged women.

Salvatore led him up on to the flat office roof, where he selected a number 4 wood. He forced his wooden tee into a nail hole on a plank. Then he proceeded to drive golf balls whizzing off the building, over the quay and into the sea, narrowly missing a docker or two on the way.

'Do you have to do that? You're going to kill somebody,' said Enzo.

'What are you supposed to say? Fore, isn't it? Fore!' he roared, as the dockers dived for cover. Salvatore had never played golf before in his life and his swing was not a thing of beauty but he improved marginally with each stroke.

'Just take her,' he said between swings.

'I am not a rapist,' Enzo protested.

Salvatore threw his eyes up to heaven and pointed his golf club at Enzo. 'It's not like that. She expects it. It's normal.'

'Normal?'

'Yes,' said Salvatore, sending another golf ball off the roof. This one hit the water at an almost horizontal angle, skimmed the surface three times and then sank. 'Did you see that!' he said, delighted. Then he looked around the bay and noticed something else. 'What's going on? Why are there no ships?'

Enzo sighed. 'I told you. This is normal.'

Salvatore rummaged in the golf bag but there were no more balls to be found. He had drowned them all.

'Could you order me some more?'

Enzo took a little vindictive pleasure in saying, 'Sure. It'll take six weeks; unless you'd like to go for a swim?'

Salvatore looked like a child whose new toy was broken. He stared down at the clubs, already tired of them.

'Lunch?' he suggested, quickly recovering from the loss.

Enzo informed Daniel that he probably would not be back in the afternoon and told him to keep a close eye on the staff, who were liable to slack off even more in his absence. Then he and Salvatore retired to Massawa's only Florentine restaurant, where even though they were the only lunchtime clients, the owner still asked them whether they had a reservation. The waiter turned on a noisy air conditioner especially for them, as Salvatore perused the short wine list. He pointed at a heavy red and they both ordered tuna steaks.

'She is just waiting to be asked. You're actually insulting her by not.'

'I really don't think that's true,' said Enzo, shaking his head.

'What do you know? I know,' said Salvatore.

'What if she says no?' asked Enzo.

'She won't.'

'How can you be so sure?'

'If she does, then hire someone else,' said Salvatore, pouring the wine.

Enzo realised that his friend wasn't taking his troubles seriously at all. 'But I just employed her. She probably needs the job.'

'Exactly,' said Salvatore, resting his case.

'So you're saying she might say no.'

'I'm not saying that.'

'But she could – it's possible?' Enzo continued.

'You're driving me insane, you know that?' said Salvatore, giving up. 'You're over-thinking the whole business. Stop thinking; can you just do that?'

Enzo nodded but he wasn't fooling anyone. He decided to steer the conversation away from his housekeeper. 'How is it all going in Libya?' he asked.

Salvatore sat back, happy to go on at length about how he made sure to keep well in with his superiors so as not to get sent to their North African colony, ever. The Italian army in Libya spent its time getting shot at and that was not for him. Salvatore was a strange soldier indeed, thought Enzo. Most men joined the army with the express hope of actually seeing some military action. The colonel then ordered another bottle of wine and as usual the staff jumped to attention for him, even though Enzo was by far the more regular customer.

When he breezed into the living room later, Aatifa had set two dinner places opposite each other as they had been the night before.

'Hello,' Enzo said cheerfully, but she only nodded.

She had immediately spotted the fact that he was drunk, but it was a rare occurrence and he wasn't about to apologise for it.

She returned from the kitchen with the meal she had prepared, a vegetable soup with courgette and red peppers. He uncorked a fresh bottle of wine and poured himself a full glass.

'Wine?' he said, showing her the bottle.

She shook her head and sat down opposite him.

'Is it not good?' she asked, when she noticed that he was drinking more than he was eating.

'It's very nice, very nice,' he assured her, having a couple of spoonfuls. 'Mmm, good.' Then he returned to the wine and watched her as she ate.

'You're happy working here?' he asked. 'It's OK?'

She nodded with a frown. 'Yes, fine.'

'Good. That's good,' he said to no one in particular.

After he had finished a third of the wine on his own, he stood up awkwardly.

'Excuse me.'

He left the room, swaying a little as he did so, and heaved himself up the stairs.

The tight space of the bathroom was too small for him in his inebriated state and he couldn't help banging noisily into things. Then he made for his bedroom and placed the two pillows side by side at the head of the bed.

He heard her downstairs in the kitchen, putting the bowls away, then the click of the lights being turned out. A moment later, she arrived at the bedroom corridor. He was waiting for her, standing in his doorway, leaning against the door jamb for support. She seemed unsure what to do but she slowed and stopped a few feet away from him. He saw her look into the bedroom and notice the change in the pillows.

Enzo was sober enough to know that if he wasn't drunk he wouldn't be able to do this. He was glad that she didn't seem scared or at least she didn't show it. Not wanting to put into words what he was asking for, he gestured, with a wave of his arm, for her to enter the room. It was not meant to be an order and he tried not to be aggressive but he could feel the uncomfortable weight of the moment. He watched her hesitate, looking from his room to her own door and safety further down the corridor. It was impossible to read what she was thinking. For a moment he wished she'd say no. It would be better if she said no. But then unexpectedly she moved past him and entered his room.

She stopped just inside the door and his heart raced as he

closed it behind them. All rational thought disappeared as he began to undo her clothes. He ignored the fact that she just stood there. Since she had walked inside he had not looked at her face, afraid of what he might see in her eyes. He felt her discomfort but he didn't care, he'd gone beyond that.

As he led her to the bed, she was still half-dressed and he had all his clothes on. She hadn't touched him once, her arms remaining rigid by her side. Her body was so beautiful, it almost made him pause. But his excitement was building too quickly. He undid his trousers and began straight away. They didn't kiss. There was no romance or intimacy. She avoided looking at him, her face turned towards the window. This was all for him. Nothing else mattered.

'Stop,' she said suddenly, putting a hand on his chest for the first time.

He kept going, deliberately disregarding what she had said.

'Stop!' she repeated loudly, giving him a sharp push in the ribs.

He fell beside her, out of breath, taken aback by the sudden unwelcome return to reality.

'What? What is it?' he said, but she was already gathering her clothes off the floor and hurrying out.

A few seconds later he heard her bedroom door slamming.

When he had caught his breath, he went out into the corridor and looked towards Aatifa's closed room. He felt bad about what had happened but decided against going to see how she was. As he returned to his bedroom, he was sure that he would be awake all night, thinking about this. But his exertions had pumped the alcohol around his body and when he lay down again, it went straight to his brain and he was asleep in ten minutes.

*

The next morning he woke up with a sore, throbbing head. He felt ashamed, but also angry at Aatifa for having made him feel ashamed. Thinking he'd avoid any unpleasantness by leaving before she got up, he dressed quickly. But he found her in the living room, already on her knees scrubbing the red terracotta floor. His cup of coffee sat on the table waiting. He had not caught the aroma from upstairs this time. All he could smell was the overpoweringly stale odour of wine coming from himself.

She stopped what she was doing, stood up and dried her hands nervously. Then they took turns to look at each other as the other one looked away. He was relieved that she didn't seem angry.

'Do you want me to leave?' she asked, finally breaking the thick silence.

He paused, trying to think but his head was slow and confused. 'I don't know. I have to go to work.'

She nodded and he turned and left, leaving his coffee untouched on the table.

He sought refuge in the bathroom at work. He took off his shirt and tie, and washed his neck and armpits in the sink to try to get rid of the stench of wine that seemed to be seeping out through his pores. After slapping cold water on his face several times, he dried himself and dressed again. Then he started to bash his head gently against the tiled wall, only stopping when an Eritrean staff member entered. The man saw what he had been doing but said nothing apart from, 'Good morning, sir.'

'Good morning,' he mumbled in return.

He sat at his desk in a foul humour, a large ledger open in front of him. Then he shouted for Daniel over the wall. A second later his assistant knocked and came in, looking worried.

'I've told you before about these entries,' said Enzo. 'They're supposed to be in the import ledger. How many times do I have to say it?'

Daniel looked over his shoulder and nodded, immediately removing the offending ledger.

'Yes, sir, of course, I'll see that it doesn't happen again.'

It was unlikely that it had been his assistant's fault and now Enzo felt guilt to add to his anger and shame. He stopped him before he got to the door.

'You're married, aren't you, Daniel?'

Daniel nodded. 'Yes, I am.'

'What are Eritrean women like?' he asked.

Daniel considered the question for a moment before he responded. 'They are like all women everywhere, each the same and each different, sent to confound us. It's better to face lions.' He smiled at the last part but Enzo was in no mood for levity. 'Will that be all, sir?'

'Thank you, Daniel,' said Enzo.

Through the blinds, he saw that all eyes were on Daniel as he returned to the main office, each person wondering if they had been responsible for the error. He was not surprised when Daniel made a beeline for one of the two young Italians who were always the first out of the front door every evening.

Enzo had no desire to do any work at all today. He didn't want to face lions either but he would have to go home and face her some time. If only it would all go away. He wished another earthquake could come to Massawa and swallow him into the ground. Thinking back over the previous night's events and seeing her face as she had run out of his bedroom, he tried to imagine what his own must have looked like. Animal.

The approaching sunset bathed the street in a pink and orange hue as Enzo reached the garden gate. The second he opened the front door he knew that she was still there, even though the house was deathly quiet. He made straight for his bedroom, hoping to delay their meeting, but when he reached the landing, he saw her. She was sitting on the end of her narrow bed, stitching holes in her old clothes. His arrival seemed to catch her by surprise and he was sure that he saw her quickly wiping away a tear. She turned towards him but he entered his room without acknowledging her.

Enzo sat down on the bed and pulled off his tie. He sensed her presence in the doorway behind him but he didn't turn around.

'Perhaps it would be better if you did leave,' he said, facing out of the window to the sea.

She had brought up the suggestion that morning, so he was just throwing her words back at her.

'I would like to stay,' she said.

He frowned. She was making it hard. The decision to fire her was not because she had rejected him. He wanted her to take some of his shame and guilt away with her. How would they be able to face each other every day, pretending nothing had happened?

'I just can't see it working out,' he said, shaking his head.

He half turned as he heard her begin to undress behind him. She didn't look up at him as he stood and went over to her.

'Are you sure?' he asked.

She didn't reply, just continued undressing until everything was on the floor at her feet. He watched her get into the bed and then he undressed too.

This time he was a little more tender; nervous that she would do what she had done the night before. She continued to look away from him but he watched her, making sure she did not become distressed. In fact, she seemed to be coldly managing what was happening to her, as if she had prepared.

When it was over he collapsed with the sheer relief of it. His shoulder and leg muscles ached after being put to use but it was a good feeling. He smiled at her gratefully but she was already getting off the bed. She scooped up her clothes in one movement, not bothering to try to hide her body from him, as though that didn't matter now. Then she paused at the door. For a second he thought she was about to say something nice.

'So I still have the job?' she said.

The question made him feel dirtier than he'd ever felt in his life.

'Yes,' he said.

She left without another word.

'I am not the man you think,' Enzo whispered.

Chapter 6

THE NEXT MORNING, Aatifa was on her way to the bathroom when Enzo emerged from his door, heading in the same direction. Even though she was nearer, she immediately turned and started to head back to her own room.

'You go first,' he said, but she shook her head.

'Please,' he insisted, waving his arm for her to go in.

The last time he made the same gesture it had all ended badly and she could see that he remembered it too. He let his arm fall limply down by his side.

'Please,' he said again, folding his arms this time and stepping aside until she went in.

Later he sat at the dining table and drank his coffee as she sat on her chair in the kitchen. When it was time for him to go, he came to the doorway, and made a point of saying goodbye. She gave him a half nod in reply which appeared to be enough for him and he left with a contented air.

When Aatifa had gone for this job she had known that something like this might happen. It was common knowledge what some Italian men were after when it came to the local women. There were some, particularly Muslims, who would not even apply for a housekeeping job. This man, Enzo, had not seemed the predatory type to her but she knew that you never could tell. In any case, she needed to earn money and no one else was going to provide it. So she had walked into the Italian's world with open eyes, steeling herself with the knowledge that she was strong and could handle whatever life threw at her. She had been wrong about that.

What had surprised her most was not his behaviour but how quickly and easily her own emotions had surfaced and over-taken her. She didn't normally allow that to happen. Her tears had come for the whole of the next day, not in floods but constant and uncontrollable. What a fool she was, to know so little about herself.

She walked briskly into the centre of town, taking a different route this time until she reached the gates of an elementary school. There, people had gathered on the sun-bleached lawn in the school garden for a ceremony. Aatifa watched through the iron railings as a group of eight-year-old Eritrean children lined up to receive diplomas from their teacher, a bespectacled Italian woman in her forties. The boys and girls were all dressed like Italian school children in knee-length blue smocks with white collars.

Aatifa could hear the teacher repeating the same line to every student as she handed them a rolled-up paper scroll, tied with a little red ribbon.

'Congratulations on completing your schooling. Congratulations on . . .'

She beamed proudly and clapped when she saw Azzezza receiving hers. Azzezza clutched it in her palm, holding back a grin that was threatening to break free.

'Thank you, Maestra,' she said.

The teacher looked down at her and touched her cheek

tenderly. Aatifa thought the woman might cry until she composed herself and picked up a new scroll for the next child. Azzezza ran to hug Madihah who was standing nearby in the purple shade of a blooming jacaranda tree. Aatifa lingered for a moment, watching Azzezza unroll the scroll for Madihah to see.

Madihah cannot read what it says, child, she thought as she watched Madihah put on a show of being impressed by the document. Then she slipped away unnoticed. As she walked back to the Italian's house, she looked forward to Azzezza showing the diploma to her tomorrow. And she thought of the words that she could use to tell the child how wonderful she was.

As usual, she had the dinner prepared for him when he came home. She was expecting all to be fine with them now but instead he stood in the living room doorway and looked at her coldly.

'I'm not hungry,' he said. 'I don't want food.'

He left the room and went upstairs. She could not think of anything that might have changed between them since she had given him her body. They had only seen each other briefly after that and he had seemed all right. In fact he had been trying to kill her with politeness. She did not understand this man; his moods changed with the wind. Since the food would only spoil, she sat down at the table and ate by herself.

Later, when he still hadn't come back, she opened the door to the back yard. The kitten was outside, waiting patiently to be let in, and he pounced on Enzo's cold dinner.

As she turned the corner into the bedroom corridor, she wondered if she might find him standing in his doorway waiting for her. But his door was firmly shut. She kept on going, relieved that his desires would not be a nightly burden.

When she awoke the next morning he was already gone.

Enzo had been the first in the doctor's waiting room, although he had not been entirely alone. There had been him and the ubiquitous Mussolini portrait. They were everywhere, each with a different pose to suit any occasion. Military poses, thinking poses, dressed in a suit, a helmet or on a horse. He had caught sight of it out of the corner of his eye, next to a poster saying that smoking was good for your teeth. He had made sure not to look directly at it in case he and the Duce got into a difficult conversation.

Opposite him now was a workman in green overalls with one arm in a rudimentary sling and a mother with a sneezing teenage boy. She was resupplying her son with fresh cloth handkerchiefs each time he exhausted the last. The workman was telling them all about his accident although no one had asked him. It threatened to be a story without end but they were saved when the elderly Italian doctor finally opened his surgery door.

'Who's first?' he said over his reading glasses.

On another day Enzo would have let the mother go first. 'It's me,' he said, holding up his hand.

In the surgery, Enzo looked down as the doctor's right eye expanded to monster size through his thick magnifying glass. His own trousers were at his knees and the doctor was kneeling in front of him examining his private parts, which were shrunken due to a mixture of cold and fear. The subject of investigation was a couple of large, angry-looking red spots; down there, where no man wants them.

'Nasty,' said the doctor unhelpfully, adding with surprising venom, 'bloody African bitches.' He shook his head, got up off the floor and went to wash his hands.

Enzo swallowed nervously as he pulled up his trousers and zipped himself up.

'Is it treatable with something?' he asked hopefully.

'Oh, there's no treatment for that, as such,' said the doctor.

Of course there isn't, thought Enzo, as his heart sank.

'You could try a net, that helps,' offered the doctor.

'Excuse me?' asked Enzo.

'It's the female ones that bite, you know.'

Enzo broke into a relieved grin. 'Mosquitoes?'

'Yes,' the doctor said. 'What did you think I was talking about?'

Enzo didn't dare tell him.

'The ones they have here are twice the size of our Italian ones. They'd nearly take the hand off you and other parts. There's malaria to consider too, always a risk.'

Enzo nodded. He had been lucky so far and the idea of contracting malaria via his genitals didn't bear thinking about. He paid the doctor and shook his hand vigorously as if he had just cured him of something life-threatening.

He arrived home after work with a spring in his step and a large bag of cloth under his arm. Just as he was about to close the front door, his neighbour, Eva, appeared at the gate. Her perfect hair suggested that she had just come straight from the hairdressers.

'Enzo, sorry to disturb you. Can I have a word?'

She walked up the garden path and immediately noticed the white cloth, bulging out of the top of the bag.

'Are you doing some decorating?' she asked.

'Not exactly, no,' he said.

'You haven't seen my cat, have you? A little thing, white? He's missing.'

'No, I'm sorry, I haven't. I didn't know you had a cat,' said Enzo, hoping she would go away.

To his surprise, Aatifa appeared in the hallway behind him carrying a white kitten. She handed the animal to him without a word and he handed him on to Eva. The kitten let out an unhappy miaow.

'There you are,' Eva said, holding the animal awkwardly. Then she sneezed.

'My housekeeper,' Enzo explained.

He studied Eva's reaction but she ignored Aatifa as if she wasn't there.

'Enzo, have you kidnapped him?' Eva said, attempting a joke.

'I've never seen him before in my life,' Enzo said seriously.

He looked to Aatifa for some help but she offered absolutely none. The kitten was now struggling to get free from Eva's bony hands.

'Well, he's found now,' said Eva, tightening her grip. 'Aren't you, you little troublemaker? Thank you so much, Enzo.'

'I'm glad I could help. Any time,' he said.

Eva left at last and he closed the door. He turned and looked at Aatifa.

'If she fed it more, it wouldn't look like a stray,' was all he got from her.

She walked back into the house and he smiled at her unexpected spitefulness.

Later, in the bedroom, she watched in amusement as he stood on top of a wooden stepladder and tried to erect the white mosquito net over his bed. 'What?' he asked.

'You're doing it all wrong,' she said.

'Am I! Well, you could help.'

Eventually he admitted defeat and held the ladder while she put the net up herself with annoying ease. The hanging white cloth waved gently in the evening breeze coming off the sea.

'Not bad at all. It looks good, doesn't it?' he said proudly.

She smiled at his pleasure in having achieved something so simple.

Enzo stared, enjoying this new side of her. It was the first time he had ever seen her smile. Stepping in close, he kissed her gently. She let him, without responding or withdrawing. Then he kissed her again, his lips pressing softly against hers. He undressed her slowly, caressing and kissing as he did so. This time too, he sought her eye contact. She seemed confused by his behaviour but began to pull off his clothes in a matter-of-fact way.

He tried to make love to her with tenderness, not rushing like before. She stared at her usual point out of the window but turned to glance at his face occasionally. When it was over she seemed unsettled. She pushed back the new net, got out of bed and began to gather her clothes.

'Wait,' he said, 'you can stay here . . . if you like.'

He wanted her to stay more than anything.

She stopped and looked at him. 'I prefer to sleep in my own room.'

He nodded, trying to hide his disappointment. Here was a rule she had made to guide them. He didn't much like it but he certainly wasn't going to give her orders.

'Wait a little then?' he suggested.

She returned slowly to the bed and sat upright, with her arms folded, so that her head wasn't touching the wooden headboard. He looked up at her from his pillow and wished that she could be more relaxed with him.

After an uncomfortable silence, he spoke. 'How come you never got married? Women marry very young here, don't they?'

She paused before answering.

'I almost did, once.'

He nodded and there was another long silence before she said, 'You are not married?'

'No,' he said. 'Once almost but it didn't happen either . . .'

'Why not?' she asked.

'We both decided that we didn't love each other. It was a lucky escape really. I'm not very good at romance.'

She smiled again and he thought how beautiful she was. He wished that he could make her smile all the time and that she would never stop.

'Where are you from?' she asked and he was pleased that she was interested in knowing a little about him.

'I'm from Genoa, like Christopher Columbus and Paganini. You've heard of them?'

She shook her head and then asked a question that seemed to have been on her mind. 'And why did you come here?'

'Oh, I had a job back home, with good prospects . . . but, well, I don't know, I hoped there might be something more to life, something different. I had a friend here, so I came. No one thought I'd last very long.'

'You like it here?' she asked, in an odd way.

'Yes, I do. Even more now,' he said, looking into the blackness of her eyes.

This was his best shot at being romantic but she seemed to take it as her cue to get up and leave. As she was on her way out, he decided to ask her something else that had been on his mind.

'What we do . . . together, I mean. You do it because you want to, don't you?'

The question seemed to take her by surprise. She gave him an unconvincing nod and then was gone.

Looking at the crumpled pillow where she had just been, he rested his hand on it softly. Their arrangement was certainly not perfect by any means but he couldn't remember ever being this happy in his life.

Chapter 7

THE WHOLE TOWN was bathed in a thick sea mist during the night, reducing visibility to almost zero. Pockets of it lingered still, in the morning, as though they were visiting spirits. Outside his house, Enzo said a generous hello to Eva and her husband, and to the gift shopkeeper, and the flower lady and anyone else he recognised. He thought about Aatifa for the whole journey and was already counting the hours until he would see her again.

When he reached the quay, he was surprised to see a familiar form tied up to the dock and his smile faded quickly. *Queen Eleonora.* The supply ship was already unloading. He had completely forgotten about her arrival and he vowed never to let that happen again. Daniel was waiting outside the office with a worried expression.

'Yes, I know, I should have been here,' Enzo said. 'I forgot.'

'It's not that, sir, there's a gentleman to see you, upstairs.'

He said it in such a tone that Enzo knew this was no ordinary visitor.

'His name is Bobbio.'

Enzo racked his brain but he was pretty sure that he did not know anyone by that name. 'What does he want?'

Daniel shrugged. 'He came on the boat this morning.'

This was doubly bad. He had not been there to meet either the ship or this out-of-towner. He went up quickly to face whoever it was.

As he entered the main office, he saw a short, balding man in his fifties through his office blinds. He could also see that he was sitting in his chair. The staff had noticed this too and as one they craned their necks towards Enzo to see what his reaction would be. As Enzo got nearer, he noticed that the man was poring over one of his own workbooks. And he was taking notes too. He was tempted to storm in there and give this Bobbio a piece of his mind, but decided he had better hold fire.

Bobbio glanced up briefly as Enzo stood in the doorway. He made no move to get up out of his chair.

'Signor Secchi?'

'Yes. That's me. Can I help you?' said Enzo, trying to be both polite and firm at the same time.

Bobbio turned to a new page in the workbook. 'I am told you are the man I need to talk to.'

'Really? What about? Look, do you mind not looking through . . . those are mine.'

The visitor was unfazed and still didn't look up.

'Bobbio is my name, from the Ministry of Italian Africa, the ministry to whom "your" ledgers belong.'

Enzo sat down in the visitor's chair. In his entire five years in Massawa, this was the first time that he had been outranked in his own office. It didn't feel good.

'These are very ordered I must say,' said Bobbio.

Enzo forced himself to smile. 'We try to provide an efficient service here.'

'Efficiency is the minimum that is expected,' said Bobbio dismissively.

Enzo studied his opponent. He was wearing a relatively new

navy blue suit, a finer quality than his own but not by much. His tie was perfectly knotted and he had not loosened it despite the fact that he was sweating uncontrollably, the way all new-comers did in the beginning. His face was an unhealthy pallor and it was hard to tell what colour his thinning hair had been before it went grey. His small eyes were green so perhaps it had been fair.

'I've been sent down here by the ministry to assess your readiness.'

'I'm sorry, readiness for what?' asked Enzo, hoping the word 'assess' meant that he was just here on a lightning visit.

Bobbio sighed and answered while continuing to write his notes. 'It is the Duce's desire to expand our empire by taking over the land of your neighbour, Abyssinia or Ethiopia, what-ever it's called. I'm sure you've already heard something about this?'

Enzo nodded, he had seen something mentioned in a news-paper months before but he hadn't taken it seriously at the time. He knew little about Ethiopia except that it was sup-posed to have some of the most fertile land in the region and that it was vast compared to Eritrea. Ten times bigger and more than three times the size of Italy itself. There was one other detail he remembered. It was almost the only African country left that hadn't been claimed by a European power.

'If the Ethiopians prove unwilling,' Bobbio continued, 'and they are being very tiresome at the moment actually, then we will bring an army through your port to convince them.'

Enzo shifted uncomfortably on the visitor's chair. 'You mean a war?'

Bobbio looked up at him finally. 'Just a little one, perhaps, if they don't see sense. And when that's over, then we will bring our people here, one million of them.'

Enzo smiled. 'You're joking?'

Bobbio raised an eyebrow. 'About what? A million, to begin with. Men, women, families, to create farms, cultivate the land, build roads and towns. In Eritrea too. All with the help of substantial investment from us, of course.'

Enzo felt a tingle of excitement. 'That's what I've been saying we need all along.'

Bobbio looked at him, apparently amused. He turned Enzo's desk nameplate slightly around.

'Well, Enzo, your wish has come true. Italy's poor will no longer have to sail cap in hand to New York and Chicago. They'll be coming here to our own colonies.' He stopped talking for a second to slap at a large fly that was biting his neck. 'Though why anyone would choose to move here is beyond me. It's not exactly civilisation, is it? Who did you cross to get exiled here?'

'I applied,' said Enzo stiffly. 'There is opportunity here for those willing to try.'

Bobbio gave him a patronising smile. 'Let's hope they are willing as you say. If I were you, Enzo, I might consider this an opportunity to get myself out of this backwater. You don't want to stay here for ever, I assume?'

'No, of course not,' Enzo replied, though he wasn't sure right now what he wanted.

Bobbio nodded. 'Indeed. Now before we begin, I must use your bathroom. Ship's food. I should have known better than to touch it.'

As the ministry man headed for the toilets, a sudden uncomfortable feeling came over Enzo. Will I be like him in ten years' time? And then a worse thought followed the first: am I already like him? He told himself he would not let that happen.

He sat down behind his desk, reclaiming his throne once again, but he couldn't stay easy for long. He stood up and paced around the room trying to conjure up an image of one million people and how busy his port would be with them.

In the main office, the bathroom door opened but instead of the ministry man, he saw Daniel walking out slowly. A look passed between the two of them and Enzo guessed that something had been said inside. Daniel went straight over to his own desk and Bobbio came out soon after.

'This way,' said Enzo and he led him outside to begin the tour of the port facilities.

From the corner of his eye, he saw Daniel staring coldly at Bobbio's back.

Aatifa made her way to Madihah's hut, bringing more of Enzo's books with her. Azzezza dutifully handed back the first encyclopedia before grabbing the new ones eagerly. She scanned them quickly. One was a large book of maps; the other, the Roman Empire book, had pictures of Caesar and galley ships and lions in the Coliseum. Aatifa could see that she had little interest in either of them.

'You don't like these?' she asked, disappointed.

'They taught us this at school,' Azzezza replied, 'to show us how great they were. But they lost that old empire, didn't they? And they don't dress nearly as well as they used to.'

Aatifa smiled at her clever granddaughter.

'What else has he got? Any music books?' Azzezza asked hopefully.

'I don't know. I will look. I am a library for you with legs, eh? He has a gramophone too with opera music. Would you like to hear it some time?'

'Oh, could I?' asked the girl, getting excited.

'Maybe, we'll see,' said Aatifa, wondering how she could get Azzezza in and out of the house unnoticed.

Madihah was cooking at the other end of the room, and she watched over her shoulder as Aatifa put her new week's wages on the table. There was a little extra included: half of the proceeds from the sale of her hut that morning to a young couple. Aatifa wasn't expecting gratitude but she couldn't resist looking at Madihah as she left, daring her to say something.

Aatifa was already striding halfway up the street when she heard footsteps running after her. She turned around, thinking something was wrong. Madihah suddenly seemed younger, reminding Aatifa of when she was a child.

'Mama . . . thank you,' she said.

Aatifa's frown changed into a smile. She took a step closer, touching Madihah's cheek tenderly and said softly, 'Little flower.'

Madihah held her hand with both of hers, pulling the palm tight to her face. Moments of closeness between them were a rare thing, and Aatifa cherished them. Not many people knew that Madihah was her daughter. They could easily be mistaken for sisters, though she thought Madihah was more beautiful than she had ever been. Like sisters, they rowed about everything, big and small, it didn't matter what. Aatifa blamed herself. She was difficult, prickly like a cactus, and she had passed this on to Madihah. Perhaps they were too similar ever to get along. She had not thought Iggi good enough for her child and she had said so, to him too. But then they had created Azzezza, the light of her life, and her baby, Madihah, was a mother now too. She let Madihah keep her hand held to her face for as long as she wanted. Who knew when they would do this again?

*

As Aatifa walked back through town, she saw people getting ready for the evening's festivities and realised that it was September 10th, New Year's Eve in the Orthodox calendar. She had forgotten about it completely, though that was not unusual. It was not in her nature to take part in such communal events but today Madihah had put her in an easy mood and she felt like doing something.

At the edge of the market she saw a middle-aged Tigre shepherd with several under-fed lambs for sale. He stood tall and straight, which made her think that he had been a warrior at one time in his life. Protruding from the top of his baggy trousers was an ornate wooden dagger handle in the shape of a large rounded X. He wore a pencil-thin moustache and his hairless chest was bare apart from a flimsy, tattered waistcoat. The top of his head was as wild as her own, except the ends of his hair had been braided from the height of his ears down and rested lightly on his shoulders. The shepherd saw her approaching but turned his head away and ignored her. She knew why, of course. She did not appear to be a person who would possess the price of a lamb. She continued on nevertheless until she was directly in front of him. Then she studied the smallest lamb in his collection, which was a beautiful snowy white. It reminded her of the bony neighbour's kitten, except this animal was destined to be food not a pet. The tiny creature would not have much meat on it to speak of but it would definitely be enough to feed two.

'How much for that one?' she asked, pointing at her choice.

She enjoyed the Tigre man's surprise. Yes, you were wrong to make assumptions about me. The man surveyed her slowly, trying to judge how much buying power she might have. You would be wise not to make any more assumptions, she thought, that would be a mistake. The shepherd turned away from her, and looked at the lamb, pretending that he did not really want to be parted from it. Then the battle began.

'That one is thirty,' he said sternly.

'Ha,' she laughed, 'do I look like a fool to you?'

'That is the price,' he replied, 'the only price.'

'Keep it then,' she said.

She turned abruptly and began to walk away.

'Twenty-five,' he blurted out after her, before she had gone ten paces.

She walked back to face him again and was pleased to see that he had no idea what to expect from her.

'Am I a child that you would rob me so easily?' she asked.

The shepherd was insulted now. 'I am not a robber of women or children,' he said angrily. 'Keep your money. I don't have need of it.'

'I intend to,' she said. 'I will go and look elsewhere for a fair-priced lamb.'

She turned again and had walked a little further this time before he spoke.

'Twenty.'

She stopped and turned to look at him but did not walk back.

'Ten,' she offered.

The Tigre man looked shocked and he wasn't pretending.

'That is not fair,' he said, shaking his head.

Now she walked slowly back to him.

'Then you tell me what is a fair price for that scrawny animal that wouldn't fill the belly of a baby.'

The shepherd looked panicked now. Aatifa felt a tinge of guilt for having roasted him on a spit but then he had allowed himself to be cooked and only had himself to blame.

'Fifteen?' he said, more in hope than with any confidence.

Aatifa shook her head. 'It is worth twelve.'

He would sell it to her now for that much if she pushed him but that would have been cruel.

'Thirteen?' he said, trying to salvage some pride.

She allowed her tough expression to slip away and gave him a benevolent smile. 'Agreed.'

The shepherd muttered unknown curses as he untied the lamb from the others. He watched her take out the money from inside her dress. She did her best to conceal the small bundle of notes with her hands as she counted out the exact amount, but he still saw that she had enough money to buy all three lambs twice over.

'Happy New Year to you and your family,' she said, as she led her tottering purchase away.

'And to you,' he said sullenly, before shouting after her, 'the meat will be tender, you'll see.'

Enzo's head was racing as he walked home. The streets were unusually busy but he was too distracted to figure out why. A million people, he kept thinking. One million. Where would they put them? They would need beds to sleep in, homes to live in, schools, hospitals, absolutely everything. Even to make the most basic provision would require a building programme on a scale that Africa had never seen. The cash investment would have to be enormous. Was Italy capable of seeing such a task through, given the state of the economy back home? Or had it all just been big talk? Grand plans thought up at a fancy dinner table in Rome that could never be realised.

Bobbio had departed earlier that evening and not a moment too soon. Everything Enzo had shown him had met with disapproval and a dismissive shake of his round balding head. He was not satisfied with anything and he kept repeating, 'This won't do at all. We'll have to make it bigger, much bigger.'

After he had said it the first ten times, Enzo had stopped getting annoyed. The office buildings, the warehouses, the dry dock, the cranes, all of them went down in Bobbio's little notebook with a black mark against each.

As the day's last train to Asmara prepared to leave the dock, Bobbio sat at the window of his first-class carriage, casting a final jaundiced eye over everything that Massawa had to offer to the Colonial Ministry. He had more of the same business to attend to up in Asmara and was flying from there back to Rome via Libya.

The whistle blew and the train jolted into life, a giant iron caterpillar shuffling away down its narrow track. Enzo waved him off but his visitor didn't notice, too busy inscribing more unflattering notes in his little book of insults. For a moment, Enzo wished that the train would choose this as the day on which to slip its rails and plunge mercilessly down the mountainside in a mess of smashed wood and twisted steel.

'Is he coming back?' said Daniel, appearing beside him at the track's end.

Enzo wondered what had happened between him and Bobbio in the office toilets, but decided not to ask.

'Not this time,' said Enzo. 'He may in the future, perhaps.' Bobbio's return to Eritrea was dependent on those grand plans he had talked about becoming real.

Daniel nodded glumly.

When Enzo arrived home, he looked for Aatifa in the living room and the kitchen but she wasn't there. He called her name up the stairs from the hall but still there was no answer. As he returned to the kitchen, he noticed that the door to the back yard was open.

Outside, Aatifa was bending over a lamb with his largest and widest kitchen knife poised behind her back. The tiny creature was tied up to an old withered lemon tree. He heard her whisper something in the lamb's ear as she covered its eyes with one hand and moved the knife steadily towards its throat with the other.

'Stop!' he shouted.

Aatifa relaxed her arm, breathed out and turned to look at him.

'What on earth do you think you're doing?' he said.

'I'm getting dinner. It's New Year,' she said.

'Dinner? I forbid you to kill that animal!' The words felt uncomfortable coming out of his mouth and he realised that this was the first time he had ever given her a direct order.

Aatifa looked confused and offered him the knife. 'You want to do it?'

'I most certainly do not.'

They stared at each other in a stand-off and he could tell that she was annoyed. The four-legged meal then licked her hand. Aatifa rubbed under its chin and said softly, 'Aren't you the lucky one?'

The reprieved animal gave a 'maaaa', then gambolled off around the yard, managing to knock over Enzo's cobweb-covered bicycle with its tether. Aatifa walked back towards the kitchen and he could hear her cursing under her breath.

'What?'

'There's nothing else to eat,' she said sharply.

'Fine,' he said firmly. 'We'll just have to eat out.'

*

The sun had gone now in the west. Only a small patch of sky still glowed faintly as they walked side by side into the old town, without speaking or touching. Bats raced in circles over their heads in search of moths; the swallows had all gone home to their nests. Around them Massawa's residents were gathering for the festivities. This was a traditional Christian festival but the city's majority Muslim population was out in force to enjoy it too.

Enzo scanned the faces in the crowd. He was the only Italian among them but no one made him feel out of place. Everywhere, adults chattered in the local languages while children played noisily around them. There were musicians too, performing on home-made wooden instruments that looked like the African cousins of guitars and violins. The atmosphere was invigorating but most of all he was enjoying the new sensation of being out with her. If there was an official dress code, neither he nor Aatifa would have passed. Almost everyone else was dressed in the same colour: the women in white robes and headscarves and the men in long white tunics with matching baggy trousers or sarong underneath. At least they had rebelled together, he thought.

He smiled as Aatifa gently touched the head of a little girl walking past, dressed in her finest clothes. She said some compliment in Tigrinya and the girl blushed.

'You want to eat now?' she asked.

Enzo looked around at the hot food stalls. 'All right,' he said warily. 'I've never had any of these things. What would you suggest?'

'Never?' she said. 'But how long have you been living here?'

'Five years,' he admitted, 'just five.'

'What have you been eating all this time?' she asked, bewildered. 'Only your food!'

'Yes – but our food is the finest in the world,' he insisted.

She shook her head and led the way to a stall. The cook, a chubby old Eritrean woman, put out two large flat pieces of bread, like thick crepes. And in the middle of each of these, she placed a steaming pile of brown, nondescript lumpy sauce. Aatifa reached inside her dress and pulled out some cash to pay her.

'No, I'll get this,' Enzo said, as he reached for his wallet in his jacket pocket.

'This is your money,' she said.

'Is it? Oh,' he said. 'Well, let me anyway. I want to.'

She shrugged and put away the money and Enzo paid the cook from his leather wallet. He could see that his gesture made no sense to Aatifa but it made him happy to do it.

Enzo watched closely as she began to eat the food with her fingers. She pulled off a piece of the bread from the outside and used this as a spoon to scoop up some of the sauce from the centre. He copied her, looking at it for a moment, before finally putting it in his mouth. Halfway through chewing he felt his tongue going numb and the roof of his mouth catch fire. He began to cough uncontrollably and Aatifa laughed. She poured him a glass of water and he guzzled it down.

'You don't like it?' she asked.

'You might have warned me,' he replied, as sensation gradually returned to his tongue. 'What's in it?'

'Lots of spices . . . and lamb,' she said with a wry smile.

Enzo mustered the courage to try another mouthful. It was easier this time as the initial shock had anaesthetised his taste buds, but the experience just confirmed what he already knew. Italian was best and he would not be altering his eating habits even for her.

'What am I to do with it?' she asked loudly, over the music.

'We could leave it in the garden? It will keep the grass low,' he suggested.

'It will grow into a sheep,' she said, shaking her head.

'Oh yes,' he said, feeling foolish. 'Sell it then, or give it away? Do you know someone who would take it?'

Aatifa nodded. 'Yes, I know someone.'

Enzo stopped eating altogether now and looked around at the passers-by.

'You want to see more?' she asked.

'Sure, why not,' he said and so she finished and they walked on.

Nearby, a dance was taking place. Two Eritrean men holding large drums made from wood and animal hide stood in the middle of several concentric circles of women. The drummers were pounding out a rhythm that alternated between a heavy bass sound on the widest, top part and a lower, lighter sound from the bottom, narrower end. Smiling women, all dressed in white robes and headscarves, danced, sang and ululated in rings around them. Some of the women held up small Orthodox crosses which were ornate and intricate at the top three points, resembling plants in bloom.

'It's not like my catechism class when I was a boy,' Enzo joked.

'You are in Africa,' Aatifa said. 'Why would it be the same?'

An old woman broke from the outer circle and grabbed Aatifa with both hands, pulling her into the moving line. Aatifa protested but the woman pushed her along and soon she was dancing and clapping with the others. Enzo waved as she completed her first full circle and as she danced away again, he thought how alive she looked.

As he watched her, he became aware of three young men

staring at him coldly from the other side of the dancers. They looked different in some way that he could not quite put his finger on. For the first time that night, he felt unwelcome. He turned away and focused instead on Aatifa who was coming around to pass him once more.

When the dance was over and the drums fell silent, everyone clapped and cheered. Aatifa joined him again and he saw that she was out of breath and sweaty for once, like he was every day, except it seemed attractive on her.

'You dance well,' he said.

'I don't think that's true,' she said, laughing. 'Let's go quickly before she catches me again.'

'Do you know those men over there?' Enzo asked, nodding towards the three men whose eyes had never left him.

'They are from Ethiopia,' she said, after one glance.

Enzo looked warily back at the trio. They continued to stare but, to his relief, they did not follow.

Aatifa waited until they were a little further on before she asked, 'Is it true what they say, that Italy wants their country too?'

'Where did you hear that?' he asked.

'It is what they are gossiping about in the market,' she replied. 'So is it true?'

For a moment he wondered if he should keep his conversation with Bobbio a secret but there didn't seem much point to that now. 'There is some talk about developing it, like we did here,' he said vaguely.

'For them or for you?' she asked sharply.

'Both, of course,' he said, surprised.

'Of course!' she said, mocking his words. 'You are very generous.'

She walked on ahead of him and he had to quicken his pace

to keep up with her. They continued on like this, side by side and in silence until some little boys came dashing around a corner carrying blazing torches on wooden sticks. On seeing Enzo, one of them stopped and placed his torch flat on the ground, right in front of him. He froze and Aatifa turned and smiled at his confusion.

'You must step over it three times and then give him a coin,' she said.

'Really?' he said doubtfully.

'Yes,' she said, 'then you will be blessed.'

Enzo stepped high over the torch three times, in awkward arched movements, being careful not to let his trouser legs catch fire.

'All right?' he asked, when the task was complete. The boy nodded, picked up his still burning torch again and stood waiting.

Enzo rooted in his pocket and gave a coin each to the boy and his friends. They immediately bolted off like flaming comets, in search of their next customer.

'Will I be lucky now?' he asked Aatifa.

'Are you not already?' she said before turning again and walking on ahead of him.

Enzo did not invite Aatifa into his room that night as he was tired. But it was sobering to realise that she certainly would not visit him on her own account. He lay awake for a while wondering what she had meant about him being lucky already. How was he lucky? To be born a European gave him a greater chance in life than she had, that was true. To be white was also a distinct advantage. To be a man too. He had a good job, and a steady income, though he had got these through hard work and discipline. He had his health; being alive at all was lucky to be sure. Had she meant any of these? Or had she meant that he was lucky to have her?

He had only just fallen asleep when he was woken by a sandstorm that had whipped up from outside the city. An angry gale-force wind assaulted the house with layer after layer of fine-grained sand. He jumped up to close his shutters before the whole room was covered in it and he heard Aatifa doing the same down the corridor. The yellow tempest raged for an hour before it blew itself out and calm was restored.

Up above them, on the mountain, Salvatore sat alone in his favourite Asmara bar. The owner's daughter brought his second beer, anaesthetic preparation for a late dinner with some high-profile guests. Then she took his overflowing glass ashtray and replaced it with a clean one. He winked at her, bringing a slight blush to her cheeks. At nineteen, she was too young for him but that wasn't the reason he left her alone. He didn't want to have to find somewhere else to drink. Checking his watch, he downed the beer in one go and left.

Main Street was practically deserted as he made his way to Cadoni's candlelit trattoria. Salvatore hated these tedious fact-finding missions from Rome, apart from the free meal that came with them. He'd never met one of his dinner companions, a civil servant called Bobbio. The other was Major Antonio Dore, a Fascist officer seconded to the Colonial Ministry. The young major had arrived in Asmara two weeks before, and he had already had the dubious pleasure. Dore smelled of ambition, quickly working into their conversation that he was related to the House of Savoy. Salvatore suspected that King Vittorio Emanuele III was probably not even aware of his distant cousin's existence.

Fascism and Mussolini had the royal stamp of approval, so

entering into the Fascist ranks had been an obvious choice for Dore. The major had confessed to using every influence he had to get this attachment to Eritrea. Colonialism and expansion were the new fashionable topics in Rome and Milan, he said. He was in no doubt that his reputation would be made here. Salvatore had smiled at that one. No one came to Eritrea to get noticed.

He entered the dimly lit restaurant and spotted the major at a table. Bobbio looked up from his antipasto as he heard the door closing behind him.

'Gentlemen,' said Salvatore with a smile. 'I see you've started without me.'

'That's because you are late, Colonel,' replied Bobbio, without a hint of humour.

The hierarchy among this eclectic group was unclear but Salvatore could see that Bobbio obviously considered himself to be the top dog. As he would have to endure these two men's company for several hours he laughed off the comment and for the rest of the evening did his best to feign interest. The topic for discussion was the ministry's grand plan for East Africa and how the mandarins in Rome thought it might best be achieved.

After an hour of this, Salvatore excused himself to go to the bathroom and stepped outside, past the kitchen, to enjoy a cigarette. When he returned he saw that Judge Muroni and his young Eritrean girlfriend had arrived. The judge's back was to him and Salvatore walked over to his own table without saying hello.

'The usual for me, Luigi,' said the judge.

'Of course, sir, right away,' said the owner and he turned to the young woman, 'and you, signorina?'

'The same for me,' the woman said, as she did every time the judge brought her here.

'Very good,' said the owner, nodding politely.

Dore and Bobbio had both turned to see the newcomers. Bobbio frowned and turned away again.

'I find the level of chaos here,' he said, pausing for the most appropriate word, '. . . disturbing.'

Chapter 8

Aᴛɪғᴀ ᴡᴀs sᴡᴇᴇᴘɪɴɢ the storm's thick residue off the front porch as Enzo came downstairs. And people were doing the same tedious chore all the way to work.

His chair had never felt the same since Bobbio had sat in it and Enzo was just wondering if there might be a spare when he heard the squeak of small metal wheels running along the cement quay outside. Getting up to investigate, he saw a small business van parked below his window that belonged to a retailer of Italian women's fashion in town. His own dock workers were helping the driver to load up a consignment of dresses that must have arrived on the ship the previous day. Enzo watched the rails gliding past with their billowing cargo. Then he went down and approached the driver for a private word.

At the end of the day, he walked home with a small bundle under his arm, covered in brown paper and tied with a piece of string. He would have preferred a more elegant wrapping but this was all there was to hand in his office.

Enzo hoped she would be pleased with his present. He had not failed to notice that she regularly repaired her own well-worn clothes. This would be something special for her, something that she would never have been able to afford herself. He recognised that this was a further step away from normal employer/employee boundaries but they had already trampled all over those.

As he neared the house, he saw Aatifa standing at the garden gate, engaged in what looked like a heated argument. The other party was a grey-haired Eritrean man, dressed in dirty, calf-length trousers and a half-open, loose-fitting shirt. The awkward way in which he held himself suggested that he was no longer in the best of health. Enzo instinctively began to walk faster towards them. The old man turned and saw him coming, then said something abruptly to Aatifa before hobbling away in the opposite direction.

'Who was that?' asked Enzo as he reached the gate, but Aatifa was already walking back towards the house.

'My father,' she said, without stopping.

The word came as a shock to Enzo. He had never considered that Aatifa would have relations. How stupid of me, he thought, of course she does.

'He seemed angry about something. What did he want?'

Aatifa looked to make sure her father had kept on going. 'Money,' she said. 'He will get nothing from me.'

She went back inside and headed straight up the stairs. Enzo followed and found her busily tidying her bedroom. But she could not hide the fact that she was on edge. On the far wall, he noticed that she had taken down one of his seascape paintings and replaced it with a simple, brightly coloured portrait of an Eritrean girl.

'Is everything all right?' he asked.

'Yes,' she said curtly.

'Anything you want to talk about? You know you can.'

She shook her head and he could see that she had no intention of discussing this matter with him.

'I got you this,' he said, holding out the brown paper package.

She stopped what she was doing and looked at the bundle with a mixture of apprehension and suspicion.

'Take it, it's for you' he said gently.

When she didn't move, he walked over to her and placed it in her hands. Then he stepped back to the doorway and waited confidently. She slipped off the string, and the brown paper parted to reveal one of the newly arrived European dresses. She looked down at his gift with a heavy frown. This was not at all the reaction he had anticipated.

'Try it on,' he urged.

Aatifa kicked off her sandals and stepped out of her own dress which seemed coarse and simple in comparison to the one he had chosen for her. He had guessed her size, which was no easy task for his untrained eye. The dress was an ankle-length, figure-hugging gown in silver silk, off the shoulder and backless down to the waist. She looked stunning in it. She still did not look happy, however, so he took her hand and brought her in front of the full-length mirror in his bedroom.

'Look, you are beautiful,' he said, stating the obvious. 'You see?'

But she was not looking in the mirror; she was staring down at the dress and touching it warily.

'What's wrong?' he asked.

She looked up finally at his reflection in the mirror. 'I am never going to be an Italian woman.'

'I know that,' he said. Nor would he have ever asked her to try. 'But it's French, from Paris.'

The difference, such as it was, didn't seem to matter to her and he guessed that Italian, French or English were probably all as one to her.

'Would you like me to take it back?' he asked, trying to hide his disappointment.

'No,' she said, 'but you didn't need to get me anything.'

'I wanted to,' he said.

He sat down on the edge of the bed, watching her as she touched the material more confidently now, studying her reflection in the mirror.

'I was thinking we could go to see my friend in Asmara, if you'd like?' he said. 'We could stay up there for a night.'

'Asmara?' she said, obviously interested.

'Yes. You've been there before, I'm sure?' he asked.

'Only once, a long time ago,' she replied.

Enzo was pleased that he could give her this too. 'Well, that's settled then.'

As the black engine of the Massawa–Asmara train ploughed its way across the plain below the mountain, the passengers in the carriages behind were being slowly roasted. The temperature on this part of the journey was always the hottest, hitting a crazy fifty degrees in mid-afternoon. Some people had already closed their windows in an attempt to keep out the heat. Enzo could feel prickly rashes breaking out on his back, but Aatifa did not seem to be affected at all. This was her first time on a train and she was enjoying it, standing up with her head hanging out of their open window, her hair being blown about by the hot slipstream.

'Look, over there,' said Enzo, pointing at some oryx grazing nearby, their black and white heads bowed to what little grass there was. In unison, the animals raised their distinctive, long horns into the air when they heard the locomotive passing.

'Aren't they beautiful?' she said. 'I love them.'

Enzo stood up beside her and put his arm around her waist.

He felt her looking at him and then down at his arm but she did not pull away.

The other passengers around them were a mix of Italians and a few Eritreans. Some were sleeping, while others were reading the *Eritrean Daily News* or using it to fan themselves. No one paid much attention to them. Mixed race couples were not an unusual sight any more.

The train began to slow down and Aatifa looked worried.

'It's only the mountain,' he explained, retaking his seat. 'We have to go up now.'

She continued to stare wide-eyed out of the window, taking in every bridge and curve while he closed his eyes on the more precarious bends. After half an hour, he began to nod off, his head resting back against the wooden seat. When he woke they were already near the summit. A dozen red-faced baboons were running alongside them, hoping for scraps of food.

'We'll be there in a few minutes,' he said drowsily.

Aatifa nodded and then got up and went to the water closet. A breeze flooded the carriage with hazy steam and when it cleared, Enzo was pleased to see her returning wearing the French dress. All eyes were upon her as she made her way back down the aisle and she flushed with embarrassment. Enzo held out his hand for her as she retook her seat, her battered sandals now visible under the hem. He wanted to say 'thank you' but he hoped she hadn't done it just for him.

From the station they headed directly for the Cinema Impero where Salvatore had arranged to meet them. Their progress was slower than it might have been as Aatifa spent the whole time looking sideways and backward at everything, almost walking into a lamppost.

'None of this was built the last time I was here,' she said. 'It hardly even had streets then.'

'You see that one?' said Enzo. 'It's like a radio.'

She looked at the large building, which was exactly the same shape as the wireless in his house, with circular windows on the front to imitate tuning dials.

'Can you guess what that one is?' he said when they passed another.

Aatifa shook her head.

'It's an F on its side, see . . . like in Aatifa but that one is for Fascism.'

'What is that?' she asked. 'I've heard people mention it.'

'It's . . . ah . . . Fascism is . . .' and then he frowned. It was supposed to be the guide to modern Italian life but he had never really understood it. 'It's hard to explain exactly. It's an idea, to make everything better.'

Aatifa stared back at the building with suspicion.

'Are you cold?' he asked, looking at her bare shoulders.

'No,' she said, 'the air is nice.'

Walking past a patch of open ground between two buildings, they came across a busy photographic unit. Two young Eritrean women in traditional dress but naked above the waist were posing for the all-male Italian team. One of the women sat astride an army motorbike with an infantry rifle hanging over her shoulder. The other stood beside her, with an Askari soldier's fez perched on her head and also carrying a rifle. One of the crew handed the standing woman a large sign to hold which read: 'Come to Africa for Italy and the Empire'.

The two women put on false smiles as the photographer snapped away, though their mouths were only in unison for one in every three shots.

'What's this for?' Enzo asked. The photographer turned and took a quick snap of him and Aatifa.

'A magazine,' he replied. 'Photo spread on our colonies.'

'Could I get a copy of that one of us?' Enzo asked. 'You're not going to print that, I hope,' and he wrote out his address for the man.

Behind him, he heard Aatifa muttering something to the two women in Tigrinya. The pair immediately took a step towards her and began to fire back a string of their own insults. One of them pointed a finger at Aatifa and she looked down at her dress.

'We're trying to work here,' the photographer said to Enzo.

As he led Aatifa away, she sank into a deep silence and Enzo began to worry that this pleasant evening was not going to turn out as he had planned.

When they arrived at the cinema, Salvatore and Zula were already waiting outside. Instead of his usual army uniform, Salvatore was dressed in a light blue linen suit that Enzo had not seen before. Zula was wearing a mid-green pencil dress and appeared affronted that Aatifa had outdone her. Aatifa did not catch this as she was staring up at the cinema's art deco façade which was studded with rows of large lightbulbs. These were bookmarked on either side by the words CINEMA and IMPERO in large vertical letters that stretched the whole height of the building.

'You must be Aatifa,' said Salvatore, without waiting for Enzo to make introductions.

He shook her hand energetically and Zula gave her a kiss on the cheek, which made Aatifa recoil slightly.

'I'm Zula, I've been dying to meet you,' she gushed.

Aatifa nodded and looked to Enzo to rescue her from this assault of friendliness. The way she was looking at Zula made him nervous. It was exactly the way she had looked at the two models only a few moments earlier.

'Right, let's go,' said Salvatore, letting the two women go in first. To Enzo's relief, Aatifa allowed Zula to link arms with her.

'You chose wisely, my young apprentice,' said Salvatore, winking at him as he paid for the tickets.

'You too,' said Enzo, 'she must be a record for you. How long is it now?'

'Oh, it just hasn't become boring yet, that's all.'

The four of them made their way into the plush interior and an Eritrean usher helped them to find seats together. The audience was a mixture of locals and Italians with everyone sitting where they pleased. While the cinema was Italian-built, the designers had taken Africa as their theme with reliefs of antelopes, palm trees and dancers on the walls. Aatifa turned around as she heard the projector bulb spark into life somewhere behind them and then the auditorium went dark.

First up was an Istituto Luce newsreel in which a man's jaunty voice accompanied images of some recent world events.

'American Amelia Earhart becomes the first woman to fly solo across the Pacific,' the voice announced, in tandem with footage of short-haired Amelia waving from the cockpit of a single-propeller aeroplane. The Italian women in the audience all applauded this and the men nodded to show that they were impressed too.

'In Germany, the new air force, the Luftwaffe, is formed.' German men were shown hard at work in factories, churning out new aircraft. 'Also in Germany, what they are calling "the people's car" is launched, the Volkswagen Beetle.' At the sight of the little insect-shaped car, everyone in the audience burst out laughing.

Next came a short reel from the Colonial Ministry on

Ethiopia. A woman with a small blade was shown cutting parallel vertical lines on the face of a screaming child. There was no live sound to go with the images, but everyone in the audience turned away. Zula winced. Aatifa looked around at the shocked faces. This scene was followed by images of Ethiopians disfigured by illness, probably leprosy. And lastly Mussolini appeared on screen, addressing a large crowd in Rome. Some Italians in the audience applauded when the Duce came on but Enzo didn't and Salvatore's clapping was half-hearted at best. The newsreel voice then talked about Mussolini's desire to add Ethiopia to the growing Italian empire.

'If he wants it so much then let him go and take it,' Salvatore said drily. Then he looked at the people in the row behind him, daring someone to comment, but no one did.

Enzo stared at the screen, realising that he had not seen the last of Bobbio. If they were announcing this in public cinemas then the 'little war', as he had called it, was probably going to happen. He looked at Aatifa beside him and saw that she was riveted by the whole experience.

The final part of the newsreel was on sport and received the biggest applause of all. 'American baseball legend Babe Ruth hits the 714th and final home run of his career before sadly announcing his retirement from the game.'

The house lights came on for a brief moment and Enzo touched Aatifa's hand. She turned and he smiled at her but if she smiled back, it was lost in the darkness as the lights faded down again. The auditorium was pitch black for a few seconds except for the flaming tips of many cigarettes. Then the screen sprang to life once more as the main feature of the night began, an Italian comedy called *I Love Only You*. Enzo and the Italian crowd were soon enjoying it and laughing along. It was a costume romance involving a case of mistaken identity, with endless obstacles being placed in the way of two young lovers. Aatifa did not take her eyes off the screen once, studying the antics of the film's female star, Milly, with interest. During a scene when one of the Italian characters was roughly arrested by soldiers, all the Eritreans laughed and cheered as one. It was an odd outburst as it was not supposed to have been funny. Enzo looked around him and saw the Italians in the audience shifting uneasily. But the moment was soon forgotten as the movie continued towards its inevitably happy conclusion.

'Alcohol time?' said Salvatore, as the smiling crowd filed its way back out on to the pavement.

'Aatifa,' called Zula from outside a shop window. 'Come and look at these shoes!'

Aatifa looked at Enzo first and then went slowly over, without pretending to be interested in any of the footwear for sale.

'I want those ones there, the red ones. Aren't they divine?' said Zula, pointing at a blocky pair of red heels.

Enzo and Salvatore strolled on at a leisurely pace.

'You think there really will be a war?' asked Enzo.

'The Duce gets what the Duce wants, doesn't he?' said Salvatore.

'But if the Ethiopians saw what we've done here in Eritrea . . .'

'They'd welcome us with open arms?' said Salvatore, finishing his sentence for him.

'We can help them, surely it makes sense,' replied Enzo.

'To you it does. Alas, the noble savage does not always know what's good for him.'

Enzo glanced behind them. He was glad that the women were only catching up now and that Aatifa hadn't heard what his friend had said.

*

In a dark, moody corner of the bar, Salvatore got drunk quickly as usual. Enzo hardly touched his wine, having resolved to stay sober given that he had his own date for once. The band for the night was a ballroom quartet, made up of elderly Eritrean men on clarinet, trumpet, piano and drums, playing old-style, easy-listening melodies.

'Would you like to dance?' Enzo asked Aatifa.

She accepted reluctantly and he led her out on to the dance floor where they both attempted to waltz. It was her first time and Enzo was no Fred Astaire but they did their best. As they moved around the floor in badly drawn circles, he tried to remember the steps he had learned for his school graduation ball. That was more than twenty years ago now and he was finding that dancing was not the same as riding a bicycle. You didn't just pick it up where you had left off. Eventually, they got themselves into an acceptable one, two, three routine and he relaxed and stopped looking down at his feet.

'I'm glad you're here,' he said, but she didn't reply.

Later on, Enzo found himself alone with Salvatore. They had swapped seats somewhere along the way and he noticed Salvatore's blue linen jacket draped over the back of his chair.

'That's a nice cut,' Enzo said. 'Where did you get it?'

'That? I had it made here in Asmara.'

'An Italian?' asked Enzo, his suspicions aroused.

'Yes, but it's OK, he's good, he's Calabrian. Had to leave his home town in a hurry. He says if he'd stayed there he'd be dead already. Everyone is using him.'

'I really need new suits,' said Enzo.

'Well, he's your man,' assured Salvatore and he wrote down the address on the back of one of the cinema tickets. 'You'd better use him quick though, before someone tracks him down here. And they will, you know, the world is a very small place now.'

Enzo looked around wondering where his date had got to.

'You want to look good for her, is that it?' asked Salvatore.

'I like her,' he admitted.

'And so you should. Let me tell you something, you'd never be able to land a woman like that back home.'

'Thanks a lot! With friends like you . . .'

'It was a joke, Enzo, lighten up, would you?' Salvatore looked at him for a moment. 'So you're happy?'

Enzo paused for a long time, longer than a happy person should take to answer. 'I am,' he said finally, 'it's just . . .'

Salvatore sighed and lit a cigarette.

'Sometimes, she makes me feel, I don't know . . . dirty.'

'What did she say to you?' asked Salvatore, laughing.

'Nothing, that's the point: I never know what she feels about me . . . or us.'

'Great!' said Salvatore. 'If she was Italian she'd be telling you what's in her head every five minutes. Is that what you want? Yak, yak, yak, till you can't take it any more.'

Enzo shook his head.

'Look, don't get too close, OK? These women are just for a bit of fun. They're not real girlfriends. You understand? It's not like you can bring her home to meet your mother.'

Enzo nodded. He knew this. 'My mother would have a heart attack.'

'Exactly. You want to kill your little old Mama?'

'No,' said Enzo, smiling at last.

'Just enjoy it and don't think so much. Fun,' said Salvatore slowly, emphasising the word for effect.

'Yes, fun,' agreed Enzo gravely, as if he had just told his

confession and this was his penance. He looked around the room, missing her.

Aatifa had been in the Ladies for fifteen minutes, taking a welcome break from the noise. It had been a mistake for her to come. She had no wish to be a part of this world, but she would stay and go through it for him. This was not because she felt she owed him but because she could see that the evening had some meaning for him.

'There you are,' said Zula, arriving beside her at the bathroom mirror.

They had both known immediately that they were completely different, and not just in age. Aatifa was from a poor rural background and Zula had spent her entire short twenty-something life in the Italianate capital. To Aatifa, Zula was a product of the colonisation and if either of them should be pitied, it was her.

'Enzo's nice, isn't he, bit of a softie,' Zula said, as she began to fix her bright red lipstick.

Aatifa only nodded and Zula looked up at her in the mirror. Their eyes didn't meet but Aatifa could sense her staring at her hair. Then Zula turned and reached out her hand to touch it.

'You know, I could help you do something with . . .'

Before her fingers even got close to making contact, Aatifa's hand shot out and grabbed Zula's wrist firmly. She held it tight and rigid in the air between them.

'Ow! You're hurting me,' Zula protested.

Aatifa released her arm, but their fake friendship was now at an end. Zula quickly packed her make-up into her handbag and left. Aatifa did not want to face the bar again, but when two Italian women came in she braced herself and went back out.

'All right?' asked Enzo, pleased to see her.

'Yes,' she lied.

Finally, to Aatifa's relief, the bar began to close and it was time for them to leave. Outside, Salvatore shook her hand and placed his other hand on top as well.

'It was lovely to meet you, Aatifa. Look after this guy. He's delicate, like an orchid.'

Enzo kissed Zula's cheek and then the two men stood back to allow the women to say their own farewells. For a moment it seemed they would have to stand there all night until Salvatore looked questioningly at Zula. She moved forward reluctantly and gave Aatifa the briefest of hugs.

When they were alone, Aatifa shivered, so Enzo took off his jacket and put it around her bare shoulders. Then he held her hand as they walked the hundred yards to their hotel.

The hotel lobby was another art deco creation, with yellow painted wood and silver metal surfaces, warmly glowing in subdued lamplight. The uniformed, middle-aged Eritrean concierge looked up from a newspaper when he saw them coming towards his desk and stood immediately to attention.

'Signor Secchi?' he enquired politely.

'That's right,' said Enzo.

'You're very welcome, sir. Could you fill this out please?'

The concierge turned the large registration book around and handed him a fountain pen with the hotel's logo on it. Enzo signed his own name quickly with a flourish of his wrist and then he paused, frowning at the page.

'Is there a problem?' asked the concierge.

'No,' said Enzo.

The register had two spaces to be filled in for all the guests in each room and over his shoulder, Aatifa could see that he had written down his own name but not hers. He looked at her now, out of the corner of his eye, in some embarrassment. Then he wrote *Signora Aatifa Secchi* and she realised that he did not know her full name. He put the pen down on the desk and the concierge read the names but made no remark.

'How long will you be staying?' he asked, as he handed Enzo the key.

'Just the one night,' said Enzo.

'Very good, sir,' said the concierge, ringing the bell for the luggage boy.

As Enzo bent to pick up his bag, the concierge turned his head slightly towards Aatifa. He stared at her figure-hugging gown and at Enzo's jacket draped over her shoulders. Then he looked down his nose at her, seeing in her what he wanted to see. His expression made Aatifa angry. And she resolved that if she ever met him again, he would not look at her that way without getting a stinging response from her in return.

'Goodnight,' said the concierge, all smiles once more now that Enzo had retrieved his bag from the floor.

'Goodnight,' said Enzo.

There is a lot to be said for anonymity, Aatifa thought, as they walked up the stairs followed by the bell boy; wearing this dress had made her stand out and she did not like to do that. Worse still, it had left her exposed to the assumptions of others, and she disliked that more than anything.

'I'd like to make a stop tomorrow, before we go,' Enzo said, hanging up his smoke-saturated jacket in the wardrobe of their hotel room. 'Salvatore recommended a good tailor, believe it or not.'

Aatifa stood at the open, double windows, looking out at the wide, palm-tree-lined main street. She had heard people describe how much Asmara had changed, but the scale of the transformation was still a shock. The Italians had made it happen, she knew, but Eritrean workers were the ones who had built it.

'Is this what your home is like?' she asked a moment later.

'Yes, I suppose; although everything is newer here. Would you like to go with me to Genoa some time?' he asked. 'Maybe we could . . . one day.'

She heard the hesitation in his voice.

'There is no need,' she replied without turning, 'if you have made Eritrea look the same.'

He walked over to her and began to massage her exposed shoulders, his fingers quickly soothing her tight muscles.

'Don't you like it?' he asked.

'It's beautiful,' she said.

'We only have one room,' he whispered as he bent and gently kissed her neck, 'so you'll have to sleep with me the whole night, I'm afraid.'

She slowly turned around into him and for the first time since they had met, they kissed because they both wanted to. They undressed each other as they moved over on to the double bed, and quickly Aatifa's pent-up tension gave way to desire. When he moved on top of her on the bed, she pushed his shoulders gently. For a second he thought she was pushing him away until he realised that she was pushing him down. So he moved down between her legs. She felt his tongue searching and she immediately began to enjoy it. He kept going until she got what she wanted, which was a lot quicker than she expected.

Enzo sat up with a look of achievement but she turned and faced the opposite way, suddenly uneasy with how comfortable it was all becoming with him. He had treated her well, all things considered, and life with him could definitely have been a lot worse. But it should not be this way between us, she thought.

Enzo lay down beside her and ran his fingers gently along the delicate contours of her back as if they were rivers on a map.

'You know I never thought I would end up with someone like you,' he said.

She turned slightly, wondering what he had meant.

'Did you, I mean with someone like me?' he asked, as he rested his head on his raised hand so that he could see the side of her face.

Aatifa smiled at the question. 'When I was young, I thought that some day a man with at least fifty goats would want me to be his wife.'

'I don't have any goats,' Enzo said, looking worried.

'I know,' she replied.

He stared at her for a moment.

'Are you happy?'

'Some people were not meant to be,' she answered.

'What do you mean?' he asked. 'Everyone deserves that . . . I'd like you to be.'

It surprised her that he seemed to care about her feelings. No one else did. Even she had stopped a long time ago. Their conversation drifted into silence and they fell asleep in that position, facing in the same direction.

Chapter 9

THE NEXT MORNING, in refreshing balmy weather, they paid a visit to the Calabrian tailor on their way to the train station. He was a short-legged man, plump around the middle and seemed a gentle, inoffensive sort. Enzo couldn't imagine what he had done to land himself on a vendetta list. Aatifa sat patiently among the piles of folded cloth while he was measured, and a jacket and trousers were adjusted to size with pins. He ordered two new suits. If he liked them, he would come back to buy more.

When they reached the house, the first thing Aatifa did was to rewrap the French dress in the brown paper it had arrived in. Then she put it under her other clothes in the bottom drawer of her wardrobe. Behind her, Enzo came into the room carrying the wages ledger. He hovered awkwardly in the doorway as he always did when he had something to say.

'I want to stop paying you,' he said firmly.

'You're firing me?' she asked, shocked.

'No!' he said. 'I'm just not comfortable that you are my employee. I don't want you to feel like a servant. I know I hired you as a housekeeper but that was before—'

'I need that money. I give it to my family,' interrupted Aatifa.

Enzo wondered who she was talking about. She had already said that she would never give money to her father. A mother, perhaps, or some sisters?

'I can still give you money, more even. Just not as wages,' he said.

'You don't want me to cook and clean any more?' she asked.

'Only as a wife might; not a housemaid. There's a difference, isn't there?'

'I am not your wife,' she said coldly.

'I know that,' he replied, wondering how this conversation had gone so badly.

'I do good work. Are you displeased?' she asked.

'No, of course not.'

'Then I will do the same as before. And you will give me the same amount each week?'

Enzo sighed. 'I will.'

He took out some notes and offered them to her. She took them and then added another of her signatures to the growing list in the ledger.

At bedtime, Enzo decided to try a different approach. While she was getting the house ready for the morning, he went upstairs and closed his bedroom door. Then, leaving all the lights on, he sat in the bed and waited. When Aatifa arrived on the landing, he heard her outside and watched her lingering shadow under the door. She hesitated for a moment before Enzo saw her shadow growing larger. The handle began to turn, so he quickly picked up a book from his nightstand, pretending to read it. He didn't look up as she stood still in the open doorway. She stalled there, unsure what to do next.

'Will I come in?' she asked finally.

'As you wish,' he said, trying to sound casual.

She deliberated for a few seconds, then closed the door behind her and began to undress. When she had her back turned, he allowed himself a little smile. She got into bed beside him, and he started actually to read the book, Dante Alighieri's *Divine Comedy*. He had never once managed to get past the opening Inferno section and on to Purgatory and then Paradise after that. He knew that he probably wouldn't this time either and was likely to remain in hell for ever. When he heard the regular breathing of the sleeping woman beside him, he put down the book quietly and turned out his lamp.

Much later, around three in the morning, he woke and was pleased to see that she was still there beside him. He listened briefly to the high-pitched buzz of mosquitoes hovering outside the net and then went back to sleep.

Aatifa heard the squeaking gate, followed by the light thud of the post hitting the doormat so she picked it up and took it to Enzo in the kitchen. He opened the largest letter first and it turned out to be a black and white print of the two of them that the photographer had taken in Asmara.

'That was quick,' said Enzo, smiling, and turning it around for her. But he saw that it was not an evening that she wished to be reminded of.

He immediately recognised the handwriting on the second letter as his sister Maria's. Its contents did not make for happy reading. Almost knocking over his coffee, he stood up quickly to check the date on a pasta maker's calendar on the wall.

'Shit!' he said loudly, and went straight out to the telephone in the hall.

Enzo could hear Zula singing along to a Fats Waller record in the background when Salvatore picked up the phone.

'Maria is coming,' Enzo shouted over the music. 'This weekend, the day after tomorrow.'

'Your Maria?' asked Salvatore.

'Yes. Her letter was late. It took for ever to get here.'

'Oh, well, that's nice,' said Salvatore. 'Zula! Turn down the music, will you?'

'She asked about you . . . in her letter,' said Enzo, lowering his voice to a normal level.

'Did she?' said Salvatore, sounding suddenly awkward. 'Yeah, you know I'm not sure if I'll be able to make it down. I've got a lot on at the moment.' He paused. 'How long is it since her husband died?'

'Seven years now,' said Enzo.

'Right, I remember, that was rough. Well, tell her I said hello. If I can make it down at all, I will, but you know how it is.'

'Yes,' said Enzo. He knew how it was and hoped that Maria would too.

Aatifa looked worried when he returned to the kitchen.

'My sister is arriving for a visit,' he explained.

'Oh,' said Aatifa, relieved and confused. 'You like her, your sister?'

'Of course I do. I've been asking her to come out for ages.'

'That's good then?' said Aatifa.

'Yes,' said Enzo, still frowning, 'it is.'

'Where will she be staying?' she asked.

'Here, with us,' he said.

They spent that evening cleaning out the spare bedroom. The contents of Enzo's Genoa boxes had for the most part outlived their usefulness. One was filled with spare hemp sheets that had been eaten by moths over the years and were now full of holes. Several contained more dusty books, all of which he had read. He wanted to dump them now since there was no more available shelf space but Aatifa refused.

'You can't do that, books are important,' she said.

'But you don't even know how to read them,' he said, managing to make it not sound like an insult.

'Somebody will,' she said. 'And they will learn from these. I will find a place to store them.'

'Fine,' said Enzo. He had more pressing problems on his mind.

Another three large boxes contained his own private notebooks in which he had made a meticulous, detailed record of his fifteen years of work at Genoa's port.

'What are these?' asked Aatifa, looking at the extensive, catalogued collection of leather-bound volumes.

'My old work, from Genoa,' he said.

'And why did you bring them here?' she asked.

There was no reasonable answer to that, he knew. Even for him it was quite bizarre, to have taken so many personal notes on top of Genoa's own official records and then to have packed them up and transported them all the way to East Africa.

'We can burn them,' he said.

'All of them? You're sure?' she asked.

'Yes,' he said, 'I should have done it long ago.'

When the room was finally cleared, they erected the cast-iron double bed that was lying in pieces against the wall. Aatifa made it up with fresh sheets and pillow cases.

'Is it big enough for three, do you think?' asked Enzo, looking at the width of the mattress.

'Three?'

'Yes, there's my sister, who isn't small, I'm afraid, and her two children.'

'And how big are they?' she asked.

'I don't know. They were tiny when I saw them last but I expect they've grown a lot since then. I could get another bed I suppose . . .'

As Aatifa put the finishing touches to the covers, Enzo hovered behind her.

'I think it would be best if we didn't let on to Maria . . . about us,' he said. 'You should sleep in your own room.'

Aatifa broke into a smile. 'You are scared of what your sister will think?'

Enzo smiled too, pleased she could make fun of him.

'No! It's not that . . . you don't mind, do you?' he asked.

'Why would I mind?' said Aatifa and she walked out with the last box of his obsolete notebooks.

Enzo waved energetically as Maria appeared at the top of *Queen Eleonora*'s gangplank, followed by her two children. The elder, Angela, was twelve now and the boy, Gianni, was nearly ten. They had both shot up since he last saw them and, if he wasn't mistaken, Maria had become a little more robust and rotund too. No one could pass her on the narrow walkway and she created a logjam of passengers behind her. She had worn black ever since she had been widowed, but he was pleased to see that she had progressed now to a dark green dress.

'I can't believe you finally came,' Enzo said, as they hugged. Then he shook hands with the children.

'Pleased to meet you, Uncle Enzo,' Angela said politely.

'Hello, Angela, Gianni. You're all so welcome.'

'The Duce says it's our patriotic duty to visit the colonies,' said Maria, 'and you never bother to come home. So it was the only way to get to see my little brother. Let me look at you.'

Enzo was embarrassed as she gave him a full-bodied forensic stare.

'You look healthy for once,' she said suspiciously. 'What's going on, Africa suit you?'

An Eritrean porter carried their luggage to the boot of the saloon car that Enzo had hired, a black and brown Lancia Augusta with more dents in the side than straight parts. He didn't own a car himself as he was able to walk everywhere he needed to go, apart from Asmara and he went there by train, right from his office door.

'Should I tip him?' asked Maria loudly, nodding at the porter.

'No, definitely not,' said Enzo, 'he gets his wages from me.'

Enzo helped them all inside the car. Then, after turning on the windscreen wipers by mistake, he drove off in a jerky fashion, still getting used to the handling of this unfamiliar vehicle.

'How was your trip?' he asked.

'Oh, don't remind me,' moaned Maria. 'I was sick four times.'

Angela giggled in the back as Gianni made a vomiting gesture behind his mother's back.

'What have you got in here?' complained Enzo, as he plonked the leather suitcases down in the hallway.

'A woman needs her shoes,' said Maria, fanning herself. 'Is it always this hot? I'm positively passing out.'

'Yes, I'm afraid so. This way,' and he ushered them into the living room.

Maria looked around, unimpressed. Then Aatifa entered from the other door carrying a tray of home-made lemonade.

'Oh, just what I need,' said Maria, grabbing a glass.

She took a sip and turned back to Enzo, leaving Aatifa standing in no-man's land behind her. Aatifa proceeded to offer drinks to the children.

'Maria,' Enzo began. 'This is—'

But Maria interrupted, 'Mama sends her regards, she's well, more or less.'

'That's good,' said Enzo, and he started again. 'Maria, this is Aatifa.'

Maria turned. 'Oh,' she said, only now giving Aatifa a closer look.

'Hello,' said Aatifa.

'Hello, Aa-ti-fa,' said Maria. 'Did I pronounce that correctly?'

'Aatifa works here . . . for me,' said Enzo.

Maria looked from Aatifa to Enzo and he could tell that she was already putting two and two together.

'Let's go out tonight, shall we?' she said. 'Is that possible? Do you have any restaurants here?'

'Yes, of course we have restaurants,' said Enzo. 'We are not in the desert.'

'Good, let's do that then. And will Aatifa come too?' Maria asked, like a fisherman casting out a baited line.

Enzo and Aatifa looked at each other, both momentarily thrown.

'Aatifa has work to do, I'm sure,' offered Enzo. 'And she can mind the children as well, can't you?'

Aatifa nodded and smiled at Angela and Gianni but they both looked back at her warily.

'Pity,' said Maria. 'All right. Well, first I need hot water and a bath.'

'I'll show you,' said Aatifa. 'This way.'

That evening, Enzo took Maria to his usual Florentine restaurant. He introduced her to the staff as his sister, visiting from Genoa, whereupon the men fawned over her as if she were one of their own family. They were given the best table in the house but as soon as they were seated and alone, Maria cast a cold, clinical eye around the place. The waiters in white shirts and black bow ties were Italian. The simple, homely decor was Italian. Even the smells wafting from the kitchen were Italian, but still she was nervous.

'They are not going to poison me, are they?' she asked.

Enzo sighed. 'They're from Florence.'

'Yes, but where's the food from?'

'Would you like me to take you to where the Eritreans eat instead?' he threatened.

'No!' she said, looking horrified at the thought.

'Relax! You'll be fine, I've eaten here plenty of times.'

'Yes, but you are practically a native now. Immune to all those deadly little bugs no doubt.'

Enzo shook his head: Italians abroad, afraid of anything new, though he had been exactly the same until recently. It was also correct that there were bugs and diseases here for which European bodies were unprepared. Before he came, their family doctor had insisted on inoculating him against smallpox, typhoid, yellow fever and cholera, but he had not heard of any outbreaks since he'd arrived.

Maria rearranged her sterling-silver cutlery and then asked casually, 'How's Salvatore?'

'He's fine,' said Enzo, 'but he's not sure if he'll be able to make it down. He's very busy with the army.'

Honesty would have been the better course as Maria looked at him coldly.

'He doesn't want to see me, does he?' she said.

'Of course he does! He said he's really going to try,' said Enzo.

'You're a bad liar, as usual. And he was always a waste of my time.'

Enzo felt ashamed, but he saw Maria putting her disappointment aside quickly.

'We could go up to see him if you like,' he offered. 'It's a long train ride but Asmara is really worth a visit.'

Maria considered this for a moment and then said, 'No, the children have done enough travelling already and we're only here for a week. We came to see you, not anyone else.'

Enzo smiled, glad that the years had not changed her. He loved Salvatore dearly but he did not deserve this woman.

'So, you dark horse, where did you find her?' asked Maria.

'Who?'

'You know who I mean. That wild-looking woman, Aatifa. She's extraordinary, those eyes, just stunning!'

'Are they? I hadn't noticed,' said Enzo, surprising himself with how quickly he had returned to lying.

Maria grinned. 'You think you can hide something like that from your big sister?'

'I'm not hiding anything,' Enzo protested, 'she's just a housemaid.'

'Fine,' said Maria. 'Be like that. Enzo's big secret.'

'There's absolutely nothing to tell,' he insisted.

Maria ignored him and focused on the menu instead.

'So, what are we going to eat?' she said. 'Anything you recommend?'

'The fish is always good. Linguine with scampi is their speciality. Don't have the beef.'

Aatifa tidied up around Gianni and Angela as they sat at the living room table. They were supposed to be doing the homework their mother had insisted on but were busy studying their new Eritrean babysitter instead.

She sensed the children staring at her, but every time she looked over at them they buried their heads in their books.

'You're from Genoa too?' Aatifa asked finally, to break the ice.

'Yes,' they both replied in unison.

'And that is school work?' she said, nodding at their books.

'Our teachers gave us tonnes of homework to bring on holiday,' said Angela. 'Can you believe it? They're completely crazy. Why is it called a holiday if they are going to do that?'

Aatifa smiled. 'What do you study at your school?'

'Oh, the usual,' answered Angela, 'you know, mathematics, Italian, music, Latin, geometry, science.'

'I hate science,' said Gianni, butting in.

Aatifa pointed at his school book. 'Is that one science?'

'Can you not read?' asked Angela, delighted.

Aatifa shook her head, unembarrassed.

'I wish I couldn't read,' said Angela, 'then I wouldn't have to go to school.'

'You'd have to go to learn how to, stupid,' said Gianni.

'No, I wouldn't. I'd get expelled for being a dunce and then Mama wouldn't have a choice. She'd have to keep me at home.'

Gianni frowned, momentarily confounded by the perfect logic of this argument.

'What does it say?' asked Aatifa.

'This bit is about how plants grow,' said Gianni. 'Chlorophyll, photosynthesis, all that stuff. It's really boring. I don't see why I need to know any of it. When I'm big, I'm going to be an archaeologist at the pyramids in Egypt.'

'No, he isn't,' said his sister. 'I keep telling him he's going to be a rubbish collector or work down in the sewers with a shovel. He already smells like he does.'

Gianni threw a pencil at her which bounced off her forehead.

'Ow!' shouted Angela, preparing to respond.

'No fighting,' said Aatifa firmly, and they both stopped, though they would not have done the same for their mother.

'Now study, like you were told,' ordered Aatifa. 'Then when you grow up you can both be whatever you want to be.'

This was something she would often say to Azzezza, but for these two privileged children it didn't sound like a fantasy. They both returned reluctantly to their homework, continuing their bickering in whispers.

'Idiot,' mumbled Angela.

'Double idiot,' replied Gianni.

Once, Aatifa thought, Enzo and Maria must have been like these two.

Appearances were maintained overnight, with Aatifa and Enzo sleeping alone in their own rooms. Enzo made sure that Maria heard his loud, 'Goodnight, Aatifa.'

For a while, before going to sleep, Aatifa sat in her favourite spot on the window sill looking out over the sea. It had already changed colour from turquoise to black, apart from a long white strip caught by the moonlight. She thought about life and opportunity and about how fate gave more of the latter to some than it did to others. She also spent some time thinking of ways in which this gap might be lessened.

Once the temperature had begun to fall the next evening, Aatifa guided Maria and the two children around a craft market where stalls were displaying Eritrean pottery, wood-work and baskets. Maria occasionally picked up items and looked at them, but showed little interest. Aatifa could tell that the previous night's sleeping arrangements had only served to arouse her curiosity.

'How long have you been working for my brother?' she asked as they walked.

'Two months,' said Aatifa.

'And what's that been like?'

'Fine.'

'A good boss, is he?' she asked, trying another tack.

'Yes,' said Aatifa.

Maria nodded, giving her time to expand on her answer but Aatifa didn't offer any more.

'It's good that he has you,' she said. 'I don't know how he's managed out here on his own all this time. He's not at all the type.'

Aatifa gave her a polite smile, unsure whether Maria was being insulting or tender towards her brother. To change the subject she picked up a slender-necked clay pot and showed it to her.

'Djebena. For coffee.'

'Yes,' said Maria, 'I saw you using one this morning. I sup-pose I'll take one of those for Mother. Will you buy it? I'm sure they'll only try to fleece me.'

The seller, a Beni-Amer woman with a jewelled ring through her nose, had not understood but Aatifa was insulted on her behalf. However, the trader took one look at Maria and proceeded to ask for a completely outrageous price. Aatifa shouted at her in Tigrinya, giving her a rapid lecture on the downside of dishonesty and the shocked seller immediately handed over the pot at the local rate.

'Quite a row you had back there,' Maria said, impressed. 'Was she really trying to rip me off?'

'No,' said Aatifa, lying for the trader, 'it is normal to bargain here.'

As they continued the tour, Aatifa felt Maria's eyes on her still. She had not been stared at so much since she had worn the silver dress. But these were not the invasive looks of men. Every time she met Maria's soft brown eyes, the Italian woman held her gaze and gave her a warm smile in return.

In the morning, Enzo took a rare day off work so that he could take Maria, Angela and Gianni on a trip around the bay on one of his coastguard vessels, giving them splendid views of the Massawa coastline and the flat Dahlak Islands to the east. At one stage their boat was passed by a British Navy light cruiser, flying the Union Jack. It was sailing south down the Red Sea coast, probably on its way to British Somalia. Angela and Gianni shouted and waved their arms and the smiling sailors in their white uniforms did the same back.

"ello!' Angela roared.

'Ciao,' an English voice shouted.

'What do you think?' Enzo asked Maria, when they had a moment alone.

'Too hot, too dusty,' said Maria. 'How much longer are you going to stay?'

'I don't know,' said Enzo, 'I haven't decided. There's still work for me to do here.'

'You do want to come back, don't you?' asked Maria.

'Of course,' he said. 'Some day.'

'Anything else keeping you here?' Maria asked.

'What do you mean?' he said.

Maria sighed and then smiled. 'I like her. You do too, don't you?'

Enzo thought about whether he should try to keep up the pretence but it didn't seem to be working so he nodded.

'It's a pity she's . . . you know,' said Maria. 'You'll have to find yourself a proper wife next.'

He didn't think she meant it in as cruel a way as it had sounded but he didn't reply. The conversation ended there as the children excitedly called them to come and look at something on the other side of the boat. They strolled over, and were completely unprepared for the sight of a pod of three large orcas bursting through the surface of the sea in unison as they headed north at a cracking speed.

'Look!' Angela said, almost crying. 'Look!' even though everyone already was.

The giants breached again in a graceful arc, gallons of water sliding down off their sleek blackness.

Gianni stared open-mouthed until he finally found his voice. 'This is the best holiday ever.'

Aatifa would have loved this, thought Enzo. He resolved to bring her out to try to see them some time. She was the only one he wanted to show this to. If there was a 'proper' wife out there somewhere waiting for him, presumably some happy combination of white and Italian, then he had absolutely no interest in meeting her.

*

Later, the children explained to Aatifa in great detail what they had seen. She didn't know what they were talking about until Angela found a picture in one of Enzo's encyclopedias.

'You saw one of these?' asked Aatifa in disbelief.

'Three,' said Angela, hopping from one foot to another.

'As big as houses they were,' added Gianni.

'Why didn't you bring her, Enzo?' scolded Maria.

'I don't know,' said Enzo, feeling guilty. 'I should have, but I didn't know those whales were going to pop up, did I? We'll go another time,' he promised Aatifa.

She nodded, looking back at the orca picture on her lap.

'Can we do it again tomorrow?' pleaded Gianni.

'No,' said Maria. 'Anyway, what are the chances of us seeing them again like that, Enzo?'

'Hardly any,' he replied, 'we were very lucky,' and he looked apologetically at Aatifa again.

On her way to bed, Aatifa paused at the open door of the spare bedroom, and looked enviously at Maria lying in the middle of the double bed. The two children were cuddled up on either side of her, both fast asleep. A standing fan purred away beside them, pointed directly at their heads. Maria, however, was still awake and beckoned Aatifa in.

'The excitement,' said Maria, 'they're exhausted.'

'They are both great children,' Aatifa said, in a low voice so as not to wake them.

'They're a handful sometimes,' said Maria, 'but still, I wouldn't be without them. Would you like to have children yourself?'

Aatifa paused, and then made a decision.

'I already have a child,' she said slowly, 'though I have not been much of a mother.'

'Oh,' said Maria, 'Enzo never said anything. A boy or . . .'

'A girl, she is grown now. I haven't spoken about her with him.'

'Ah.' Maria nodded. 'But I bet that's not true about you not being a good mother. You love her?'

Aatifa was startled that this could even be asked. 'I do.'

'Well, that's all they need from us, isn't it, to be loved?'

Aatifa nodded. She hoped that it was true.

'And where does she live, your daughter?' asked Maria.

Foreseeing questions that would be difficult to answer, Aatifa said briefly, 'With family.'

'And do you get to see her much?'

'As often as I can,' said Aatifa.

'But don't you mind not living with her?' Maria persisted, unable to resist the temptation to mine for more details.

Aatifa searched for the vaguest answer she could give in reply. Then Angela began to stir beside her mother and she took this opportunity to slip out quietly.

'Goodnight,' she whispered.

Aatifa walked on down the corridor and found Enzo standing in his doorway. He raised his finger to his lips for her to be quiet and he offered her his hand. She looked at it and put her own hand in his without hesitation.

After a full week of sightseeing, restaurant dinners and shopping, the day of Maria's departure finally arrived. She spent the entire morning packing up the children's belongings, which they had managed to disperse all over the house, and then Enzo carried the suitcases outside to the hire car.

'Time to go,' shouted Enzo from the garden gate, looking at his watch.

Aatifa stood by in the hall, waiting to say her own farewells.

'Well, Aatifa,' said Maria, smiling at her.

Aatifa held out her hand, but to her surprise Maria moved in and gave her a warm hug, followed by a firm kiss on both cheeks.

'Perhaps we will meet again,' said Maria, 'who knows? But if not I am very glad that I met you.'

'It was nice for me too,' said Aatifa.

As the children followed their mother out, Aatifa stopped them and handed each a present of a wooden toy. Gianni's was a circle of tiny painted chickens on a wooden base. She showed him how to twirl it gently so that each chicken would bend and peck the wood, one after the other. He ran out to show it to his mother while Angela unwrapped her gift, a small wooden lyre with multi-coloured threads decorating its handle.

'Oh, it's lovely. Thank you,' Angela said. 'I'll miss you.'

'Some day you will rule the world,' said Aatifa, embracing her and bringing a blush to the girl's cheeks.

She accompanied Angela out to the car and waved them all off. A movement caught her eye on the way back in and she was sure she glimpsed Eva hiding behind her net curtains next door.

Back in the living room, Aatifa retrieved Gianni's science book from where she had hidden it. Azzezza will love this, she thought. She had almost not taken it from the boy's bag, but in the end she did, in order to create opportunity where none existed. It was not stealing exactly. She had given a wooden toy in return. A fair exchange, even though only one party had been aware of the transaction.

Chapter 10

TWO PLEASANT WEEKS of peace and routine followed, when it seemed to Enzo that life could really not get much better. Then one still morning Bobbio came back unannounced, this time arriving on the Asmara train, accompanied by Major Dore. Enzo didn't have a chance to get up before he burst through his office door and slapped a bundle of papers triumphantly on his desk in front of him. No one bothered introducing him to Dore.

'What's this?' asked Enzo.

'Ships,' said Bobbio with a broad grin on his face. 'Diplomacy has been exhausted, surprise, surprise. It's the military's turn now.'

Enzo flicked through the pages in growing astonishment. 'All of these?'

'All,' said Bobbio, making himself comfortable in the visitor's chair.

At least he is letting me keep mine this time, Enzo thought.

He got up, papers in hand and walked over to the door. 'Daniel!' he shouted. 'Call all the staff together. Right now.'

When all the stragglers had made their way in from the quays, they gathered in a semicircle around Enzo in the main office, some sitting in chairs, others standing behind them.

Bobbio and Major Dore watched silently from Enzo's office door.

'You've all seen the list by now,' said Enzo. 'What it means is that we will soon be busier here than we have ever been before. With immediate effect, I am cancelling all holiday leave.'

Some of his staff might have been tempted to groan at that part, but they were all acutely aware of the two outsiders.

'I want all of you to clear your desks of everything else and get some rest too,' continued Enzo. 'Finally we are getting a chance to show what we can do. Let's be ready.'

He looked over at Bobbio for approval of his little speech. The ministry man gave him a little nod as if to say that it wasn't outstanding but it would do. Then for the rest of the day the three of them camped in Enzo's office, poring over a large map of the region and going through all the finer details of what lay ahead.

The plan, such as it was, was simple. 'A quick movement of many men to the front,' explained Bobbio, 'a quick invasion, swiftly followed by a quick victory. Then we will send most of the men home, keeping just enough of a garrison in Ethiopia to allow the real colonial work to start.'

No military problems were foreseen. Enzo's role was to ensure the smooth running of his port. Luckily neither of his two visitors knew the first thing about shipping, so at least he could expect to remain master of his own harbour. The major and Bobbio planned to set up their own offices in Massawa, mercifully away from the port, but Enzo knew that they would be breathing down his neck from now on.

At dusk, when they had finally done for the day, Enzo stood alone on the dock and looked out to sea. The port was empty and the water was unusually calm, without a ripple or a breeze. Further out an Arab dhow at full sail glided away in the golden light of sunset. This sight reminded him of one of his favourite seascapes, *The Bay of Naples* by Aivazovsky. He took it all in, knowing that it was not going to remain like this for very much longer. Then he turned for home.

He chose not to discuss the coming events with Aatifa. There was no official reason not to tell her but he kept silent anyway even though the burden of it grew with each passing day. On the fifth and final night, he lay awake, while she slept peacefully beside him, unaware of what was sailing their way. The ships would already be through the Suez Canal by now, he guessed. He dozed off fitfully, and each time he woke he checked the time on his watch. Then at four in the morning he got up as quietly as he could, gathering his clothes and shoes and carrying them out to the bathroom to get dressed in there. He felt an urge to wake her then and explain everything, but he decided against it and slipped out of the front door, closing it gently behind him.

Half an hour later, he stood with Bobbio, Daniel and Major Dore on the roof of his office as a red dawn made a cloud bank appear like hot coals above them. He had not been up there since that day with Salvatore, but thankfully no one asked about the set of golf clubs that were still lying where Salvatore had abandoned them. There were more impressive things to look at. One after another, three huge troop carriers came into view on the horizon, powering towards his harbour. It was a thrilling display of Italian military might. Enzo looked over at Daniel and was pleased to see that he seemed to be excited too.

'History in the making, gentlemen. Now everything changes,' announced Bobbio. 'It's over to you, Enzo.'

'Whatever they throw at us, we are ready,' he replied.

'Good, I'm glad to hear it,' said Bobbio, smiling for once, as he and the major went back inside.

Enzo continued to watch the approaching vessels. Even one of these would be more traffic than they had ever had in any one day.

'We can handle it, sir,' said Daniel.

'I know,' said Enzo, trying to convince himself.

They had to cover their ears then as the three ships signalled their arrival with simultaneous blasts from their sirens. Aatifa would be awake now, Enzo thought. No one in town could have slept through that. He imagined her pushing open the bedroom shutters, revealing the armada in the bay below. Seeing the size of these hulks, she would not need to ask why they were here or what they carried on board. And she would know that he had kept this news from her.

Thousands of mostly young Italian soldiers in grey-green uniform, carrying knapsacks and rifles, began to disembark from the first arrival, the luxury liner *Conte Biancamano*. Along with these men came tonnes of military supplies and machinery. But to Enzo it didn't feel like the beginning of a war at all. The atmosphere was more like a party, with laughter and smiling, giddy faces. He immediately put himself in the thick of it, delighted to see so much new Italian blood arriving at long last. He shook hundreds of hands until his right arm was sore.

'Welcome, welcome, hello,' he said, to anyone within earshot.

To his surprise some of them didn't know what country they had landed in.

'No, this is not Ethiopia,' he explained. 'You're in Eritrea.'

'Aren't they the same thing?' asked one soldier.

'No, not at all,' said Enzo, pointing at the ground. 'Eritrea, where we are now, is already part of Italy.'

He was relieved when Salvatore arrived to survey his new recruits.

'Welcome, boys. Heroes one and all,' he said.

'They don't know anything,' said Enzo. 'They don't even know where they are.'

'Really!' Salvatore laughed, and stopped the next youth to pass him. 'Hey, soldier, where are you?'

'Africa, sir.'

'There you go, see, he knows. It doesn't matter anyway. They're only paid to fight.'

'Surely there won't be a war now,' Enzo shouted over the noise, 'when the Ethiopians see all this?'

'It depends on how proud they are, doesn't it?' said Salvatore.

Enzo's smile faded as he remembered the looks on the faces of the three Ethiopians he had seen watching him on New Year's Eve. They had been proud men, who were not afraid to look him in the eye.

There was a commotion above them on the gangplank as a baby-faced private tried to rescue his round infantry hat which had just been stolen by one of his colleagues.

'Hey!' he protested. 'I need that.'

'For Italy and the Duce! Come and get it, Paolo!' said the hat thief, as he sent the private's hat spinning high up into the air.

'Duce, Duce, Duce,' they all shouted.

Private Paolo pushed past the soldiers in front of him, racing to grab his hat before it was trampled beyond all recognition.

Near the bottom of the gangplank, Enzo saw Dore scanning the new arrivals. A large group of blackshirted Fascist militia were next to disembark. When they touched land, some of the officers greeted the major warmly.

Then everyone with a query, large or small, descended on Enzo all at once.

'Where's the ammunition warehouse?' 'The oil depot?' 'The repair yard?' 'The communications building?'

Daniel and the rest of his team fielded questions too. It looked chaotic because of the sheer number of men but the operation was proceeding smoothly. Enzo spotted Bobbio surveying the scene from his office window. Perhaps he was impressed; it was hard to tell.

A giant truck pulled up alongside Enzo.

'Where can I park this lot?' asked an engineer. 'I've orders to triple the building space here.'

'Over there,' said Enzo, shocked. 'Did you say triple?'

By the time night fell, and the reflection of the harbour lights was shimmering on the surface of the water, Enzo was still on the dock, coordinating the last of the men and supplies.

'We did it, sir,' said Daniel, smiling as he wiped sweat from his brow with a handkerchief.

'Yes, we did. Well done, Daniel.' Enzo knew that it would not have gone so easily had Daniel not been there. He suddenly felt an immense pride in their achievement. 'But we've got to do it all again in a few days.'

Even though he was more tired than he'd ever been in his life, Enzo walked home in good spirits. His back ached from standing for so long and he looked forward to a soothing bath and the soft touch of Aatifa's skin. Up ahead of him he spotted some newly arrived blackshirts who were already drunk, and trying to coax a young Eritrean woman into their car.

'Come with us,' one of them said, 'it'll be fun.'

How they had got their hands on a private car so quickly he

didn't know. At first the conversation with the woman seemed playful enough. They were all smiling but when she continued to refuse, two of the men grabbed her by the arms and forcibly dragged her into the back seat.

'I don't want to,' the woman shouted, 'let me go.'

Enzo thought about intervening even though he was still fifty yards away. Then one of the young men saw him and stopped dead, staring down at him. Enzo felt a creeping fear as they faced each other, as if the man were waiting to see if he would do anything. Their silent stand-off was only broken when the man's colleagues shouted at him to hurry up. He jumped back in the car which then sped away, skidding around a corner and out of sight.

When he arrived at home, he was relieved to see Aatifa. She was annoyed with him, he could tell, but he walked directly over to the front window. He could hear distant sounds outside of fast driving and drunken shouting but they were not on their street.

He turned away from the window. 'I don't want you to go out on your own at night for a while.'

'Why not?' she asked.

But he just turned back to looking up and down the road. Standing there in his little house with its neat garden, he felt suddenly small and weak. He wished instead that it was a castle that could protect them. The most unexpected thing of all was that it was his own compatriots who had made him feel like this.

'We must go and help her,' Aatifa said, when he finally told her in the bedroom.

'They are long gone now,' he replied, 'there is nothing we can do.'

'The police?' she suggested.

'I don't even know who they were,' he said, which was true.

Besides that, he was reluctant to make an official complaint against any Fascist officer. It wasn't a wise thing to do. He also wasn't sure he would be able to describe the young woman in a way that would distinguish her from any other Eritrean woman.

'I'm sure it's nothing. Just some play-acting,' he said, hoping that she would let it go.

He went to the bathroom and when he returned and was folding his clothes, he asked casually, 'You saw the ships?'

'Yes,' she said, 'why didn't you tell me they were coming?'

'I don't know,' he replied, 'it must have slipped my mind.'

Chapter 11

Though he did not tell anyone, this would be the first real military action Salvatore had ever seen. The Great War in Europe had ended in 1918 and he had managed to avoid that madness through a timely diagnosis of tuberculosis – actually his smoker's cough combined with a sizeable bribe to an unprofessional doctor. He had joined the army only after the Armistice was signed. It seemed a safe bet that the world would not be stupid enough to do such a thing again.

After serving in various garrison towns around Italy, a colonial posting was the next step for a rising officer like him. His superior by then was an old drinking partner and he made sure over a game of poker that he was sent to Eritrea and not Libya or Somaliland.

Now, as he was busy organising his new troops for the coming advance, part of him was actually looking forward to what lay ahead. He would finally be able to say that he had been in a war. And thankfully, the odds in this one were overwhelmingly in their favour. It would not be like fighting the mechanised armies of Germany and Austria as they had done alongside the other allies in the Great War. Indeed even to class this as a proper war seemed to be another case of Italian exaggeration. But at the very least it would provide him with some good after-dinner stories.

Salvatore walked back towards his barracks' office, having dealt with an overcrowding problem in the billets. Turning a corner, he encountered a young soldier, who appeared to be lost.

'What are you looking for, Private?' he asked.

'The armoury, sir,' the private said, saluting.

'What's your name, son?'

'Private Paolo Monni, Colonel!' he shouted.

Salvatore hid a smile. 'The armoury is that way,' he said, pointing in the opposite direction to the one in which the private was heading.

'Yes, sir, thank you, sir.'

Private Paolo was about to go when instead he said nervously, 'Sir, can I ask you a question?'

'Of course,' said Salvatore, sighing. 'What is it?'

'They're not armed like we are, sir? The Ethiopians, I mean. Just spears and such, isn't that right? They say it'll all be over in a day.'

'Who told you that?' asked Salvatore.

'Some of the other privates were talking, sir. Is it true what they say?'

Salvatore frowned. It would be better to tell him the truth now, rather than have him find it out on the battle-field.

'Not quite true, no,' he said. 'Unfortunately they have rifles too. Antiques, probably, but it would be a mistake for us to underestimate them. Forty years ago at Adwa we did and they killed four thousand of our soldiers.'

The private turned even paler than he already was.

'But we are putting a giant, modern army in the field, son,

and we are prepared,' Salvatore said, attempting to reassure him. 'Your friends are not so wrong. Two weeks at the most.'

'Yes, sir,' said the private, 'thank you, sir.' He did not look convinced, but saluted once more and shuffled away.

The young man's fear had succeeded in making Salvatore feel nervous for the first time. He shook his head and walked on, hoping to reach the safety of his office without being way-laid by any more frightened privates. He had almost made it when he was surprised to see Judge Muroni, dressed in a three-piece cream suit, sitting outside his door. The old man was plainly agitated.

'Judge, what are you doing here?' he asked.

'A word, Colonel, if you have time?' said the judge, standing up.

'Of course,' said Salvatore, and indicated that they should go inside his office.

'Have you heard?' asked the judge, looking around him for eavesdroppers.

'Heard what?' replied Salvatore, as he closed his door behind them.

He poured them both a drink from a bottle of aged Irish whiskey that he'd bought on a recent trip to Cairo.

'They are making it illegal. The law is already written. There's no way I can stop my wife coming out now.'

'I'm not following you,' said Salvatore. 'Making what illegal?'

'What we are doing . . . with them,' replied the judge. He could see that Salvatore still didn't understand him so he added in a whisper, 'The women.'

'What! That's ridiculous,' said Salvatore, thinking that the judge must be overreacting to some half-heard rumour. It wouldn't be the first time. Then he saw the old man's hand shaking as he gulped down his whiskey and realised that he was serious.

'Can they even do something like that?' he asked.

'They already have,' the judge lamented, 'that's what I'm trying to tell you.'

'But why would they bother?' said Salvatore.

'They are saying that it gives them notions that they are equal to us. Breeding dissent. Undermining our authority. Anyone who has a relationship with a native woman is to be considered an enemy of the state.'

'Enemy!' Salvatore laughed. 'Now you're really kidding?'

'It's no joke,' said the judge, shaking his head. 'Not to the ministry anyway. It's to be a crime now, with everything that entails.'

Salvatore tried to analyse the implications of this news. He wondered if the ministry weasel whom he had met in Asmara had anything to do with it. Then he remembered who else had been in the restaurant that night.

'They asked me if I knew anyone,' continued the judge. 'You were the one who introduced me to my girlfriend.'

The last part was said in an angry tone that Salvatore didn't like.

'As far as I remember you didn't need much encouragement,' he snapped back.

The judge nodded apologetically. 'Yes . . . I know, I know. What are we going to do?'

'I don't know, let me think,' said Salvatore, pushing the bottle towards the old man.

They already knew about the judge and his woman; that much was clear. So why had they spoken to him but not mentioned her? Then he realised. They had been giving the judge a forewarning, probably because of his senior position, and he had just been too dim to see it.

As he walked to work, Enzo was attracted by the noise of a disturbance outside an apartment building. A small crowd of Italians and Eritreans had gathered around a shabbily dressed Italian civilian who was trying to beat an Eritrean woman. He was slapping her face whenever he could get a good hold of her while she struggled to get away from him. The man seemed wild with rage, his eyes bulging, but no one was intervening. Enzo began to elbow his way through the spectators, determined to put a stop to it. But before he could do anything, two policemen pushed ahead of him and arrested the man. Then they hauled him away, despite his loud protests. The Eritrean woman stood up now, holding the side of her face. It was already starting to show signs of bruising although nothing too serious. She raised her scarf up over her head and hurried off. Enzo, impressed that the police had sorted it out so efficiently, continued on his way.

Aatifa led the lamb through the house towards the front door, its tiny hooves skidding on the hall tiles. It was sturdier now, having eaten every single blade of grass and leaf in the back yard, along with the leftover vegetables Aatifa had given it from the kitchen. 'Maaa,' it said to Eva, on her knees in her rose garden. Eva looked up with a start and gave Aatifa another suspicious look.

They passed through the old town, seeing young soldiers everywhere. Aatifa kept a careful eye out for the men in black shirts Enzo had described but she saw none.

'Come and look,' she called when she reached the hut and Madihah, Iggi and Azzezza all came out to see.

'Here, it's for you,' she said triumphantly to Madihah, who could hardly believe it.

Iggi looked venomously at both the lamb and Aatifa and made no comment as he returned inside.

'Oh, can we keep it?' said Azzezza. 'Please!'

Aatifa laughed. 'You are just like a man I know.'

'You can keep it for one day,' said Madihah.

'Two,' bargained Azzezza.

'But only two,' insisted her mother as Azzezza happily grabbed the lead from her grandmother.

Inside, the adults discussed the arrival of the troops and the coming war but the conversation was short-lived.

'What business is it of ours if they want to go to Ethiopia?' said Iggi.

Aatifa wanted to say, 'You're a fool if you think it isn't,' but she held her tongue for Madihah's sake. She also wanted to enjoy the benefit of her four-legged gift for at least a while longer.

The troop carriers were due to return later in the week with more new arrivals but for the moment the quays were quiet and Enzo and his staff had some welcome breathing space. Enzo enjoyed the luxury of being able to work undisturbed at his desk. But just as he had settled into his usual routines, the telephone rang. At the other end of the line he could hear the sound of scuffling, mixed with a parrot's excited squawks, and in the distance a woman yelling abuse in Tigrinya.

'Enzo?' said Salvatore loudly.

'Yes,' he said. 'What's wrong with Zula?'

'Oh, she's down on the street,' said Salvatore. 'She didn't want to leave. I'm throwing her clothes out of the window. Look out!' he shouted. 'Green high heels.'

This was followed by another rapid string of abuse from Zula.

'Why are you doing that?' asked Enzo.

'It's time to get rid of your girlfriend too,' Salvatore replied sternly.

'What?' said Enzo, hoping he had misheard.

'Just do it! Today! Hey – keep the fucking noise down!'

Enzo could hear Zula spitting out more abuse at an unhealthily high pitch.

Salvatore came back on the line once more: 'I'll explain later.'

The connection went dead. Enzo waited for a full two hours but Salvatore did not call him back. Eventually he tried to ring him but his calls went unanswered. He gave up trying when the operator began to get irritated. The problem with having only one friend in the world was that there was no one else he could call.

Later, as he was leaving work, he saw Major Dore pinning up a new notice in the foyer. Enzo stepped back up to the top of the stairwell and peered over the banisters. When he heard the front door swinging closed, he crept down slowly to examine the board.

It didn't take him long to spot which one had been added. The headline read: 'Royal Decree by Law Number 880'. A few of his own staff passed him on their way out and he pretended to be engrossed in another notice about income tax. Once the coast was clear again, he scanned the decree rapidly, focusing on the important words. OUTLAWED ... RELATIONSHIP OF CONJUGAL NATURE ... 1 to 5 YEARS ... PRISON. It could have been a practical joke. But with the arrest he'd witnessed that morning and Salvatore's call, he knew that it wasn't. Some illustrious names caught his eye at the bottom of the page, Vittorio Emanuele, Mussolini and others.

There was a time, not so long ago, when he too had thought that these relationships were wrong, although he had never considered them criminal. Now, however, someone much more senior than he was obviously felt differently and had acted on it. His world was being turned upside down by some faceless bureaucrat, with the King's and the Duce's approval.

All the way home Salvatore's advice rang in his ears: 'Get rid of her, get rid of her.'

He sensed a peculiar electricity in the air and wondered if it was just him or whether there really was a storm coming.

He saw Aatifa at work in the kitchen but he turned immediately and pulled the living room curtains closed, even though it was not yet fully dark outside. She came in to set the table and he took one look at her face and knew that he would not be able to do it.

'What's wrong?' she asked.

'Nothing,' he lied.

His head was racing with thoughts of actions and their consequences but she was the only detail that was clear and certain in his mind.

'We need milk and bread for the morning. You didn't bring any, did you?' she asked, oblivious to their place at the centre of a new world.

He shook his head.

'Now everything changes,' Bobbio had said. Enzo wondered if this was what he had meant.

'I'll get it then,' she said, taking some money from a jam jar on the bookshelf.

'No!' he said, too loudly.

She sighed. 'I can take care of myself. Must I be a prisoner every night?'

He wished he could say yes, so they could remain here in their sanctuary.

'I'll come with you,' he said.

Enzo opened the front door and looked up and down the street. There was still the last half light of dusk.

'I'll go first,' he said. 'I'll wait for you at the corner.'

Aatifa looked at him, waiting for an explanation that he did not give.

The ground was wet now. A light shower had come down in the last few minutes, clearing the air. Enzo picked up a rarely used black umbrella from the coatstand and took it with him. He stopped at the garden gate and turned back to her.

'Stay here for a few minutes and then follow.'

He waited for her at the end of the street, convinced that every pedestrian who passed was watching him too closely. Above him he heard seabirds calling as they headed inland, away from the coast. A storm was coming, for sure.

'Walk behind me,' he said when she arrived beside him.

She looked ready to kill him now. 'What?'

'Walk behind me,' he repeated and headed on, looking in every direction for signs of spying eyes.

Aatifa slowed until she was ten paces behind him.

'Why are you coming with me if we are not going to walk together?' she asked.

He didn't reply, just put a finger to his lips.

As they turned a corner near the market, Enzo saw a group of military policemen ahead, chatting under the awning of a bar. He considered turning around and going by another route but that might only draw attention. The rain returned in single, punctuated drops and he opened his umbrella. He watched Aatifa from the corner of his eye, as they both walked separately past the bar, but the policemen didn't pay either of them the slightest attention. Enzo began to relax though he still maintained their distance, fifteen yards apart. The rain then switched from a shower to a heavy downpour, bouncing off the pavement. Behind him, Aatifa was getting drenched to the bone. He felt her stare on the back of his head, burning into him, and he was ashamed.

When they finally got home, he fetched towels for her as she stepped out of her clothes. They were so wet that a large puddle formed at her feet on the hall floor. She sneezed repeatedly as she dried herself.

'I'll run you a bath,' Enzo said.

As Aatifa was recovering in the steaming water, he brought her in a whisky mixed with hot water and sugar. She took it from him and sipped it angrily.

'What was all that about?' she demanded.

He paused, trying to think of a good way to put it but there was none.

'It is illegal now for me to have a relationship with you,' he said.

Her eyes widened and he could see that she hadn't been expecting that answer.

'Why?'

If he could have hidden all this from her he would have, but he knew that would not be possible.

'They say I am lowering myself and damaging the prestige of Italy,' he said, closing his eyes. The words sounded even worse coming out of his own mouth.

'And for me it is supposed to be an honour!' she said sarcastically.

'Do I make you feel that way?' he asked, hurt.

She paused, then shook her head.

'I could go, if it is better for you?' she offered.

'It is not better for me,' he said quickly. Then he sighed and added, 'But we will have to be careful. You can't be seen here at night. You'll have to stay away from the windows and don't answer the door or the telephone. It's fine during the day, it looks normal then.'

Aatifa stared down into the bathwater. After a few moments she looked up at him and said, 'You people make stupid laws. Who could write such things?'

Enzo thought for a moment and then said sadly, 'A man like me probably.'

Chapter 12

FOR SEVERAL DAYS, they adjusted to this new routine. He or she would close all the curtains at the front of the house in the early evening and then they stayed in. This was not so great a change since they had only ever been out twice together, but it was hard for both of them not to feel trapped. Twice a week the great troop carriers came and went, delivering their heavy cargo of soldiers. An army half a million strong was assembled until Eritrea seemed fit to burst at the seams. The train schedule from the port to the plateau increased to forty times a day. The carriages were always full going up and the tracks never silent.

Ever since he had seen the Italian arrested for beating the Eritrean woman, Enzo had kept a sharp eye on the newspapers for any mention of it. And sure enough today there it was at the bottom of page six. A court hearing had been set for noon for what would be the first public outing of the new law. Enzo told Daniel he was taking an early lunch.

As he slipped into the back of the courtroom, the hearing was already well under way. The large room was similar to courtrooms everywhere, stark and uninviting with cold polished surfaces. A place reserved solely for justice and punishment. The seats were long, uncomfortable wooden benches over a grey and white terrazzo floor.

Judge Muroni was on the bench, so Enzo sat down quickly behind a tall man. Then he watched the proceedings over the man's right or left shoulder, depending on who was speaking. He and the judge did not actually know each other, but there was still a chance that he might remember having seen him with Salvatore. The accused was in the middle of answering questions, and obviously felt he did not deserve to be in court at all. The prosecutor, a short wiry man, was dressed in a flowing black cape over his suit and stood with his nose permanently in the air as he tried to make himself taller than he was. He walked back towards his seat to check some notes and, for the first time, Enzo noticed the other man sitting at the prosecution's table. Bobbio. Enzo thought about leaving; he did not want to have to explain his interest in this trial. But then the defendant began to raise his voice, appealing to the whole room.

'Does a man not have the right to discipline his own servant?' he said indignantly.

'The question is not what you did but why you did it?' said the prosecutor, turning back to face him.

If the defendant had been a wiser man he would have shut up there and then.

'She kept running off to her black boyfriend. I told her before . . .'

'So you beat this woman out of a jealous rage, is that it?' said the prosecutor, directing his voice to the judge.

'I suppose,' said the defendant, 'if you want to put it that way, I don't know, but do you think I should have to put up with that sort of thing?'

'From his own lips, your honour,' said the prosecutor smugly.

'What does it matter?' said the man, quite bewildered now. 'I was within my rights.'

'You are not on trial for beating this woman,' the prosecutor explained patiently. 'You are on trial for the crime of having a relationship with her. One proof of which is a fit of jealousy as you have just described.'

'You can't be serious,' the defendant said, turning to the judge for assistance.

'That's all, Your Honour,' said the prosecutor, sitting back down beside Bobbio.

The man looked as though he were ready to do serious violence to his lawyer. 'I didn't know,' he said, pointing at him. 'He didn't explain it properly.'

'All right, I've heard enough,' said the judge. 'Tommaso Aloi, the court finds you guilty of this crime and sentences you to twelve months in prison.'

'Wait!' cried the hapless defendant.

'Take him away,' ordered the judge to the bailiff.

'Please! I'll get rid of her . . .'

Enzo watched as the struggling man was hauled away by two guards. Bobbio shook the prosecutor's hand and Judge Muroni nodded to the two of them before he left the chamber. It didn't take a genius to figure out that the three of them had sat down and discussed the outcome of this case beforehand. The law had been written and a public example was being made. When everyone stood, Enzo left quickly.

Outside, Enzo pulled himself together and started to look at the positives. He was never going to beat Aatifa in the street or anywhere else for that matter. And who else knew that she was more than just a housekeeper? Salvatore, Zula, his sister Maria. None of them was going to inform on him, so there was no real danger if they continued to be careful. Looking at it that way gave him a new confidence. They were still masters of their own fate.

There had been another unexpected but not unpleasant side effect from the whole business. Every night since their relationship had been made illegal, they had each made love to the other as if it might be their last time. They did the same that night again and in the morning too. He had given everyone, including himself, a few hours off because of the parade.

He lay admiring her as she napped beside him. When she was clothed, she seemed such a strong woman because of the way she moved around and worked. But naked she was different. There was no muscle to be seen, and she was tiny and fragile compared to him. It was a joy to get to know her body and what she liked. He would try to do only those things and find new ones too.

She had also changed from the person who in the beginning would just allow him to do what he wanted without responding herself, to the generous lover she was now, who gave and took as she pleased.

'I am a dangerous criminal and you are my accomplice,' he said with a grin when she opened her eyes.

She laughed. 'You don't look very dangerous to me.'

'I am!' he protested. 'This is just my disguise.'

'Should I be scared of you?' she asked.

'Never,' he said, getting out of bed and reaching for his clothes. 'So are you coming to see?'

Her smile faded, but she nodded and got up too.

It seemed for all the world like a victory parade before the fact. A brass band played. Crowds of Italian civilians lined Massawa's streets, waving flags and cheering. In front of them, row after row of troops marched past on their way to Ethiopia. Enzo spotted Bobbio and Dore on the other side of the street, so he stepped a few feet away from Aatifa, letting the crowd fill the space between them.

Colonel Salvatore led the next regiment, riding on a grey mare, in his full dress uniform, complete with ceremonial sword. On seeing Enzo, he reined his horse to one side.

'How do I look?' he asked, as the infantry marched on without him.

'Impressive,' said Enzo, amused by his vanity, even now as he was heading off to war.

Salvatore was surprised to see Aatifa standing nearby. 'You did get rid of her, didn't you?' he asked, under cover of the brass band.

'Not yet. I will,' Enzo said half-heartedly.

'You have to, you know that?' said Salvatore, becoming serious for once.

Enzo nodded, not wishing to discuss it here.

The last of the Italian infantry column passed, and it was the turn of a hundred Eritrean soldiers. The Italian crowd and some Eritrean locals applauded and cheered them on. These men wore their own uniform of billowing khaki trousers, matching tunic, and a red tasselled fez on their heads. They were called Askari, the Arabic word for soldier.

Aatifa began to walk quickly alongside them.

'Iggi!' she shouted angrily. One of the soldiers turned to look at her.

Aatifa started to berate him in Tigrinya but Iggi kept on marching in step with the others. Enzo looked around nervously and saw that her shouting had caught the attention of Bobbio and Dore across the street.

'Did you understand her?' Salvatore asked, smiling.

'No,' said Enzo.

'Why are you helping them do to others what they have already done to us?' Salvatore translated.

Enzo turned back to Aatifa, shocked.

'Quite a woman you've got there,' said Salvatore. He grabbed the reins of his horse, which was growing restless now. 'I'll see you in a week or two, if I'm still alive. And don't forget to get rid of her.'

'Good luck and keep your head down,' said Enzo, suddenly worried for his friend. 'They'll probably aim at the officers.'

'No matter,' said Salvatore with a smile. 'I'm bullet-proof.'

He rode on after his regiment, giving Aatifa a little ironic salute as he cantered past her. She had finally stopped following Iggi and he marched on until he was out of sight. She turned around and saw Enzo staring at her angrily.

They walked some distance apart back towards the house, but once they had reached a secluded alley, away from prying eyes, Enzo stopped her.

'Who was that man?' he demanded. 'You seem to know him very well.'

'He is one of my family, that's all,' she said dismissively, 'and it is my concern who I talk to, not yours.'

'It is mine when you draw attention to us like that,' he said.

Aatifa didn't answer this but Enzo believed her when she said that the Askari was a relative. She had never lied to him before as far as he knew. In fact she never had any problem telling him the truth, no matter how hurtful he might find it.

'Don't you see what we have done for this country?' he asked angrily. 'What we have built? There are jobs for everyone. Prosperity. We will do the same in Ethiopia, if they'll let us.'

Aatifa waved her hand to indicate that she did not want to hear any more of this, which made him even angrier.

'Before we came here there was nothing; you want to go back to that?'

Aatifa jabbed a finger at her chest. 'We were here and we are not nothing.'

'I didn't mean it like that,' he said, annoyed that she had managed to put him on the back foot.

'What you have built, you did for yourselves, not for us. And now you use us to make war on our neighbours.'

'They chose this war,' Enzo protested.

'Ha,' she replied.

'In the long run, what we are doing will benefit everyone,' he insisted.

She shook her head and said, 'Tell me, those Ethiopians who die now, what benefit will they get?'

Enzo was disappointed. 'You hate us then, is that it?'

He had said 'us' but they both knew that he meant 'me'.

Her eyes filled with tears. 'I hate that you are so greedy,' she said and walked on quickly, leaving him standing there alone.

Chapter 13

THE HOT SUN rose over Northern Ethiopia as Salvatore and his men continued their advance along the mule track between Brachit and Adigrat. Vegetation was scarce here and there were no trees or shade of any sort under which they could seek respite from the heat. The major confrontation that they had been led to expect in the first few days had not materialised. Every five minutes, Salvatore would scan the horizon with his binoculars but there was no sign of anyone wishing to oppose their claim to the country. They had not seen action yet, or any Ethiopian forces at all for that matter and that suited him just fine. He was now more concerned about being killed by the fierce heat or by the myriad insects taking lumps out of him than by anything else. Unfortunately, the grey mare underneath him was a magnet for anything that buzzed.

His company was a mix of Askari and Italian infantry, which included the nervy private whom he had encountered back at the barracks. Among the native troops, he recognised the man that Aatifa had been shouting at, Iggi. Bringing up their rear was a light tank that trundled along reasonably well over the rough terrain. As soon as they had crossed the border from Eritrea, paved roads had vanished into dust.

'Where are you, you bastards?' muttered a corporal behind

him. 'Maybe they are just going to give it to us without a scrap. They must know they can't win against us, eh?'

'That would be good, wouldn't it?' said Private Paolo beside him.

'All this is a waste of bloody time,' continued the corporal. 'We should be having our feet up, with a beer.'

Salvatore smiled in agreement. Above them they heard the hum of engines drawing closer. They all looked up in the sky and saw four of their own air force's biplanes flying in formation as they headed south.

'Give 'em hell,' roared the corporal as they all waved and cheered.

Salvatore was grateful that he was on the side that possessed aircraft and tanks.

It was mid-afternoon when he spotted smoke up ahead. There was no wind so it was floating straight up into the sky. It was black too which probably meant fuel oil. As they rounded a rocky hill he saw that it was coming from one of the Italian biplanes that had crash-landed some distance away. Perhaps it had been shot down but more likely the engine had failed due to some mechanical problem caused by the heat and dust.

He ordered his troops to halt, looked through his binoculars and saw the pilot frantically trying to put out a fire near the propeller. Suddenly the man stopped, spotted something to his left, and ran towards the cockpit. A group of Ethiopian horsemen had arrived and as Salvatore watched, they formed a circle around the stricken aircraft. They were dressed in white robes, not uniforms, and over their shoulders they carried what looked like oversized antique rifles.

Salvatore gave the command for his Askari to move forward but the wreck was up on a ridge and it would take several minutes to get there. Meanwhile, the terrified airman had stood up in the cockpit and was training his rifle on the riders. There was no way to warn him as a tribesman to his side aimed and shot him at close range. The force of the bullet threw him out of the aeroplane and he tumbled down on to the lower wing, where he lay motionless. An angry murmur rose from the Italian soldiers behind Salvatore. Then, above them on the ridge, one of the Ethiopians dismounted and raised his curved sword in the air. Salvatore closed his eyes and looked away as the pilot's corpse was decapitated in one swift movement. Distracted by the sound of someone throwing up, Salvatore turned and saw Private Paolo retching on the ground. He wiped his mouth with the sleeve of his tunic, then stood up, embarrassed, and shouldered his rifle.

Salvatore raised his binoculars once more, just in time to see the Ethiopians galloping away in the opposite direction. A cloud of dust rose up behind their horses' hind legs. One of the riders was carrying something with him, secured to his saddle. It took Salvatore a few seconds to realise that it was the pilot's severed head.

When Enzo arrived home from work, the house was eerily quiet. The only sound was the returned kitten, calling to Aatifa from the yard outside and scratching at the back door.

'Hello?' he shouted up the stairs but no answer came.

There were no signs of cooking in the kitchen either and he immediately feared the worst: she had left him. Since the day of the parade, they had slept in their own separate rooms and had hardly spoken two words to each other. The situation had become so bad that he wondered whether they still had a relationship to keep hidden.

In her room, he saw that some of her belongings were still there including that picture of a girl on the wall. Perhaps she didn't care about these few things and had just abandoned them.

As the night wore on, he stood for hours looking out of the front window, until it became too dark to see. Then he went up and sat on her bed, feeling completely lost without her. Finally he lay down and curled up, still fully dressed. He found comfort in the familiar smell of her from her sheets and pillow. Aatifa made her own lavender oil and he had seen her use this in her hair. If he kept his eyes closed and breathed in, he could pretend that she was there beside him. And that was how he managed to fall asleep.

Daylight had only reached a hazy blue outside when the sound of persistent knocking woke him. Running down quickly, he tripped and had to grab hold of the banisters to save himself. He yanked open the front door, but outside was a young Eritrean woman whom he had never seen before.

'My mother asks for your help,' she said.

Enzo nodded and averted his eyes. She looked distressed, but all beggars did and it was impossible to tell the ones who were genuinely in need. He rooted in his pocket for a few coins and handed them to her. Then he began to close the door as she looked down in confusion at the money sitting on her palm. The door was almost shut when she spoke again.

'No, please . . . I am Madihah, and my mother is Aatifa.'

He froze and slowly opened the door again. Looking at her properly for the first time, he could see the resemblance in her nose and eyes.

'Where is she?' he demanded.

It had taken him a while to rouse the elderly doctor from bed at this hour, but now they had him up, dressed and grumpy. The early morning air was heavy with damp as Madihah led them through the maze of streets. As they waited to allow the ungainly doctor enough time to catch up, Enzo quizzed her about her family tree. The answers he received were hard to believe.

When they finally bent their heads to enter Madihah's hut, Enzo saw Aatifa trying to comfort a feverish little girl. The breathless doctor frowned and took over straight away. Aatifa stepped back, giving him room to work and made her way over to Enzo.

'You're a grandmother! How is this possible?' he asked angrily, managing to whisper and be too loud at the same time.

Aatifa nodded in a matter-of-fact way to Madihah. 'She is my daughter' – and then she nodded to Azzezza – 'and she is her daughter.'

'Why didn't you tell me about any of this?' he demanded.

'Because you never asked me. Did you think my life just revolved around you?' she snapped.

Enzo avoided her eyes. It was true.

'Where is the father . . . of your daughter?' he asked.

'Gone. He was never a father,' she said dismissively.

The doctor glanced around from where he was sitting on the bed and beckoned Enzo over. Now that he saw Azzezza up close for the first time, even he could tell that she was very ill. The girl looked up at him weakly and he was surprised that she seemed to know who he was.

'You are the man with the books,' she said softly.

Enzo didn't know what she meant but he nodded anyway. The doctor stood and came close to him so that no one else could hear them.

'She has dengue fever,' he said. 'I'll give you medicine that will help a little but most of all her temperature needs to be kept down. That's critical.'

'And she'll be OK?' asked Enzo, but his heart sank when the doctor looked unsure.

'For you and me this would be serious. For one so little, well, in some cases this doesn't end well.'

Enzo looked at Aatifa and Madihah at the other side of the room. They were both staring at him anxiously, trying to read his reactions.

'Hopefully we caught it in time,' said the doctor, 'but it's going to be rough for her. I'll come again tomorrow.'

When the doctor left, the women moved back to the girl's side. Enzo had never seen Aatifa this worried before so he put off asking her any more questions for now. The women exchanged a heavy look when he told them the name of the illness.

'But he said that she should be fine,' Enzo lied.

Aatifa felt Azzezza's forehead and saw that she was still burning with fever. Then she turned and caught Enzo looking at his watch.

'You should go now,' she said sharply.

He should have been at work already; there were more ships due that morning. He hesitated, then said firmly, 'No, I'll stay. I'll go and get some ice.'

Enzo quickly foraged around his house, grabbing some towels and a large metal bucket. He was just on his way out again when the telephone rang. He contemplated not answering but it didn't stop ringing.

'Oh you're there, thank heaven,' said Daniel, relieved.

'Something's come up, I won't be in today,' Enzo said. It was the first time he had said these words in five years.

'But Signor Bobbio is here to see you,' Daniel whispered nervously.

Enzo pictured Bobbio trying to eavesdrop on Daniel's conversation.

'Whatever it is, you handle it,' he said, 'you're well able to, Daniel. Tell him I'm sick, make something up, anything, all right?'

Daniel took a deep breath at the other end of the line. 'Yes, sir,' he said doubtfully.

Enzo left an Italian bar in the old town carrying the metal bucket, which was now laden to the brim with chunks of ice. Balancing this from the handlebars of his rusty bicycle, he headed back towards the Eritrean area. On the causeway two policemen on foot patrol noticed him. He must have been a peculiar sight, but he kept his head down, and just carried on.

When he arrived back at the hut, Madihah quickly wrapped some of the ice in a towel and handed this to Aatifa who put it on the child's forehead. The frozen pieces began to melt instantly, water running down over Azzezza's face. Aatifa dried it off and then looked up at Enzo. He tried to smile reassuringly but no one took any comfort from it. The women continued to apply more and more ice until the bed was soaking and it was all gone. Then Enzo picked up the empty bucket and left to get more.

He had done several trips by the time the moon had risen over Massawa bay, giving light to the streets between the Eritrean huts where no lampposts had ever been.

Elsewhere, many miles away, the same moonlight illuminated the white tents in Salvatore's camp. The night air was damp as he walked between them, assessing the morale of his troops. Some of his men played cards, sitting around crackling, resinous wood fires. Others joked with each other, pretending nothing had happened that day. A few were writing letters home to loved ones, an activity that had increased noticeably since the incident with the Italian pilot.

Salvatore spotted young Private Paolo sitting on his own. The innocent, childlike look that he had had only a few days ago in Asmara was gone.

'All right, Private?' he asked.

'Yes, sir,' said Paolo as he straightened up.

'Not playing cards?'

'No, sir, I didn't feel like it.'

Salvatore nodded and started to walk on.

'I'm sorry I was sick today, sir. I just couldn't hold it back.'

'Forget it,' said Salvatore, 'it can happen to the best of us.' He made another attempt to move on.

'They shouldn't have done what they did, sir, to that poor pilot.'

'No, they shouldn't,' agreed Salvatore. 'But we'll make them regret what they did, don't you worry.'

Private Paolo nodded. 'It's a pity for the family too, you know, having to bury him without—'

'Yes,' said Salvatore abruptly, eager now to end the conversation. 'The pilot's commanding officer will be writing to them.'

The private nodded and Salvatore walked on.

In another part of the camp, well away from the Italians, the Eritrean soldiers smoked and ate around their own fires. Salvatore stopped behind a tent, out of sight, and lit a cigarette. He listened as one of the men recounted family memories of Italy's last military excursion into this territory. Salvatore knew all about this from his military school days. It had been forty years ago, before most of them were born but then, as now, the Italians had brought Eritrean Askari with them. Some of them were probably the grandfathers of these new recruits. The

Ethiopians had won that round through a combination of overwhelming numbers and Italian military incompetence. Thousands of Italian soldiers were killed or captured but he knew that the victorious Ethiopians had taken particular exception to the Eritreans who had fought alongside their European masters.

'What did they do to them?' asked one of the Askari around the fire.

The teller of the tale was enjoying frightening them all with the gory details. 'From those whom they did not kill, they cut one hand and one foot and left them in a pile on the battlefield.'

Salvatore looked around at the array of frightened faces. He smiled wryly when he saw that one of these was Iggi. You should have listened to Aatifa, he thought.

'It's true,' said another man, 'I know. My mother's father was with them. For the rest of his life he hobbled around with a wooden crutch and he could not work with just one hand, only beg.'

This kind of talk was really not good for morale. Salvatore threw away his cigarette and prepared to intervene. But he was saved the bother as a senior Askari with a grey beard stood up.

'Enough of these stories,' he said loudly. 'We must only fight like wild men and not allow anyone to make prisoners of us.'

The storyteller nodded and kept any more anecdotes to himself.

The war back then had ended with that battle at Adwa, making Ethiopia the first African nation to defend itself successfully against colonialism; at least for a while. It had been a great humiliation for Italy and Salvatore had heard older officers speak of it bitterly. In return for the release of all Italian prisoners, Italy had been obliged to sign a treaty recognising Ethiopia as a sovereign nation. Since then, Ethiopia had become a proud member of the League of Nations, set up after the Great War so that there would be no more wars. But, Salvatore noted, none of the other League members was coming to its aid now.

The hut was lit by two candles, sending flickering double shadows on to the walls as the flames wavered in the night draught under the door. Aatifa lay sleeping beside Azzezza, whose fever had lessened, though it still had not released her. Enzo and Madihah sat opposite each other on the dirt floor. Above her, hanging on the wall, was a rudimentary portrait drawing of a man which had perhaps been done by a child. Enzo recognised the subject as the Askari from the parade.

'My husband, Iggi,' said Madihah, following his eyeline.

'You are the family she gives her money to,' he said.

Madihah smiled. 'We used to fight about it. We didn't speak for a month. My mother always aims higher than she can reach.'

'I'm sorry, I don't understand,' said Enzo.

'You Italians say that our children can only study for three years,' she said, with no animosity in her voice.

Enzo had not heard of this rule before. He imagined there must be a good reason for it.

'Azzezza needs clothes and other things,' Madihah continued, 'but when she was no longer allowed to go to school my mother insisted on using her money to hire a private teacher for her instead, one afternoon each week. She says that if one day we are to govern ourselves then our children must be educated.'

Enzo's eyes widened.

'So my daughter can read and write and knows mathematics and history but she has holes in her shoes.'

Enzo looked over at the sleeping Aatifa. Once again, he realised he hardly knew this woman at all. He was a bit player in a plan she had cooked up to educate the girl. And it would all be for nothing if she didn't pull through this. For a brief second he wondered whether, if the girl died, Aatifa would leave him. He was immediately ashamed of himself.

After sitting together in silence for a long time, Madihah drifted into exhausted sleep. Enzo followed soon after her, leaning his head back against the wall of the hut.

All was quiet then for what could have been five minutes or an hour. Once, Enzo felt a light movement passing in front of him, which made him open one eye lazily, but he thought nothing of it and went back to sleep.

He was woken abruptly by a shout. 'Where is she?' cried Aatifa.

Azzezza was gone.

They bolted for the door as one. Outside, there was no sign of the child or anyone else. Enzo made for the nearest corner but the streets were deserted apart from a couple of skinny mongrel dogs. Aatifa and Madihah ran the opposite way but, looking back over his shoulder, he saw them both returning quickly to where they had started. Enzo ran on to the next street and thought this one was empty too until something caught his eye on the ground.

A moment later, he walked back, carrying Azzezza, outstretched and limp in his arms.

The gun battle began at first light when boulders were pushed down a hill to trap the tank. Then a rifle shot missed Salvatore's left cheek by a whisker. As he and his men took cover behind anything they could find, he allowed himself a smile. Enzo had been right. They did aim for the officers first. Once they had all taken up good positions, he ordered his men to return fire at will.

From the sounds in front of them, an Ethiopian force of perhaps some fifty men had them pinned down from a cliff above. Salvatore considered it wiser to stay put and just shout instructions and encouragement to his men. He expected their tank would prove decisive in this fight. However, minutes after the battle had begun, the tank's side door burst open and the frightened crew jumped out. As they fled for cover, they shouted that the enemy's bullets were passing straight through their armour as if it were a tin can.

About thirty feet away, Salvatore saw Private Paolo and the corporal hiding behind a large rock. The two of them were arguing about something as the corporal busily prepared his rifle. Salvatore guessed that the private was trying to persuade his superior to keep his bloody head down. But the corporal was having none of this. He raised himself off the ground to a half-standing position, aimed and fired twice. Then he waited another second, perhaps to see if he had hit his intended target. A smile broke out on his face just before a bullet ripped into his chest and he slumped down, head first, over the rock they were sheltering behind. Paolo frantically tried to pull him back down by the end of his tunic but the man was awkwardly positioned.

'Private, stay where you are,' shouted Salvatore.

It was too late. Paolo was already standing and pulling at his fallen colleague. He almost had him free of the rock when another bullet hit Paolo sideways across the bridge of his nose, throwing him backward, the dead corporal tumbling down on top of him.

The Italian infantry and Askari kept returning fire and were beginning to gain some ground, but Salvatore could see that the Ethiopians were now preparing to disappear as quickly as they had come.

'I can't see, I can't see,' Private Paolo repeated over and over as he kicked and pushed his former colleague off him. Then he stood up, stumbling about between the rocks, his hands half covering his bloody face. Against his better judgement, Salvatore got up and ran to help.

Enzo sat on the ground outside the hut in the warm morning sunlight. He was exhausted, unshaven and had slept in the same clothes for two nights in a row. The locals gave him funny, amused looks as they headed off to their jobs in town. Some were in suits and looked better than he did.

Madihah came out of the door beside him and inhaled the sweet, fresh air. 'The fever has broken,' she said.

When he had found the girl lying motionless in the middle of the street, he had thought that it was all over. But he discovered that she was still breathing and he reckoned that her high temperature must have made her lose consciousness. They had all worked hard through the whole night to reduce the fever and eventually it had begun to drop.

'Take a break,' Enzo said to Aatifa when he went inside. 'I'll keep an eye on her.'

Aatifa had not left Azzezza's side since they had brought her back to the hut, nor allowed herself to fall asleep again. She had even drawn blood on her arms from pinching herself to stay awake. Even now, he saw that she was reluctant to leave the child.

'Go on, I'll call you if she needs you,' said Enzo, and she finally went out.

Enzo had been sitting beside her for only a few moments when the girl woke from a deep sleep. She was still too weak to move but her eyes surveyed the room, trying to remember where she was. Then she noticed him and he looked down at her and smiled.

'You won,' he said softly.

She half smiled. It was too much of a strain to do anything more. Then she closed her eyes once more.

A few hours later, she woke again and, using a wooden spoon, Aatifa fed her some fresh soup that Madihah had made. A little of her energy was returning and she could sit up now, propped against a pillow. She was still not the colour of the living.

'I'll go then,' said Enzo, standing in the doorway, his usefulness to them now at an end.

Aatifa nodded without looking around at him. He was surprised that she had nothing at all to say to him after what they had been through together. Madihah seemed surprised too, and gave her mother a withering look. Aatifa ignored them both.

'Thank you,' said Madihah.

'If you need anything, you know where to find me,' said Enzo.

The doctor had said that he would visit Azzezza again that day and he trusted the man to keep his word. No doubt he would be presented with a fine bill for the privilege but he would have gladly paid anything.

As he pushed his bicycle through the sewer-lined streets, he went over the events of the previous two nights. He could see how much Azzezza meant to Aatifa, and the child had seemed to him to be a special sort, like Angela and Gianni. Aatifa had

taken the housekeeping job with him to get the money to educate this girl. And in the beginning he had clearly just been a
means to an end. Is that why she had slept with him, to keep
her job? He didn't want to believe it but he knew that it was
true. Yet he hoped that things were different now and that he
had become important to her. Not just a provider of money.

The question of who Madihah's father was entered his head
but he pushed it away quickly. He could not bear to imagine
Aatifa having been with another man. On the causeway, he
cycled past some of the same local residents that he had seen
that morning. They were returning home now, perhaps on
their lunch breaks. He paid more attention to them this time,
particularly the ones in suits. How was it possible to live there
and still be so well turned out? The shirts were clean and
pressed, the shoes polished. The hut he had spent the last hours
in had neither electricity nor running water. For these men to
present themselves fit for an office job must take a great effort.
And being a veteran of sartorial trouble himself, he was
impressed by such discipline.

When he thought no one was looking, he smelled under his
arms and was immediately repulsed. There were sweat stains
too, he saw, which was even worse. He could go home first but
that would delay him even further. No. He would go straight
to work and tidy himself up as best he could in the office toilet.

He could tell that all was not well even before the docks had
come into sight. Several streets on the way in were backed up
with a noisy logjam of military and civilian trucks. The pavements were laden with onlookers, irate residents and people
trying to go about their business amid the unwelcome chaos.
Enzo abandoned his bicycle against a wall and elbowed his way
slowly through the crowd until he finally managed to get on to
the quays. There the bedlam was even worse and the reason for

it was immediately obvious. His staff were struggling to cope with truckloads of wounded Italian soldiers, hundreds of them, on their way to be shipped home. Something was clearly going wrong in Ethiopia. In his meetings with Bobbio and Dore, they had made no provision for such an eventuality. Everyone had assumed, himself included, that they would just walk in and take over the country. After all, why would the Ethiopians bother putting up much of a fight if they knew that they were going to lose?

He moved forward as best he could, finding a way through the stretchers that lay on every available piece of ground. Some wounded infantrymen cried out for assistance from army medics, who were doing their best to cope.

'Are you a doctor?' asked one, but Enzo shook his head.

He felt as if he had just stepped on to the battlefield itself. It was all so different from the first day when these boys had come; no one was laughing now. The amputees were the hardest to look at but nearly every man had a serious wound. Some were so bad that they were clearly not going to survive the journey home. A sudden thought gripped him and gave him a cold shudder. What if he came across Salvatore here, in some bloody state?

Behind Enzo, an open-topped army jeep was beeping its horn insistently. It gradually manoeuvred its way up the quay towards him and he saw that the rear passenger was Bobbio.

'Where the hell have you been?' the ministry man shouted as he stepped out of the jeep. 'Don't you know there is a war on?'

'It'll be sorted now,' said Enzo, remaining calm because he knew that he needed to be. Ignoring Bobbio, he turned around and started barking orders.

'Get those crates unloaded,' he shouted at some dockers. 'Clear that deck.'

He grabbed two overwhelmed policemen by the elbows, and with both hands he pointed at a stretch of the quay that was littered with wounded men and parked trucks.

'You see that?' he said.

The policemen nodded.

'That is the road in and out. I want you to clear it all the way down, and keep it clear all day. If anyone blocks it, arrest them.'

The policemen nodded enthusiastically, relieved that someone had a plan.

'Sir, move that vehicle, now!' one of them shouted at Bobbio. He looked at Enzo, and then got back in his jeep and drove away.

It did not take long for Enzo to get into his stride. He knew his port like the back of his hand and he was damned if he was going to let it fail this test. Slowly the stalled trucks began to move in to collect the newly arrived supplies. When they were full, they were immediately shifted back out to make room for the next trucks. Once everything was off-loaded from the docked ship, the laborious process of getting the wounded on board, one by one, could begin.

'It's good to see you, sir,' said Daniel. 'I'm sorry about all this, we tried our best.'

'No,' said Enzo, 'it's my fault, I should have been here.'

He noticed raw swelling bruises on either side of Daniel's face and a crack through one lens of his glasses.

'What on earth happened to you?' Enzo asked.

'Oh, it's nothing,' said Daniel, trying to hide his injuries with a turn of his head.

A minor collision between two trucks called him away and Fabio, the young clerk from Bologna, filled Enzo in.

'It was that Major Dore,' said Fabio. 'Punched him, the bastard.'

'Why?' asked Enzo.

'He overheard Daniel giving instructions to a truck driver and he just went mad. Said: "You do not give orders to us." So Daniel said, "Well, you tell him then." And that's when the major hit him, right across the face. He landed hard on the ground too, poor guy.'

Enzo felt like hitting someone himself. The major was not around but Enzo was not going to let this go unanswered.

It took six solid hours before the quayside was transformed from chaotic to busy, but functioning. Enzo needn't have worried about his slovenly appearance because by late afternoon everyone else was in the same state. Finally, when he had a moment to draw breath, he sat down on one of the mooring bollards. But he was not left alone for long.

'Sir, you'd better come and have a look at this,' Daniel said.

Daniel led him down to the furthest end of the quay where a pile of large wooden crates was sitting in front of a warehouse. Each one was the height and width of a man.

'What are they?' asked Enzo.

Daniel shrugged and handed over the paperwork. Enzo read it but the words did not leave him any wiser. On the top of each crate, there was an ominous stamp in large green letters: 'DANGER POISON'.

'He's in charge of it over there,' Daniel said, as he nodded to a young naval officer in a sparkling white uniform. The man was sitting in the shade of the warehouse wall, staring down the quays at the wounded men.

When he saw that they were talking about him, the sailor got up quickly.

'At last! Can I go now?' he asked optimistically.

Enzo handed the paperwork back to Daniel. Then he forced open the lid of one of the crates with a crowbar and had a look inside. Nestled in beds of straw were dozens of metal canisters, each the size of his forearm. He looked from them to the paperwork again and then lastly at the naval officer.

'It says here that they are Iprite,' he said. 'What is that exactly?'

'I don't know,' the naval officer replied. 'We just got orders to deliver it here.'

'Well, what is it used for?' asked Enzo, irritated.

The officer shrugged, in no mood for an inquisition. 'Search me, I don't know.'

'Fine,' said Enzo, and he turned to Daniel. 'Impound them all.'

'What! You can't do that,' said the naval officer.

'I just did,' said Enzo, walking away. 'We do not allow poisons in without special authorisation.'

'We'll store them here,' said Daniel, pointing into the warehouse. 'If you get authorisation, you can have them back.'

'But I have orders . . .' the sailor protested loudly. 'This is going to cause trouble.'

Enzo replied while stepping away backward, 'I am in charge of this port and they are not going anywhere.' Then he turned and kept on going.

Enzo returned shipside in time to oversee the embarkation of the last batch of wounded young soldiers. At least the fighting was over for them, he thought. He watched as one more army truck turned on to the quay and drove the whole way up, unobstructed. It parked beside him at the gangplank and he helped the driver to assist those who could walk to clamber down. One young infantryman, with bandages wrapped around his eyes, waited inside.

'I've got you,' said Enzo, as he took the private by the arm and encouraged him gently down on to the ground. 'What's your name?'

'Paolo – I mean, Private Paolo Monni. Where am I now, sir?'

'You are in Massawa,' said Enzo, 'at the port and you're going home.'

'I can smell the water,' Paolo said, nodding.

'That's the Red Sea and before long, you'll be smelling the Mediterranean too. You stick with me, all right?'

'Yes,' said Paolo, 'thanks.' He held on to Enzo's arm and let him lead him slowly forward.

'Please, nobody seems able to tell me. Do you know if I will be able to see again?'

Enzo looked over at a harassed medic nearby. The man shook his head gravely, before indicating the path of the bullet with his finger.

Enzo looked back at Paolo. 'They are going to do the best they can for you, son. I'm going to bring you up the gangway now, on to your ship, all right?'

'Yes,' said Paolo, turning his head about.

Enzo held his arm tight with both hands and led him up.

'It wasn't anything like I expected,' said Paolo, 'the war, I mean,' and then he became concerned. 'Will you be going there too?'

'No,' said Enzo, smiling, 'they don't want me. I am not a soldier.'

'Good,' said Paolo, relieved for him, 'that's good.'

'I bet you'll be glad to be back with your family again?' said Enzo.

'Yes, I can't wait,' said Paolo. 'Do you think they will recognise me?'

'Of course they will,' Enzo assured him.

'There are only my parents. I'm not married. I don't expect I will be now either.'

Enzo tried to think of a reply that would make the private feel better but he could not find the words.

Salvatore felt responsible for the boy. This was a new experience for him as he usually did not allow himself to get emotionally involved with anyone. But the boy was different.

First of all, he was too young to have been there. He may have been twenty-one on paper but he was certainly not yet a man. Someone close to him should have said he couldn't go and helped him avoid the class of 1914 draft. Salvatore wished he had Paolo's father in front of him right now. He would tell him straight what he thought.

But the boy's father was not here. Instead, in front of him, in his tent, there was a bottle of whisky, through which he was making serious headway. He was tired and shaken, had already seen his fill of armed conflict, and wished most of all for a quick end to this stupid war.

Another idea had also been taking shape in his mind. It had begun after the incident with the pilot and had culminated with what had happened to the boy. It had taken root inside him and now it held an irresistible appeal. The whole concept was simple and could be summed up in one word: revenge.

Outside his tent, he heard a vehicle. He didn't budge. It was probably just another angry, impatient dispatch from Rome. He would read it and then throw it in the bin to keep all the previous dispatches company.

The flap door of his tent was pushed open, without a request for permission to enter, and Salvatore felt his pulse quicken as he recognised the tough, imposing figure of General Graziani. Famous for his part in the Libya campaigns, Graziani was commander of the Italian forces on the southern front in this one. He should have been hundreds of miles away from here with his own regiments, so Salvatore knew straight away that he was not the bearer of good tidings.

'General, I am surprised to see you. I had no word,' he said, standing up.

'Are you? You shouldn't be,' said the general, his glance taking in the half-empty bottle of whisky and Salvatore's shoddy appearance. 'I am here to relieve you of your command, Colonel.'

Such a thing had never happened to Salvatore in his entire career, so he was unsure how to respond. He resisted his initial inclination to fire a string of expletives at his superior officer.

'You expected this, I suppose?' said Graziani.

'No, General, I can't say I did,' admitted Salvatore. 'We have been doing our utmost here. It's just a pity that results have not come quicker for us.'

'I see no results at all, Colonel,' said Graziani. 'We have stalled, wouldn't you say?'

Salvatore decided not to attempt a defence of his tactics. In any case, he had only been following the orders of another idiot general from the northern command. Once upon a time, he himself had been the biggest military hat in the whole of Eritrea but there were unfortunately many hats now. This problem would be solved with another promotion, he thought, but that was for another day. Right now it was his current position that was in need of protection. Walking out from behind his table, he offered the general his chair, and stood to attention.

'I await your orders, sir.'

The general was pleased with this performance. He made himself comfortable in Salvatore's chair and looked at the inviting bottle on the table in front of him.

'Do you have another glass, Colonel?' he asked.

Enzo stayed on the quays for the whole night until all the supplies and wounded were gone. Now there was not a single stretcher or vehicle left on the dock, just the peace of the sea and the sunrise. He stood, surveying a job well done, when he heard a voice behind him.

'Better,' said Bobbio.

The ministry man had managed to walk silently within ten feet of him.

'You look terrible. What did you have?' he asked.

For a second, Enzo did not know what he was talking about but then he remembered that he was supposed to have been sick.

'African bug,' he replied.

Bobbio didn't ask for further explanation. There were plenty of illnesses to choose from.

'It's harder than they thought . . . this war,' said Enzo.

'Perhaps there was a little underestimation, yes,' Bobbio conceded. 'But the result will be exactly the same.'

Enzo nodded and then braced himself before saying what had been on his mind all day.

'Your Major Dore struck one of my men today.'

'Really?' said Bobbio, apparently surprised to hear it.

'Yes,' said Enzo. 'Daniel.'

'Ah, that Eritrean of yours,' said Bobbio, as though this explained everything.

'It would be good if he didn't do it again,' said Enzo, with understated but unmistakable anger in his voice.

Bobbio studied him for a moment, analysing his tone and expression for any hint of personal offence. Then he nodded once, granting this round to him.

'I'll talk to the major,' he said as he walked away, before adding over his shoulder, 'Welcome back, Enzo. And do look after yourself. It seems that you are needed.'

Enzo allowed himself a smile. He would never warm to this man but it did please him that Bobbio valued his work. And he had to admit that it was still important to him too.

Chapter 14

THERE WERE MORE Italians in Massawa now than there had ever been, Aatifa thought, as she headed through the old town. And not just soldiers but civilians too. She found herself having to go around groups of them as she looked for the gift shop where she had first seen Enzo's employment notice.

She paused and wondered if she had taken a wrong turning. The street was similar but different somehow and then she realised what it was. The old shop was where it had always been, but some workers were now erecting a new name above the window, as an Italian in a grey shop coat set up a display underneath. There was no trace of the former Eritrean owner apart from his discarded, broken sign on the ground nearby.

Aatifa found him well away from the main thoroughfare, down a narrow, curved alley. He was doing his best to set up his usual displays outside an old Turkish building that was one-third the size of his former premises. He recognised her immediately and smiled.

'I know you,' he said, 'you work for that Italian gentleman.'

'Yes, that's right,' she replied.

'Nice man, nice man,' he said, before frowning. 'The new Italians are not so nice; always in a hurry and rude.'

'Why have you moved here?' she asked.

'A man wanted my old shop, for its position. Good passing trade it had, all day long. They came and told me I had to leave. It was not a choice to say yes or no. This is the way of the world, so here I am,' he said, shrugging. He looked at her, his head on one side, and then smiled.

'Now, beautiful lady, you are looking for something?' he asked. 'All my old stock is here, somewhere. It's not yet arranged but if you know what you are looking for perhaps we can find it together?'

She smiled in return and followed him into his wonderland of objects.

Having worked for more than twenty-four hours without a break, Enzo was just glad to be home. He did not expect to find Aatifa there, so he was surprised and delighted to find her in the kitchen, already immersed in her usual routines.

'How is she?' he asked.

'She is mending,' she said, before turning her back on him and continuing what she was doing. It seemed this was all she had to say to him.

He sighed, then went and eased himself down into a soft leather armchair in front of the living room window. Here, the weariness that he had kept at bay began finally to overtake him. Behind him, the curtains were already closed even though it was still a couple of hours before sunset. The room inside was dimly lit by a single lamp that gave out a warm, gentle glow. He closed his eyes for a moment, and might soon have been lost to a deep sleep except that he sensed her near him. It took some willpower to prise open his heavy eyelids, but when he did, he found her standing in front of him. She offered a small, carefully wrapped package.

'What's this?' he asked.

She held it out closer and he took it without getting up since his legs were now not responding to commands. When he opened it, he found a beautiful, old silver lighter inside. It had flamboyant engravings on it of an abstract design that seemed neither Italian nor Eritrean. He guessed that its origin was somewhere further east, perhaps India or China. Aatifa studied his face carefully to see if he liked it.

'Thank you,' he said. 'It's really lovely.'

He smiled to show that he wasn't just being polite and she seemed pleased.

'Are you hungry? The food is almost ready,' she said.

She hurried back into the kitchen where he could hear the volcanic sounds of water boiling over and vaporising on the flame.

Enzo held the lighter in both hands, tracing the curved lines of the engravings with his finger. It was easily the most welcome present he had ever received. Not because of what it was but because she had given it and that she had felt a desire to do so. This was her way of drawing a line under recent events, he guessed. She was not someone who needed to discuss matters from every possible angle. For her it was done and they could go on as before and that was all he wanted. He decided he would not badger her with invasive questions about her life, although he had many that he would like to have answered.

Resting his head against the seat once more, he slipped away into a contented sleep.

Around midnight, he woke abruptly to find himself sitting in exactly the same position in the armchair. While he was out cold, Aatifa had turned off the lamp and placed a blanket over his legs. The room was only receiving stray light from the kitchen now and some pale blue moonlight penetrating around the living room curtains. The reason he had woken soon became apparent. Someone was knocking loudly on the front door. Enzo jumped up. A visitor this late was not a good sign. He saw Aatifa standing out in the hallway with an angry expression on her face.

'Will I tell them to go away?' she asked.

'No,' he said, 'you stay out of sight.'

She did as he asked, turning out the kitchen light and positioning herself behind the door. No one would see her there unless they were intent on searching the house.

In the hall, Enzo saw the silhouette of a tall figure through the glass panel at the side of the door. Opening it six inches, he peered out and saw Salvatore standing there. He had turned up before looking rough after a night or two's heavy drinking but now he was covered in dust too. Salvatore looked him up and down and Enzo realised that he must look just as bad.

'What have you been doing, Enzo? You're a complete mess!' said Salvatore.

'I was just thinking the same about you,' said Enzo. Then he broke into a smile. 'Is the war over?'

Salvatore shook his head sadly. 'No, not quite . . . Are you going to invite me in or will I stand out here all night?'

Enzo opened the door wide for him and Salvatore wiped his army boots on the mat.

'It's all right,' Enzo called as they entered the living room.

Salvatore looked around, confused. Aatifa appeared out of the darkness into the lamplight.

'Hi, Aatifa,' he said, smiling. He gave Enzo a sideways glance.

'Hello,' said Aatifa, standing awkwardly in the doorway.

'Have we any wine?' asked Enzo.

She nodded and went into the kitchen to get some.

'You know, sometimes I think I don't know you at all,' said Salvatore.

Enzo ushered him over to the table and a moment later Aatifa returned with a bottle and two glasses. Then she left them alone.

'You can't keep her, you know that?' Salvatore said when she was gone. 'It isn't possible.'

'We'll see,' said Enzo defiantly.

'Well, don't say that I didn't warn you.'

Enzo changed the subject. 'How is it down there?' he asked, pouring two generous glasses of wine.

'Hectic, hectic but it's going well,' Salvatore lied. 'Not long left now, they hope.'

'They?'

'The generals. We are falling down with generals now,' he said, without trying to disguise his bitterness.

'So why are you here?' asked Enzo. 'Shouldn't you still be there, doing whatever it is you do?'

Salvatore frowned. 'I came to pick up something at the port but it seems that you have impounded it.'

He pulled out some folded-up paperwork from inside his tunic. Enzo recognised it immediately.

'Iprite?' said Enzo, becoming suddenly serious.

'Yes. They sent me to get it.'

Enzo assumed he was referring to the generals again. 'You know what it is?' he asked.

Salvatore didn't answer though Enzo could see in his eyes that he did.

'It's mustard gas, I looked it up,' said Enzo. 'Banned under the Geneva Protocol, which we signed.'

The colonel nodded. 'Listen to me, Enzo, this is not a good time for your red tape.'

'I have no choice,' insisted Enzo. 'There are strict regulations on the import of poisons that I am obliged to follow.'

'Do not make an issue of this,' warned Salvatore, 'for your own good.'

'It's already an issue. I can't allow it, I won't allow it,' said Enzo flatly.

It had been quite a shock that afternoon when he had managed to get a moment to read up on the substance inside those metal canisters. If he had known what it was earlier that morning, he would not have allowed it to touch land. The crates would already be sailing back to Italy.

In his office on a bottom shelf he had found a dusty but pristine copy of the Geneva Protocol of 1925. It was the first time in his career that he had ever had the need to read it. The protocol's stated purpose was to put a stop to the deployment of chemical or biological weapons in warfare, after the Germans had used gas to devastating effect in the Belgian trenches. He noted that it did not ban Iprite's manufacture or transport, so technically the protocol had not yet been breached. However, it did explicitly forbid its use, so how and why had a consignment of the stuff found its way to Massawa?

'What if I told you that Mussolini himself had ordered this?' said Salvatore, playing his trump card though he did not seem to be taking any pleasure from doing so.

'Mussolini?' Enzo had the feeling that he was being backed into a corner.

'Personally,' said Salvatore.

'But what possible reason could . . .?'

Salvatore sat back, his serious expression fading, and he gave Enzo a relaxed smile.

'You think our army needs help like this?' he asked, waving the papers dismissively. 'Of course it doesn't. This is just a precaution.'

'Why bring it here then?' Enzo asked, still trying to find some logic in the whole business.

'I know! It's silly,' agreed Salvatore. 'They are wasting your time and mine. It's meant to be an insurance policy probably, that's all, one that will never be used. Trust me. That stuff will never come out of its boxes. We'll ship them off to some warehouse at the border and then they'll be shipped right back again in a few weeks' time.'

'It seems an awful lot of trouble to go to, for nothing,' said Enzo.

'You're right,' said Salvatore, 'you're absolutely right, but ours is not to reason why.'

Enzo looked at his old friend, searching his eyes for a sign of deceit, but there didn't seem to be one. However, the whole conversation had made him uneasy, and he couldn't stop himself asking a question that he knew could be taken as an insult.

'So you'll give me your word?'

There was a split second's hesitation and a look of annoyance flashed across Salvatore's face, but it disappeared as quickly as it had come.

'Of course,' he said, 'if it makes you feel better. When they come back, you can count them, Enzo, all right? Now please, sign the bloody paper quickly or they'll think I have deserted.'

Out of the corner of his eye, Enzo spotted Aatifa peering round the kitchen door. He wondered what she had overheard and whether she would have understood much anyway. Thankfully, Iprite and mustard gas were not part of her world. Her head disappeared again as Salvatore placed the release form in front of him. Enzo paused for a moment before signing the crumpled paper and handing it back. Then he followed the document's journey as the colonel folded it roughly and stuffed it inside his tunic. Once he could no longer see it, Enzo felt a sudden urge to ask for it back.

'Right, my friend, I have a war to win,' said Salvatore, taking a long thirsty slug of his wine.

As he stood, he knocked over the remainder of his glass, splashing one hand and sleeve with the deep red liquid.

'What a clumsy idiot,' said Salvatore, looking embarrassed at the spreading mess he had made on the tablecloth and on himself.

'Oh, it's nothing, forget it,' said Enzo. 'The bathroom is—'

'No, the kitchen will do,' interrupted Salvatore, and he walked across the room and in through the door.

As Enzo soaked up the spilled wine with a cloth, he heard the sound of running water and of hands being washed clean. Then there was silence. He continued cleaning up the mess but when Salvatore didn't return, he walked over to where he could see into the kitchen.

Aatifa was sitting on her chair. Salvatore stood in front of her. His right hand was reaching out slowly, to touch the side of her face. Aatifa looked startled, but did not move away. As for Salvatore, he seemed distracted and troubled. Before the tips of his fingers could touch Aatifa's cheek, his eyes met hers and he dropped his hand slowly. Then he noticed Enzo standing in the living room, staring at him.

'Time to go,' said Salvatore, giving both of them a half-hearted smile.

When Enzo returned from showing him out, he saw that Aatifa had been disturbed by whatever had passed between them.

'Did he say something to you?' he asked.

'No, nothing,' she said, before adding, 'but he is not like he was the night we met.'

'No, he isn't,' agreed Enzo.

'What did he want?' she asked.

'He was just collecting something at the port, that's all. He needed my signature,' said Enzo.

He was relieved that she did not ask what it was.

Salvatore smoked a cigarette, while watching some furry moths dive-bomb the harbour lights. Behind him, Eritrean dockers were busy loading the newly released wooden crates on to two army trucks. In the semi-darkness, an operator almost let one fall from his forklift but managed to recover the balance just in time.

'Hey! Be careful with those,' Salvatore shouted angrily.

The general had been furious when he heard the delivery had been delayed. He had been intent on causing serious trouble for whoever was responsible, until Salvatore had volunteered to sort it out. He knew that Enzo had to be behind it. His beloved bureaucracy was always bound to get him into trouble one day. Salvatore had flown hundreds of miles just to save Enzo from himself but he would never tell him that. Enzo would probably not have taken it very well and anyway, it was enough that he had done it. It gave him a good feeling and he was not having many of those in this cursed war.

When the trucks were fully loaded, he turned to one of the young army drivers. 'Strap them down well. I want to get back in one piece.'

'What are they, sir, explosives?' asked the driver, looking at the boxes nervously.

'No, not explosives,' said Salvatore. 'Now come on, hurry up. I've got a pain-in-the-ass general waiting for me.'

The two drivers kept their mouths shut from then on. But they took their time, despite Salvatore's impatience, making doubly sure that the crates were securely tied to the sides of the trucks.

'Ready, Colonel,' said the driver when the job was done.

Salvatore stared out at the sea and didn't reply. He was thinking about how much he envied Enzo. He had got rid of Zula without a second thought. But what if he had been the one to meet Aatifa first? Could he have had the same connection with her that his friend obviously did? Then he was overwhelmed by a feeling of emptiness as he realised that he couldn't imagine what such a connection might feel like.

'Sir?' the driver repeated. 'We're all set.'

Salvatore threw his cigarette into the water, and boarded the lead truck. As they drove away, he watched Enzo's Eritrean dock workers growing smaller and smaller in the side-view mirror.

Chapter 15

BEFORE HE LEFT for work in the morning, Enzo did what he now hated doing more than anything else in the world. Opening his wallet, he took out Aatifa's salary which was due that day. Each note was stamped in red: 'Not For Use Outside the Colonies.'

He found her kneeling on the kitchen floor, furiously scrubbing the tiles with a hard brush as though she still needed to justify her place in his house. Standing up, she took the money and counted it, then divided it and gave some notes back to him.

'I did not work for three days,' she said.

'Don't be silly, keep it.'

'No,' she insisted, 'I will only take what I have earned.'

He put the money away reluctantly, knowing that it was pointless to argue with her when she was in a stubborn mood. Then she took the wages ledger down off the bookshelf and signed her name once more.

I have turned her into a bureaucrat, he thought ruefully.

As she put the ledger back, he said, 'You know I could help . . . with your granddaughter, if you like?'

'What do you mean?' Aatifa asked, looking suddenly uneasy.

'I don't know.' He shrugged, thinking it out as he went

along. 'Maybe I could pay for extra lessons for her, or she could do something else . . . Learn music even; does she like music?'

Aatifa's eyes lit up for a second. Then he saw the light fade as quickly as it had come and she shook her head.

'Why not?' he asked, unable to understand why she would turn down such an offer.

'You brought the doctor and that was enough,' she said.

'But I'd like to do more,' he persisted.

'No,' she said, raising her voice to indicate that she did not want to discuss it further.

'But that doesn't make any sense,' he said, getting annoyed with her now, 'you have the chance to give her more.'

'These things are for me to do, not you,' she said bluntly and left the room.

'Think about it at least, won't you?' he called after her.

At times such as this, her obstinacy infuriated him. Try as he might, he just did not understand her. How could she give him a present of a lighter but refuse to allow him to give anything to Azzezza?

He left without saying goodbye but regretted not doing so all the way to the office.

On her way to check in on Azzezza and Madihah, Aatifa headed for the girl's former elementary school. She needed to tell the teacher that her granddaughter had been ill and that she was not well enough yet to do their usual once a week private lesson. The giant jacaranda tree in the garden was no longer in bloom and most of its leaves had turned brown and fallen to the ground in a circle around the wide trunk. Aatifa walked up the driveway and was about to enter the front door when a new batch of six-year-old Eritrean pupils came outside. The Italian teacher was with them too and an Italian Fascist officer she had never seen before. Aatifa stayed to one side as the children gathered on the lawn. There were no parents, and no diplomas were being given out today. Instead the teacher looked on, with her arms folded, as the officer began to teach her charges how to perform the Fascist salute in the correct manner. The round-faced man was in his mid-forties but did not have the physique of a military officer, his body well padded with an extra layer of fat. Sporting a short but bushy moustache, he was dressed entirely in black from head to toe: cap, shirt, tie, trousers, even black leather gloves, which he had just taken off and was holding in his left hand.

'Like this, children,' said the officer and they all watched him obediently. 'Stand upright, as tall as you can, raise your right arm out.'

None of the children moved an inch and the officer turned to the teacher.

'Do they understand me?'

'Yes, they do,' she said, and she turned to her pupils. 'Do as the officer is showing you, children.'

Aatifa could tell she was not comfortable being a party to this exercise.

The officer now decided to stand in front of them, with all the children at his back.

'All right, everyone ready?' he said. 'With the palm of your hand facing down and all your fingers tight together, like mine are, see? Then one swift movement, straight out and slightly up.'

The children all followed suit with varying degrees of success. Some of them were looking sideways at the teacher, obviously wondering why she wasn't joining in too.

'Very good children, very good,' said the officer. He turned around to face them again. 'This salute is the new way to greet people you meet and will replace shaking hands which is both unhygienic and bourgeois.'

The officer frowned at the wide-eyed faces looking back at him.

'Do they understand *bourgeois*?' he asked the teacher.

'I'll explain it to them later,' she replied curtly.

'Now let me see you all do it together,' said the officer. 'On three. One, two, three, GO.'

Aatifa looked on in horror as the children all did the Fascist salute in perfect unison.

'Beautiful,' said the officer, delighted with himself. 'Bravo!'

'Now, children, back inside for class,' said the teacher, clapping her hands.

'You can all practise this at home, in front of a mirror,' said the officer as they filed past him in pairs.

The teacher turned and caught Aatifa's eye. She was embarrassed and Aatifa decided that now was not the best time to talk to her. She headed out of the gate. Azzezza might not be at school any longer, but at least she was not learning this type of lesson.

Aatifa looked to the bed as soon as she entered the dim light of the hut, and was delighted to find it empty. Azzezza was up and walking around slowly, one hand touching the mud wall for support, in an effort to stretch her stiff legs. Madihah was on the other side of the room holding a long-handled straw brush, trying to encourage a thin green grass snake to move in the direction of the door. Aatifa noticed that her daughter seemed upset, so she helped her by blocking off the harmless serpent's escape routes. When it finally slid outside, they sat down together.

'He does not even know that she was ill,' Madihah said, her face lined with worry.

Since the day he had left, they had received no word at all from Iggi and they had no means of contacting him either. He should have been at home with his family, Aatifa thought, instead of running off and pretending to be a soldier with the Italians.

'He will be home soon enough,' was all she said to her anxious daughter.

When Azzezza was out of earshot, Madihah shook her head and whispered, 'No, he is dead, I'm sure of it. What did he know about war? He probably died on the first day.'

Aatifa thought that her daughter was better off without this man and had no great desire to see him return. But she certainly did not wish him dead.

'He is alive,' she said, 'you would have felt it if he had gone.'

Madihah knew this was nonsense, but she took comfort from it anyway.

Azzezza turned back towards them, continuing her exercises with determination, one light, tentative step after another. Aatifa thought again about what Enzo had said to her that morning. She would give everything she had to this child without a moment's hesitation but to take it from him would be different. Rejecting his offer was an instinctive reaction and she was tempted to believe that because of this, it must have been the right choice. However, the more she had mulled it over since, the more she wondered whether she was being irrational. Azzezza was her weak point, she knew, the way through her defences. It had taken an emergency to push her into asking for Enzo's help; to do it on a regular basis would be a much bigger step.

'What?' asked Azzezza, catching sight of her grandmother's distracted stare.

Aatifa shook her head and smiled. 'You should rest now and not overdo it. A little each day.'

Enzo walked home in the cool of the evening after a day at the port that had been reassuringly uneventful. On his way, he was surprised to see his neighbour, Eva, sitting in a smoky bar. She was alone, in that her husband wasn't there, but she had plenty of male company. Around her was a group of eager young Italian soldiers, all trying to entertain her with their jokes. When she took out a cigarette, three of them tried to light it for her at the same time. Eva laughed at them coyly and then lit the cigarette herself. My God, she's teasing them, thought Enzo. Who would have guessed? And he wondered where she had told her husband she was going.

At the house, he found Aatifa sitting with her legs pulled up to her chest, on the sill of her bedroom window. Her intense expression didn't change even when she noticed him in the doorway. He decided to wait and see if she had anything to say.

'I was too young to give my daughter what she needed,' she began, while still looking out of the window towards the open, endless sea. 'In the beginning I didn't even want her . . . I am ashamed to say that, but it's true.' She looked up to see if this admission had made him think less of her but it hadn't.

He was tempted to tell her that he would never judge her, but he was afraid that if he spoke too soon it might bring an abrupt halt to this rare opening up from her.

'I have tried to make it up to her ever since, when she lets me; and now I want my granddaughter to have every opportunity she can.'

Enzo stepped a little further into the room and saw that she had been crying.

'I thought about what you said,' she continued, 'and it hurts that you can help her more than me. I wanted to be the one to do everything for them, but I cannot because we are not equals.'

He moved over, right beside her now, brushing away a stray, runaway tear with his thumb.

'No,' he agreed. 'You are better than me.'

Aatifa smiled and shook her head. 'You are a funny man.'

'Let me do this,' he whispered softly, 'for you. I'd like to. I would do anything for you.'

She looked up into his eyes and could see that he meant it.

The silence of the valley was broken by the hum from a squadron of five Italian aeroplanes flying in formation against a deep blue sky. Synchronised and graceful, their V shape from a distance could easily have been mistaken for a flock of migrating geese. Just north of the Tekezé River, which was wide and deep after the rainy season, Salvatore observed a large regiment of uniformed Ethiopian soldiers preparing for an Italian attack. They were a peculiar sight: barefoot infantry, and a mixed cavalry of horse and camel. Despite having had some modest success with their guerrilla campaign, the Ethiopians had been unable to keep the invading forces from edging ever closer to the capital Addis Abeba. Open conflict could not be put off any longer. Through his binoculars, Salvatore watched as the Ethiopian troops first heard then saw the aircraft approaching them. Their animals became jittery and difficult to control but their commanding officer ordered them to hold their ground.

Above them now, the lead aeroplane released a string of metal canisters from its undercarriage which then dropped steadily towards the men below. Each of the following pilots repeated the same procedure. Then the squadron split and turned in two groups, left and right, until they joined up in formation once again, heading back the way they had come. As the sound of the aircraft waned, the only noise left was from the dozens of shining canisters whistling through the air. Some gently bounced off each other and twirled away in opposite directions.

Salvatore saw the riders getting increasingly uneasy, probably expecting that bombs were about to land in their midst. When the canisters all exploded a hundred feet above them in mid-air, doing no damage whatsoever, a cheer went up from the Ethiopian soldiers. The explosions had left a huge layer of liquid that had formed in a split second after the detonation. This seemed to be suspended, weightless and floating in the air. As quickly as it had formed, the liquid fell like a light summer shower on the infantry and cavalry below. The men looked at each other, laughing, as if wondering why the Italians had chosen to throw water at them. Then almost immediately the laughter ceased. Cries erupted from every direction as the men's skin and throats began to burn, even through the wetness of their clothes. Some tried to rub themselves dry or tear off their tunics in a desperate bid to escape the pain. It was not pleasant to watch but Salvatore did not look away once. The burning did not discriminate between animal and man, and many horses and camels collapsed or threw their riders. One in ten was destined not to leave the battlefield alive, but death did not come quickly for them. Most endured several minutes of agony, until asphyxiation finally took them, the end coming as a release.

A smaller group of two hundred Ethiopian riders had been left untouched by the downpour. Their commanding officer immediately ordered a charge against Salvatore's infantry which was now advancing towards them from the opposite end of the valley.

'Get ready,' ordered Salvatore, as he saw them coming.

The horses rode at a canter, dwarfed by the trotting camels alongside them. Then they picked up speed until they were at full gallop, racing along the gorge. Even Salvatore had to admit they were an impressive sight.

At the Ethiopian cavalry officer's signal, his riders opened fire at a hundred paces with a motley collection of rifles, killing a dozen Italian soldiers. Then Salvatore's infantry returned a fierce volley which felled a quarter of the rapidly advancing Ethiopians. What remained of the cavalry slammed into the Italian front line. And then the fight descended into a bloody close-quarters struggle with rifles, pistols, bayonets and swords. Salvatore, on foot, fired all around him, killing several of the attackers, only pausing when he had to reload his revolver. He saw that Iggi was to his right behind the rest of the Askari but he hadn't seen him fire a single shot. His face seemed paralysed with fear.

'Fight, fight,' ordered Salvatore, when he saw that he was doing nothing. 'You want to die?'

Iggi nervously raised up his rifle, aimed and killed an Ethiopian soldier who was rapidly approaching Salvatore's back. After that, he followed Salvatore wherever he went, the two of them moving as a pair through the battle.

Almost all the chargers were dead in minutes. It had been a suicide mission. No prisoners were taken because the battle continued until there was no one left to fight. Afterwards, Salvatore looked around at the array of bodies. They were mostly Ethiopians but there were dozens of Italians and Askari too. Many had fallen in contorted positions with tortured, frozen expressions, while others seemed just to be resting peacefully. There were wounded horses and camels too, which his men were now shooting to end their suffering, the mercy of this act out of place with all that had gone before.

Salvatore began to search among the dead, looking for a familiar face. When he found the Ethiopian cavalry officer, he drew his sword from its sheath and bent over the body. His long, thin ceremonial blade had not been designed for the use he now put it to and he had to struggle at his gruesome task. Then, hands covered in blood, he stood and raised the dead man's head triumphantly in the air, holding it by its matted hair. Sensing someone nearby, he looked around and saw Iggi staring at him in disbelief. A change came over him then, and he felt himself returning to reality. He slowly lowered his arm and looked at the object he was holding. Repulsed, he let it tumble to the ground beside the body from which it had been taken. He looked once more at Iggi, and then turned and walked away from the carnage, leaving his sword standing upright in the ground where he had last used it.

Chapter 16

THE 'LITTLE WAR' took until the end of the following spring to reach its conclusion. It was clear that the Ethiopians had not been swayed by thoughts of the benefits that would accrue to them if they had meekly accepted Italian rule. Instead they had put up a fierce resistance to the very idea. Enzo did not have much sympathy for their cause. Suffering had been inflicted needlessly, on both sides, because of their short-sighted refusal to see that the Italian way in Africa was the right one. And as a result, they had delayed the development of their own country by a full six months.

The extended conflict had also turned into an unforeseen money pit, one that Italy could ill afford. Italian East Africa now extended all the way from Eritrea in the north, down through Ethiopia and on to Italian Somaliland in the south, a vast territory of seven hundred thousand square miles that made it one of the biggest colonial players in the region. Now that the Italians had won militarily, Enzo knew they would have to win over their new citizens with that promised investment. Once the Ethiopians saw their own conditions improving, he expected they would recognise that they had been hasty in their initial rejection of Italian governance.

*

Enzo had not seen Salvatore since that odd night in his house but he had heard that he had come through it all unscathed. A telephone call, he felt, would not be a satisfactory welcome home after all that his friend had been through, and he decided that he would travel up to Asmara to greet his return in person. The choice of whether or not to invite Aatifa to come with him was not a difficult one. She was still stubbornly attached to her anti-war stance, though he hoped she might come around to his way of thinking sooner rather than later. There was also the risk that the two of them travelling together might arouse suspicion in anyone looking out for such things.

He arrived in Asmara on the first train, having shared the journey with several American journalists. These men had laughed and joked among themselves the whole way up and had taken photos out of the window of everything that moved.

'I didn't know they had camels here,' one said, 'did you?'

On Asmara's main boulevard, the green, white and red bunting and the brass band had all been set up since the early hours. Waiters from the bars and cafés were standing around in anticipation of a busy day ahead, but there was still no sign of the troops. A newspaper seller told him that they were not due for several hours yet. So he decided to kill the time by stepping into the cool of the Cinema Impero for a matinee screening.

As always the feature was preceded by a newsreel and this one was, naturally, all about Italy's triumph. It showed a huge crowd gathered in Piazza Venezia in Rome as Mussolini declared victory. Thousands upon thousands of men and women were there, not soldiers but ordinary people, a sea of smiling, cheering faces. Enzo was delighted and proud to see so many of his fellow Italians back home getting excited about events in his part of the world.

'The Duce was called back to the microphone by the crowd, time after time,' said the voice-over, which was even more jaunty than usual. 'And he told them that what they had won with blood, they would now have to fertilise with work.'

In the darkness, Enzo nodded. This was exactly what he thought too.

Then the five-foot King with his elongated moustache was shown strolling around his royal gardens as the voice-over continued: 'King Vittorio Emanuele will now be adding a new title to his name, Emperor of Ethiopia.'

The previous, now deposed Emperor, Haile Selassie, had fled to Europe. He had lost control of his country but he was still using his old royal title, refusing to recognise his demotion.

During the reel change for the main feature, the lights came up and Enzo saw that there were only white Italian faces beside him now. On his way in, a prominent new sign in the foyer had directed Eritreans upstairs. It had not been there on his last visit. If it had he would not have been able to sit beside Aatifa. He looked up to the gallery above and there a dozen Eritreans sat stony-faced watching the screen. The musical introduction for the main movie was disturbed by the muffled sounds of the brass band and cheering outside. Enzo and most of the other Italians got up and left.

It took his eyes a moment to adjust from the dim auditorium to the extreme sunlight outside. The dizzy feeling soon passed and he walked with dozens of other people in the direction of the bandstand. Some sections of the regiments were still marching in columns into town. But order in the ranks had quickly broken down for those ahead of them as the young men eagerly dispersed to the various watering holes. Italian civilians shook the newly arrived soldiers' hands while Eritrean women and children tearfully greeted their Askari men. Enzo witnessed an Askari man obviously delivering some bad news to a young Eritrean woman. She started wailing and shaking uncontrollably, but her cries were drowned out by the sounds of celebration.

Among the other Askari, Enzo spotted Madihah's husband, Iggi. He watched him scanning the Eritrean faces in the crowd, but his family was not there. He had still to complete the journey down the mountain before he would be reunited with them. Enzo walked in Iggi's direction and could see that this was making the man nervous.

'Your daughter,' said Enzo, 'Azzezza.'

Iggi looked startled that this Italian stranger should know her name.

'She was sick. Very sick actually,' continued Enzo, 'but it's fine now, she's better.'

Enzo would have explained it all to him but he didn't get the chance. Without a word, Iggi began to push his way past people out on to the road, and run towards a fleet of trucks. Enzo set off after him, but Iggi had already flung his kitbag on to the back of one of the trucks and hauled himself up behind it. The driver revved the engine, slammed the vehicle into gear and it took off in a cloud of black smoke towards the Massawa road.

At least he would be reunited with his wife and daughter sooner than expected, and one of them would explain why that Italian man knew so much about his life.

When the truck turned a corner, out of sight, Enzo walked on down the main street in the direction of Salvatore's favourite bar. Sure enough there he was, at a small table on his own, having a long cool beer. Something struck Enzo as odd. While the bar was overflowing with dozens of soldiers, no one was sharing Salvatore's table. Instead the colonel had his head down and appeared not to be in the mood for conversation.

'Hail the conquering hero,' said Enzo.

Salvatore looked up, annoyed, but when he saw who it was, he smiled.

'It's you! My God,' and then he shouted to a waiter, 'A beer for my friend here.'

'You're alive,' said Enzo, as he sat down beside him.

'I told you,' said Salvatore, 'bullet-proof.'

Enzo's beer arrived in seconds. The bar staff were just filling glass after glass and lining them up in a row for easy delivery.

'How was it?' he asked.

Salvatore frowned. 'War is never pretty, or so I'm told. Hopefully I won't get to experience it again. Once is more than enough.'

'Why did they fight for so long, that's what I don't understand?' asked Enzo, but Salvatore just shook his head. 'I'm glad you are back in one piece anyway.'

'Me too,' said Salvatore, looking down into his beer. 'Not everyone was so lucky.'

'I know,' said Enzo, 'I met some of the wounded going home.' Then he raised his glass and toasted, 'To no more wars.'

The colonel nodded over to the group of Askari that Iggi had been with moments earlier. They were now spilling out from an Eritrean bar down a side alley across the street.

'They fought well, that lot. You'd be surprised how much gusto they put into slaughtering their own.'

'Did you see much action?' asked Enzo. The boyish part of him was eager to hear stories of real-life adventure.

'A bit,' was all that Salvatore offered.

Enzo supposed it was too soon to be asking for such anecdotes; Salvatore would tell him all at a later time. 'I haven't seen you since that night,' he continued. 'You remember? You had me worried there for a while.'

Salvatore looked up at him sharply, searching his face for something. Then he said, 'Look, Enzo, those crates won't be coming back to you.'

The shock hit Enzo hard.

'We used it?' he said, hardly believing the words coming out of his own mouth.

Salvatore avoided his eyes and did not reply. He didn't need to.

'We were always going to, weren't we . . . all along?'

'The decision was not mine,' said Salvatore, angry now. 'I didn't have a choice and neither did you. Orders were given and that was that.'

Enzo remained silent, burdened by a conscience heavy enough for both of them.

'We would have won anyway,' said Salvatore, knocking back some more of his drink.

This only made Enzo feel worse; to have used gas unnecessarily, when they were not even staring at defeat. It made no sense. He pulled himself together, and looked at the young soldiers who were laughing and slapping each other on the back. Then he shifted focus on to the Italian civilians who were still on the streets, congratulating the returned men and waving flags in the air.

'They don't know,' he said.

'Do you think any of them care?' said Salvatore dismissively.

'I sincerely hope that some of them would,' replied Enzo.

Salvatore gave a cynical shrug. 'The empire is rising, Enzo,' he said bitterly. 'And here's a word of advice: change all your money into gold. When empires fall, you can always buy bread with that.'

'Did you know?' asked Enzo. 'In my house? Were you lying when you gave me your word?'

'Wake up,' Salvatore snapped. 'You think there is a difference between killing them with gas and killing them with bullets? They still end up the same, just dead. You understand, Enzo? Dead.'

'At least they stand a chance,' Enzo replied. 'And how do we end up? Tell me that. We are supposed to be the civilised ones.'

An awkward silence descended between them, in the midst of all the raucous laughter and chatter. Salvatore emptied his glass and signalled impatiently for the waiter.

'All the fun has gone out of this place,' he said finally. 'You want another drink?'

Enzo shook his head. His first beer was still standing warm and uninviting in front of him. 'It has become more than fun for me, I'm afraid,' he said, standing up.

'I told you not to get involved, didn't I?' said Salvatore.

'Yes. Yes, you did,' said Enzo. 'It's no one's fault. It just happened . . . Too late now.'

And he turned and walked away, leaving Salvatore as he had found him. Alone in a crowd.

Enzo made his way through the groups of grinning soldiers and back down towards the station, not knowing or caring when the next train was due. On his way he passed another crowd of people who had gathered for the opening of a newly built Fiat service station. Even though he wanted to be by himself, the sight of it made him stop too. Designed in the popular futuristic style, it had been built in the shape of an aircraft. The roof projected out on both sides like two large wings, each supported by temporary wooden beams. As he watched, a young Italian man ordered them to be taken down and there was a sharp intake of breath from the crowd. The two roof wings jutted out so far from the main structure that it seemed they might collapse as the supports were removed, but the structure remained defiantly solid.

'Bravo! Bravo!' the crowd shouted.

'Italy is changing the world, ladies and gentlemen,' the young man shouted back at them, which brought more cheers and another round of enthusiastic applause.

As a car was driven in for the first ceremonial fill of petrol, Enzo left them to it.

The train station was empty since the next departure was not for another hour so he sat down on a wooden bench on the platform and waited. They had indeed changed the world, he thought. They had created an African empire for themselves, one way or another. He wondered if those one million Italians would come now as Bobbio had said.

As for the gas, he assumed the government would try to keep it a secret. It would be hard to hush it up since there would be victims and witnesses. But they controlled Ethiopia now, and it was highly unlikely the Duce would grant them a free press in which to report it to the world. Who would care anyway? Would anyone? The other colonial powers were not going to shout too loudly about foul play lest an accusing finger might be pointed in their direction too. No, it would be a crime without punishment, and those who had had any hand in it would just carry on as though nothing grotesque had actually happened.

Do I bear any responsibility? he asked himself. Through inaction, certainly. And will I just carry on like the others, pretending that nothing had happened? The answer did not make him feel proud.

When he closed his front door, the quiet calm of the house was a welcome relief, as if by this simple action he was able to keep the real world from entering. He would have liked to pour everything out to Aatifa but he was too ashamed.

'I met Iggi up there,' he said, 'he should already be home by now.'

She seemed to greet this news with mixed feelings.

'I'd like a drink,' he said, suddenly feeling a driving need to let loose after such a day. 'Would you like one?'

'All right,' she said, without much enthusiasm.

'What would madame like?' he said, in a mock waiter's voice. 'We have red or red.'

'Red please,' said Aatifa, smiling at his performance.

'Excellent choice, madame. Coming right up. Cook!' he shouted into the kitchen. 'What have you for our guests tonight?'

No answer came from the kitchen and Aatifa grinned and whispered, 'Pasta.'

'He says pasta, will that do?'

'I suppose it will have to,' she replied, and it lightened his mood to see her laugh.

'I'm sorry, that's all we have,' said Enzo, 'we're just training him in. Sit, I'll serve. Sit, sit,' he said, pulling out a chair for her. Then he lit some tall, slim candles with his silver lighter. 'If we can't go out together, we can at least make it nice in here. And may I say, it's always a pleasure to welcome you to our humble restaurant.'

Next he put on lively music on the gramophone, choosing a Strauss waltz, and finally he served the food and poured the wine. After downing his own first glass in one straight gulp, he poured himself another and began to refill her glass to the brim.

'No! Enough,' Aatifa protested, covering her glass with her hand.

Two bottles later, of which he had drunk the lion's share, they danced wildly around the floor. Enzo was well beyond his alcohol threshold now and was speaking his mind. Though not so freely that he would mention what he had discovered earlier. He spun her around the floor faster and faster, until she was dizzy and they were both sweaty and out of breath. It gave him great pleasure to see her enjoying herself. Like him, she was not one to let herself go very often.

'We should be dancing in the street in front of everyone, not hidden away in here,' he said loudly. 'It is our Italian disease, you know, to complicate life with rules and regulations. I should know. I am an expert in that line. I am the King of Boring Bureaucrats, the Emperor of Fools.'

'You are not a fool,' she shouted, thinking he was making a joke, and he thought how little she really knew him.

'Madame is too kind,' he said, giving a theatrical bow, 'but I'm afraid you are greatly mistaken. If you knew me well, you would hate me . . .'

Aatifa looked confused by the turn in the conversation. He embraced her again and they waltzed at increasing speed around the room, bumping into a table lamp and knocking it over on to the floor. Gasping for air and laughing, they separated. Aatifa knelt to retrieve the lamp and Enzo went to fix the curtains, which had been pulled apart.

He had them almost closed when the silhouette of a person

on the street caught his eye. Eva was standing motionless at the garden gate, looking in at him. He wondered how long she had been there and whether she had seen him and Aatifa dancing around like lunatics. She turned and continued on into her own house. Perhaps she had been out flirting with the young soldiers again, he thought. He was not the only one with secrets.

Over the weeks that followed, Aatifa noticed that Iggi had come back from the war a more confident man. He never spoke about his experiences, at least not to her. But he was determined to continue working for the Italian military for as long as they wanted him. His enlistment seemed to have given him some purpose and direction where there had been none before. And even though Aatifa did not approve, his change of character was welcome. There was also the added bonus that his regular trips away with his regiment meant that she would get to spend more time with Madihah and Azzezza without him.

Money was no longer such a stressful issue. Both of them now earned steady salaries. But Madihah still gave her a knowing smile when she told her that Enzo wanted to pay for extra tuition for Azzezza.

'If he wants to, why not let him?' she said. 'Isn't that what you wanted all along anyway, that she should learn all she can?'

Aatifa nodded, frowning. She wondered if she had been silly to worry over it. 'I'll let him do it then, it's all right?' she asked.

'Yes,' said Madihah, 'of course, is there a reason not to?'

Aatifa thought about this one last time, and then she said, 'No . . . there isn't.'

'How long will he do it for?' asked Madihah, but Aatifa only shrugged her shoulders.

He will do it for as long as we are together, she thought. And how long that would be was unanswerable.

Chapter 17

WITH RELATIVE PEACE restored once more in the region, most of the Italian troops returned home via the port. Enzo had welcomed them with open arms when they arrived, but he was more than glad to see them leaving. It was as if a great storm had been and gone. He hoped there were not more to follow.

The single outstanding issue in his life was that he had not spoken to Salvatore in months, not since that victory day in Asmara. Enzo was still angry with his friend – and at himself too, for being so trusting. But he knew that what Salvatore had said was true. Neither of them had any real power. If he had dug in his heels at the port it would only have served to delay the inevitable. He could not overrule Mussolini's orders any more than Salvatore could overrule his generals. But this did not make him feel any better about his own involvement and the feeling of shame lingered. It was a stain that he expected would never be completely washed clean.

A new post-war normality took hold of his working day. It was busier than before, with a marked increase in the number of supply ships transporting goods to their vast new colony, but the frenzied hysteria was gone. Regular office hours were observed once more, with the same young clerks back to waiting by the exit door to punch out on the stroke of seven o'clock.

Then one morning the monotony was broken when the tide brought a highly unusual cargo to Massawa: two hundred Italian prostitutes. As the colourful parade disembarked, the young women were greeted with wolf whistles from the Italian dock workers. The Eritrean staff looked on wide-eyed, enjoying the view, though they didn't dare whistle themselves. The Eritreans had never seen so many young Italian women here. They could have been forgiven for thinking that all Italian females were middle-aged and married because they were the only ones they had ever encountered. Now here was physical proof that this was not true, in the form of shapely legs and pretty and not-so-pretty faces. All of them painted regardless with a thick layer of make-up.

A short, rotund, middle-aged woman with a hooked nose and a hard expression was in charge of them. 'Come on, girls, move along,' she barked at a couple of her charges who had strayed to flirt with the dockers.

'Will you be staying in town?' asked one slightly stunned man.

'No, love, we're not stopping,' said the madam, 'we're bound for Ethiopia, where I'm told we will be the only white women for a thousand miles. You're welcome to visit the girls there if you'd like.'

And with that bitter disappointment, the dockers looked on longingly at what they would never have.

'Back to work,' shouted Enzo.

The young women formed a long line up the stairs into his office. Enzo did not trust his young clerks to do the job in a professional manner, so he took it upon himself to inspect their identity papers. Keeping conversation to a bare minimum, he checked each one thoroughly and then stamped them with his customary precision. It was a blessing that he was not responsible for any medical checks. He shuddered to think what else these women might be bringing into the colony, apart from their luggage. Business must have been pretty bad at home to make them come such a long way in search of new clients. Since there were so few Italian women here and there were still so many young soldiers, these travelling saleswomen would have a captive market. Though they would not quite have it all to themselves. There were places where the Eritrean equivalent plied their trade and, highlighting the hypocrisy of Law 880, the use of these services by Italian men had not been made illegal.

A red-haired, freckle-faced young woman was next to present her papers. She did not seem at all the type to be a prostitute. She looked more like someone's girlfriend, or daughter, ordinary and plain.

'Name?' he asked her.

'What would you like it to be?' she said coyly, spoiling his first impression.

'The one your mother gave you,' he replied sternly.

She smiled, relieved that she didn't have to put on an act for him.

'Valentina,' she said.

'Your date of birth?'

'April 23rd 1917,' she replied.

Just nineteen, he thought, only a child. For a moment he considered giving her a lecture on life's pitfalls, but she was old enough to make her own decisions.

'Occupation?' he asked, momentarily forgetting that he had decided not to ask any more of them that question. He had already been on the receiving end of a wide variety of answers, the majority of which he was not inclined to preserve in ink.

'Never mind,' he said, holding up his hand. He wrote down 'Waitress', and put an asterisk beside it so that he would remember that she was part of this specialist group.

He heard the unwelcome sound of Bobbio's voice outside, greeting the women as he walked past them down the line: 'Ladies, so good to see you.' The ministry man had become an irregular visitor to his office, once a fortnight at most.

He knocked once and entered, looking flushed and delighted with himself.

'Hello, Enzo,' he said, though he only had eyes for Valentina. 'Don't mind me, carry on, no rush.' He closed the door behind him and stood waiting while Enzo stamped Valentina's papers.

Enzo handed the documents back to her and would have wished her good luck had Bobbio not been there. Instead he just gave her a little nod to indicate that everything was in satisfactory order.

'Thanks,' she said and made for the door.

'Welcome to Italian East Africa, my dear,' said Bobbio, with a slight bow of his bald, sunburned head.

'My idea,' he said, when she was gone. 'To keep our boys away from temptation with all those native women.'

'How clever,' said Enzo, without trying to disguise his sarcasm. These days he found it hard to muster even a decent level of politeness for their meetings.

If Bobbio had noticed his tone, he didn't seem to mind. 'Enzo, I want you to take a little trip with me next week.'

'Where to?' Enzo asked with a sinking feeling.

'Ethiopia,' said Bobbio. 'Something I want you to look at. Thursday morning. I'll pick you up at seven.'

'But isn't it still dangerous?' Enzo asked, trying to think of any way out of this.

'Not where we're going, it's fine,' Bobbio said with a patronising smile. 'And the rest of the country will be as well soon enough. Just a few diehards making noises, that's all.'

'There are no ships in Ethiopia,' protested Enzo. 'It's landlocked. Why would you want me to go all the way there?'

'Because there's an unusual job that requires your skills,' said Bobbio, who was in such an annoyingly good mood that Enzo's reluctance wasn't irritating him even slightly. 'I'll explain on the way. Seven now, don't forget.'

He opened the door and let the next young woman in. 'He's all yours, my dear.'

Ever since the victory in Ethiopia, Bobbio had worn a permanently smug grin on his face, as though he had been responsible for it. In fact he had stayed as far away from the fighting as was humanly possible. No doubt his star had risen since then in the eyes of the ministry and he was probably expecting a return call to Rome any second, with a promotion thrown in too. At least, Enzo thought, that was something they could both look forward to.

The next young woman entered and sat in the visitor's chair. Enzo held out his hand for her papers without bothering to look up. 'Name?'

On the appointed day and with a distinct lack of enthusiasm, Enzo forced himself to rise before dawn. Aatifa got up too and made him coffee even though he had told her not to bother. When he had mentioned the previous week where he was going, her response had been only silence. Now as he sat drinking his coffee, she leaned against the kitchen doorway, watching him with her arms folded.

'Why are you going there?' she asked finally. 'To see the lands you stole?'

'Please . . . don't,' he said, standing up and gathering his things. 'I haven't stolen anything.'

'I don't want you to go,' she said with genuine concern.

'I don't want to go either,' said Enzo, 'but I have to. I don't have a choice.'

He walked over and kissed her cheek. She didn't respond. But then just as he reached the door, she called after him in a tender voice, 'Be careful.'

'I always am,' he said, turning around, happy to be parting on good terms. 'I'll be back very late tonight, so don't wait up.'

They flew for two hours in clear skies, on board an air force, three-propellered Caproni 101. It had room for eight passengers but they were the only two on board this particular flight. Hardly any conversation passed between them as they chose to sit opposite each other at window seats to take in the views. In any case it was difficult to hear anything at all above the constant noise of the throbbing engines. Then as soon as the pilot shouted out that they had crossed the indistinguishable border into Ethiopia, they began their descent to land.

'We're not going far then?' shouted Enzo, buoyed by the thought that their journey might be a short one.

'You'll see,' was all Bobbio would say.

An army driver with an open-topped car was waiting for them on the dusty airfield. He held the back doors open for them like a proper chauffeur.

'Would you like to tell me where we are going now?' Enzo asked.

'Ever heard of Axum?' asked Bobbio.

Enzo nodded. It was somewhere he had considered visiting

before Aatifa and before the war. The ancient Kingdom of Axum had existed for over a thousand years but as with most of the once great civilisations it had been overtaken by others and had disappeared like a shadow in time. As far as he knew there was little trace of it left.

The driver took them along narrow and uninhabited country roads though there was little difference between the supposed driving surface and the off-road part. Both seemed to be made of the same fine brown powder. About half an hour into their journey, in the middle of nowhere, they passed a giant cloth billboard that had obviously been recently erected. It featured Mussolini's face with the Fascist icon beside it, a bunch of sticks bound together, symbolising the party's slogan: 'strength through unity'. Someone had decided that this out-of-the-way place was a good location for it, but it was a bizarre sight in this arid country setting. Bobbio stood up and did a mock Fascist salute and then roared with laughter at his own sense of humour.

Enzo tapped on the driver's shoulder, and pointed at a mountain range in the near distance, 'What mountains are those?'

The driver turned and shouted, 'The Adwa Mountains.'

Enzo and Bobbio stared at the peaks, which were now half in sun and half in dark shadow. This had been the graveyard of thousands of their fellow countrymen when they had first fought in Ethiopia at the end of the last century; though a greater number of Italians had met their end in this new war. Enzo had read a figure of ten thousand, with four times that many wounded. And they had been the victors. In all probability, the butcher's bill for the losing side was many times higher.

They continued on past a small lake, where a few dead

camels lay decaying near the waterside. There were some other partial skeletons nearby which Enzo hoped were animals too.

'The water's poisoned now,' explained Bobbio. After a short pause he added, 'We could not lose to a bunch of Africans for a second time, could we?'

Enzo chose not to reply.

The journey continued across the same rough terrain. The two of them bounced around in the back seat and swallowed so much dust and flies that they were obliged to cover their mouths as best they could. The driver had come equipped with a pair of driving goggles and a scarf to wrap around his face, though he still needed to wipe the caking dust off the lenses after every mile or so.

Finally, they passed under the shade of some old olive trees and out into an open area surrounded by low-lying hills. An extraordinary sight now lay before them. The valley was full of giant man-made obelisks, though most of them were no longer standing, knocked down, perhaps, in an ancient war or by an earthquake. Huge chunks of sculpted stone littered the ground. The driver led them over to one that had probably been the biggest in its day, but which was now broken into five half-buried pieces. Enzo stared at it in awe. It must have stood at least seventy feet tall, maybe eighty. A massive granite structure, it was decorated with false door reliefs at its wide base and what seemed to be false windows the whole way up. A semi-circular shape crowned its pinnacle.

'Hard to believe they had a civilisation that could do something like this, isn't it?' said Bobbio, standing now on top of one of the pieces.

'How old are they?' asked Enzo.

'That one is third century AD,' said the driver, reading from a piece of paper. 'Axumite, whoever they were. It doesn't say.'

'All this used to be their kingdom,' said Enzo. 'Maybe they left us these, so that we wouldn't forget them.'

Bobbio shrugged and pointed along the five pieces. 'This one, the Duce wants to put up in Rome.'

'My God!' said Enzo, letting his shock get the better of him. 'Doesn't it belong here, with the others?'

'It's broken!' said Bobbio. 'They all are. They obviously didn't build them very well . . . and anyway, everything in this country is ours now, to do with as we please.'

There were already several obelisks in Rome, Enzo knew, that had been taken from Egypt in the days of the Roman Empire. The first one to arrive, the tallest in the world, once belonged to the temple of Amun at Karnak before it was re-erected in the Circus Maximus. Mussolini, it seemed, was intent on reviving the dubious traditions of Augustus and Caligula.

'Transport is your thing so can it be done or not?' asked Bobbio.

'If we try to move it, the risk of further damage is . . . can we just tell him that it can't be done?'

'Sure, you tell him, go ahead,' said Bobbio, and he and the driver shared a smile. 'Are you saying you can't do it? Because this is going to Rome one way or another, either intact or in a thousand little pieces, so you decide.'

Enzo sighed and started to study the obelisk carefully. He walked around the five pieces several times, touching them, trying to guess their weight and solidity. The ancient Romans had put the Egyptian obelisks on to large ships, sailed them up the Nile, out into the Mediterranean and from there on to their new home. That route was not an option this time around. The British had not objected too strongly to Italy's takeover of Ethiopia, but it was highly unlikely that Mussolini would be asking them politely for permission to sail his obelisk through their Egyptian colony.

The more Enzo looked at the problem, the more convinced he became that it was possible. He thought about lying, but then this precious remnant of a lost civilisation might end up being irreparably damaged if some fool approached the job in the wrong way. And he wanted that least of all.

'We would have to dig around them carefully,' he said, pointing at the buried parts of the structure, 'and get ropes or steel cable under the ends. Bring up our biggest cranes. Then we could lift each piece on to the back of trucks. They'd have to be large ones to take the weight. Plus they'd have to drive all the way to Massawa on those roads. But if they got that far we could winch each piece on to a ship at the port.'

'And then in Rome they put it back together?' Bobbio looked doubtful. 'Will it work?'

Enzo suspected his concern was more to do with the maintenance of his reputation in Rome than with any new-found archaeological passion.

'It's a big job but yes, with care, it can be done,' said Enzo, 'and hopefully we can limit any new damage.'

Bobbio turned to the driver. 'Arrange it.'

'Yes, sir,' said the driver, heading back to the car to make notes.

'You know, technically this is looting,' said Enzo, when their guide was out of earshot.

A look of anger flashed across Bobbio's face before he broke into a grin.

'It would be, if we weren't the rightful owners,' he said, holding out his hands. 'But luckily we are.'

Bobbio studied Enzo for a moment, noting that he wasn't seeing the funny side.

'We'll have to do something about that conscience of yours, Enzo,' he said, 'it's not an asset for people like us; and I'd hate to see it block your way.'

Enzo no longer cared about his way being blocked. Any promotion would mean a return to Italy and there would be no way that he could hide Aatifa back there.

'Well, that was easier than I thought,' said Bobbio. 'Let's go and celebrate.'

'Shouldn't we be starting back?' said Enzo. 'It'll be dark soon.'

'Oh, we're staying the night, didn't I say? I've something to do in Addis Abeba in the morning.'

'But I can't,' protested Enzo.

'Well, you'll have to walk home then,' said Bobbio. 'Don't worry, your precious port will manage without you until tomorrow.'

Chapter 18

THEY DROVE BACK to the airfield and boarded the same aeroplane, which Bobbio seemed to have commandeered for the day. Then they took the scenic route down to the Ethiopian capital, skirting the spectacularly dramatic Simien mountain range with its jagged volcanic peaks and deep green valleys below. As they passed over it, Enzo saw a pair of eagles soaring majestically just underneath them. But he kept this sight to himself, not wishing to share the pleasure of it with his companion on the other side of the aisle. They continued on southwards over giant Lake Tana, which was dotted with dozens of islands and reed boats. At the far end, they crossed its massive falls, the roar of which they could actually hear over the propeller engines, as it expelled tonnes of water down into the river below.

'That is the source of the Blue Nile,' the pilot shouted.

Even Bobbio was impressed, Enzo noticed. Perhaps he thought he now owned this too.

It was early evening when they arrived at the airport, just outside Addis Abeba, where a new army driver was waiting for them. Bobbio fumbled in an inside pocket of his jacket and gave the man a handwritten address on a scrap of paper. The driver smirked when he recognised the location but he wiped it from his face immediately when he looked up and saw Bobbio giving him a stern look.

Across the runway, Enzo spotted a squadron of Italian air force bombers, getting the once-over from a group of engineers and pilots.

He was excited about visiting Addis for the first time. There was no sign of Italian influence in the architecture here unlike in Asmara, although he suspected that was all about to change. Many of the structures were just single-storey blocks with corrugated-iron roofs. Mud covered the roads, apart from a strip of tarmac down the centre, and there were neither pedestrian pavements nor streetlights.

An occasional building seemed to have an Indian influence and Enzo noticed that quite a few of the shopkeepers were Indian too. Many of the streets were punctuated with blackened gaps where a building had burned down and all that remained was a charred mess of scorched wood. They passed groups of Italian soldiers standing watch at most of the major intersections but they appeared relaxed as they stood there chatting and sharing cigarettes. Around them, the local Addis residents were calmly going about their daily business. It reminded him of what it had been like in Italy when he was a young adult at the close of the Great War and how everyone there had had to adjust quickly to post-war life.

'How is it here?' Bobbio asked. 'Any trouble?'

'No, sir,' said the driver, 'it's all quiet now for the most part. The damage that you see, we didn't do all that. Our air force did some, but after their Emperor scarpered the Ethiopians looted the city for three days before we arrived.'

Bobbio nodded and smiled, satisfied with this piece of news. 'We will rebuild it, bigger and better, eh, Enzo?'

'Yes,' he agreed. They would do that much at least.

Soon there would be construction sites all over town with Italian architects in charge and this work would provide many new jobs for the locals. Though he couldn't help wondering if a building programme alone would be enough to repair the less visible damage caused in the bitterly fought war.

After a few more minutes, they pulled into the tree-lined driveway of a grand stone mansion. Standing in its own grounds, it had a manicured lawn to the front, with blooming flower beds guarded by sculpted lions.

'This used to belong to a duke from the Emperor's court,' said the driver.

'Ex-Emperor,' corrected Bobbio.

'Yes, sir.' The driver grinned. 'This one is an ex-duke now too.'

Enzo had no idea why they were here, but began to get a sinking feeling when he saw a scantily dressed woman saluting an army officer at the large wooden front door. Bobbio hopped excitedly out of the car.

'Enzo, I will rely on your discretion about this,' he said, 'as a colleague.'

Then he hurried up the granite steps, fixing what little hair he had on the way.

Bobbio had never called him a colleague before or anything close to it. Enzo followed the ministry man in through the front door and it didn't take him more than one look to work out what type of business was trading inside. Several women dressed only in lingerie walked past them and Enzo recognised some of their faces from the queue into his office. Business was brisk tonight with many off-duty Italian officers already there, from a wide mix of ranks and regiments. Enzo presumed that the discretion rule applied to them too.

A few of the women unfortunately recognised him and started pointing and giggling.

'It's him,' said one, 'from the port.'

'Come to get your papers stamped, love?' quipped another.

Enzo had never been in one of these establishments in his life, even in Genoa. He turned to look for the exit, but was waylaid by the same middle-aged madam with the hard face.

'Evening, gentlemen,' she said. 'What can we do for you?'

'We need company for the whole night,' Bobbio announced.

'Of course, sirs, we can take care of that for you,' she said. 'Follow me.'

'This will be my treat,' Bobbio whispered.

The madam led them into a small room off the hall. Inside, there were a couple of red couches against a wall and not much else, apart from an empty stone plinth near a window. Enzo had noticed two other vacant plinths in the hallway on the way in and guessed they had been occupied, before the change of ownership, by busts of Ethiopian nobility. No doubt replacements with the Duce's distinctive forehead would appear on them before long.

'Sit down, gentlemen,' ordered the madam and clapped her hands in the doorway. Enzo couldn't see how he was going to get out of this. A selection of six half-dressed women strolled in and stood in front of them. None of them seemed particularly interested in being picked. Bobbio, who had taken on a sleazy, predatory demeanour, chose almost immediately, pointing at a very young blonde woman. The blonde looked at Enzo, annoyed, and he realised that, of the two of them, the women probably considered him the better option. This was no reason to feel flattered, he knew.

'Hello, my dear,' Bobbio said, forgetting all about Enzo. He put his arm around the young woman and she led him away.

'Your turn,' said the madam.

'Could I just rent a room?' he asked hopefully.

The woman's face clouded over. 'No, you can't. Do we look like a hotel?' She waved her arm at the remaining women. 'You're not happy with these girls? What's wrong with them?'

The women all stared at him as though he had just personally insulted each one of them.

'No, it's not that at all,' he said, embarrassed.

'Then choose!' she snapped.

At that moment, another young woman entered: red-haired Valentina. She gave him a surprised smile.

'I'll take her,' said Enzo, pointing at her.

'You two know each other?' said the madam, her suspicions aroused.

'No,' they said in unison.

She didn't appear to believe either of them but said, 'Val, this gentleman requires a bed for the night; you see that he is comfortable.'

'This way,' said Valentina. As they started up the plushly carpeted stairs, she turned to Enzo and whispered, 'You're a long way from home.'

'I know,' said Enzo.

Passing some closed doors on the upstairs corridor, Enzo tried not to think about what Bobbio was getting up to on the other side of one of them. Valentina stopped at an open bedroom and waved for him to go in first. The large four-poster bed had been re-made since its last use, but Enzo doubted that anyone would have gone to the trouble of changing the sheets. He wasn't sure that he would be able to bring himself to sleep in it.

As soon as Valentina had closed the door behind them, he blurted out, 'I don't want to do anything.'

'Oh. You want someone else?' she asked, seeming not to care either way.

'No! I want you . . .' Enzo said, 'to stay I mean, but that's all.'

'OK,' said Valentina. 'And what are we going to do?'

'Sleep,' he said. 'Just sleep.'

'Really?' she asked, her eyes lighting up. 'I haven't had a full night's sleep since we got here. You know, work, work, work.'

She sat down on the edge of the bed and he stood as far away from her as possible. But when he saw her trying to ease her stiff neck by rolling it around, he said, 'I can fix that, if you like?'

He knelt behind her on the bed and started to massage her shoulder muscles.

'Oooh,' said Valentina, feeling the tightness loosening. 'Where did you learn to do that?'

'I've been practising on someone,' he said.

'Ah.' She nodded. 'Someone special?'

'Yes,' he agreed. 'She's very special.'

'Are you sure you don't want anything? She'll never know and I won't tell.'

'No,' said Enzo, 'but thank you.'

He turned his back quickly as Valentina whipped off all her clothes and dived under the covers; though the unfamiliar blue whiteness of her body did make him stare just a little.

'Ohhhh,' she said, closing her eyes and hugging the pillow, 'this is so good, you've no idea.'

Sitting down in an armchair, he took off his sweaty shoes and socks. He lay back and rested his eyes but couldn't sleep. And then Valentina started to snore loudly.

Later, when the house was quiet, he put his shoes back on, crept silently out of the bedroom and went downstairs. The madam was still up, engrossed in her bookkeeping on a table in the hallway.

'Problem?' she said casually, that kind of thing obviously being a nightly occurrence.

'No, no problem. Do you have a telephone that I might use?' he asked.

She pointed with her pencil to an alcove under the stairs and said, 'I'll have to add it to your bill.'

'That's fine,' he said. 'Do you think I'll be able to get through to Massawa from here?'

She shrugged. 'You can try, but I wouldn't bet on it.'

Getting hold of the new Italian operator in Addis took several tries. When the man did finally answer, he told Enzo that there was only one line available to Eritrea so far and that it was reserved for important calls only. Enzo assured him that he was ringing on a most urgent matter. The wait to be put through took so long that he began to think that the operator had forgotten all about him. Eventually there was a persistent crackling sound and then the telephone at the other end began to ring. It kept on ringing and no one answered.

'Do you want me to try another number?' asked the operator.

'No,' said Enzo. 'That's the only one.'

The urge to tell Aatifa that he missed her would have to go unsatisfied, but he hoped that she knew it anyway. Since the day they had first met, all those months before, they had never been this far apart. Once when Azzezza was sick, they had been separated for a couple of nights, but the distance between them now made it harder to bear. He wondered if she would be jealous or angry if she knew that he was sharing a bedroom with another woman. He hoped so.

He also wanted to tell her that everything was going to be all right now in Addis and Ethiopia. That the local people he had seen here were getting on with their lives. And that the future, with the promised Italian investment, would hold only good things for them. He was glad he had come after all just to have seen that much with his own eyes.

'Why didn't you answer it?' Madihah asked her mother in the hallway of Enzo's house.

'I'm not supposed to,' said Aatifa, looking down at her from halfway up the stairs.

'It could have been him,' Madihah suggested, 'couldn't it?'

Aatifa shook her head. 'He wouldn't call. He knows I wouldn't answer.'

Madihah nodded and followed her up the stairs, while the gramophone in the living room continued to play Paganini's violin Caprices. Aatifa had not forgotten her promise to let her granddaughter hear some of Enzo's music. They entered Aatifa's bedroom where Azzezza was sitting on her window sill, looking up at the stars.

'That's my favourite spot too,' said Aatifa.

'You like living here?' asked Azzezza.

'I suppose.' Aatifa shrugged. 'It's fine.'

'It must be nice to have your own bedroom,' the girl continued.

Madihah gave Aatifa a knowing smile, which she ignored.

'Where would you like to live?' asked Aatifa. 'In a hut or in a house?'

'I like our hut,' said Azzezza. 'But it would be nice to have a toilet, like he has, and not a bucket.'

They could all agree on that one.

'Is he a good boss?' asked Azzezza. 'Is he nice to you?'

Aatifa did not need to think before answering.

'Yes, he is,' she said.

Chapter 19

Enzo and Bobbio met each other in the morning, coming out of their respective rooms on the upstairs landing. Both of them had washed and shaved and were free of the dust that had cloaked them the day before. Bobbio looked on jealously as Valentina kissed Enzo on the cheek; his own companion was already making good her escape down the corridor. In the foyer, Bobbio settled up for both of them as he had said he would and while Enzo waited for him, he was sad to see Valentina standing in the side room, already on view for some newly arrived officers.

Unseen birds chirped away around the grounds as they came outside into the pleasant morning sunshine. The same driver was waiting to collect them at the bottom of the steps.

'We'll definitely be going home today?' asked Enzo.

'Yes, yes,' assured Bobbio, 'don't worry. I just have to show my face at this thing and then we'll be on our way.'

His appearance turned out to be at an event outside the Guenete Leul Palace, formerly the residence of Emperor Haile Selassie. He had recently vacated it in quite a hurry as he fled first to Djibouti and from there on to London. Now it was home to the newly installed Italian Viceroy of East Africa. Armed Italian guards let them in through the impressively ornate front gates which were topped by a pair of stone lions that would not have looked out of place on the driveway of any European royal.

In front of the two-storey palace, a crowd of Ethiopians had gathered to hear a speech from the Viceroy. Enzo and Bobbio just caught the tail end of it and joined in a round of polite, unenthusiastic applause. Then they watched as some of the poorer-looking Ethiopians were led up to their new white-suited Italian leader, who handed a small gift to each one of them.

'Alms for the poor,' explained Bobbio, 'my idea too. Keep the natives happy and show them who's boss at the same time. Stay here, I won't be long.'

As Bobbio walked off towards the Viceroy's group, Enzo suddenly caught sight of Salvatore standing on the steps of the palace, keeping a watchful eye on the assembled crowd. The days that they had not spoken to each other had slipped into months, each man managing to get on with his own life without need of the other. But despite all that had happened between them, Enzo was glad to see his old friend. Having perhaps sensed his presence, the colonel turned and found his face on the edge of the crowd. Salvatore's first inclination was to smile but it didn't last long and he just nodded coolly. Then the Viceroy returned to address the crowd once again.

Enzo had seen the Viceroy's picture in the newspapers but this was his first close-up view. He was a tough-looking man in his fifties, with a hawk-like face, and Enzo's first impression was of someone who did not suffer fools gladly. Before becoming Viceroy Graziani, he had served in the Ethiopian war as a general.

The people in the crowd were mostly peasant farmers, Enzo saw, but there were also some Ethiopian dignitaries. The latter were dressed in ornate shawls and held up richly embroidered umbrellas to ward off the sun. Perhaps one of these was the duke whose house now had the dubious distinction of being a brothel. None of them looked particularly interested or happy to be there, even the ones who had received alms. The whole event seemed staged.

Then suddenly the sunny calm was shattered by the boom of two grenades exploding within seconds of each other. Both had landed close to the Viceroy, throwing him violently backward. These first two were quickly followed by more explosions. Enzo saw one of the attackers, a young man, throwing his grenades from just behind the Ethiopian dignitaries, who seemed as shocked as anyone that this was happening. Another young man had managed to penetrate the palace itself and was launching his grenades from a balcony above the steps. One of these exploded right beside an Italian general, who collapsed instantly. Then as quickly as they had started, the explosions stopped, their angry violence replaced by an eerie silence. The Viceroy and the general were surrounded and dragged back into the building by their aides. Enzo searched the rattled faces of his fellow Italians and was relieved to see that Salvatore had somehow managed to emerge without a scratch.

'Get him!' shouted Bobbio, as he saw one of the grenade-throwers pushing and shoving his way out of the courtyard.

Enzo could see the indecision on the faces of the frightened Ethiopians in the crowd; unsure whether to run, which might make them seem like accomplices, or to stay. The Italian soldiers and police had their guns trained on them, wary of another attack. Some of the troops gave nervous sideways glances at Salvatore, awaiting his order.

Salvatore raised his arm and Enzo, seeing what was about to happen, shouted, 'No!' But no one heard him. All eyes were on Salvatore's hand, poised in the air. He let it drop and the soldiers and police opened fire into the crowd, making no distinction between the poor and the dignitaries or between the attackers and the innocent. Many fell in the first burst of shooting. Those who did not frantically tried to escape only to find their way obstructed by the bodies of people who had been standing beside them only seconds before. By the time Salvatore shouted, 'Cease fire,' dozens were already lying dead or seriously wounded.

Enzo looked on in horror as the injured cried out, raising their arms for help. He turned angrily away from the carnage towards the perpetrators and saw Salvatore staring coldly at the same scene. Their eyes met for a moment, but the colonel turned away and walked quickly back inside the palace.

The attitude of the soldiers guarding the road junctions had noticeably changed as Enzo and Bobbio were driven at speed out of the city. Word of the attack had spread quickly. Enzo could already see groups of Ethiopian men being rounded up by Italian soldiers down some of the side streets.

'Dirty animals,' said Bobbio, staring out of the window. 'They say the Viceroy will survive. He's a damned lucky man. General Liotta has lost one of his legs.'

He did not once mention the innocent Ethiopians who had just been cut down in front of them for the crime of being in the wrong place at the wrong time. Enzo's own question of the previous day had been answered for him in blood. The erection of some new, finely designed buildings was not going to change the hearts and minds of these people. They were never going to accept Italian rule voluntarily.

It was the early hours of the morning when he eventually arrived home. He was haggard and depressed, but relieved to be free of Bobbio's company. After they had taken off from Addis, the ministry man spent the entire flight ranting on about how this attack would ruin his chances of an early return to Rome. The house was unlit and silent as he entered and he wondered for a nervous moment if news of the massacre had already travelled here. This was unlikely. It would take several days at least to filter through and even then, only the Italian injuries would be reported in the newspapers. Walking up the stairs, he saw that Aatifa's door was open and that moonlight was reflected on the tiled floor inside. His own bedroom door was closed so he pressed the handle down gently and stepped slowly into the pitch darkness. It took his eyes a few seconds to adjust before he saw her outline, curled up on the bed. He stood and watched her for a moment, her slow relaxed breathing, her unfurrowed brow. She had not wanted him to go on the trip and he wished now that he had listened to her. But part of him was glad that he had witnessed it with his own eyes; he might not have believed it possible otherwise. After undressing, he crawled up beside her on the bed and began to kiss her face tenderly. She stirred and smiled without opening her eyes, recognising his familiar touch on her face. Then she put her arm around his neck and pulled him down next to her.

'I missed you,' he said, wrapping his arms around her and holding her as tightly as he could without hurting her.

Enzo got up at dawn and left Aatifa sleeping peacefully. An hour later, she arrived downstairs, wearing his dressing gown and yawning. He was sitting at the table, waiting for her, and she saw that he had prepared her a cup of coffee.

'Thank you,' she said, smiling.

She sat down opposite him, picking up the cup and blowing

on the top to cool it. She took a long, welcome sip and only then did she notice his troubled expression.

'What is it?' she asked.

He had never spoken about any of these things with her. But he wanted to now; he needed to talk about it with someone, and there was no one else. She would be angry, he knew, but then so was he.

'Something happened yesterday in Addis . . .' he said.

She frowned and put down her cup, waiting for him to say more.

'There were a lot of people at a ceremony, Ethiopians, farmers mostly . . . and then the Viceroy was attacked . . . some grenades were thrown, not by the farmers, by others in the crowd . . . two men, I think . . . it wasn't clear . . . it was total chaos . . . he survived, the Viceroy, I mean, but after . . .'

He was too ashamed to go on, hardly able to look her in the eye. But he didn't need to. She had understood, or at least could guess enough of it.

'How many?' she asked.

Enzo shook his head. He had no idea how many had been killed. Once the shooting had started there were people running and falling in every direction.

'How many?' she demanded, raising her voice.

'Too many to count,' he said, looking up at her again.

She paused, avoiding his eyes. Then she asked, 'What did you do?'

He was shocked at her question and did not reply.

'What did you do to stop it?' she repeated loudly.

'I stood and watched! Is that what you want to hear?' snapped Enzo, angry that she was interrogating him. He was not the one who had pulled the trigger.

'What do you think I could do?' he continued. 'I am just a

civil servant. I keep ledgers. I stamp pieces of paper. I tell ships when they can and can't sail. This shooting, the gas, I am not responsible for any of it . . .'

Aatifa's eyes were wide now, fixed on him. 'What gas?'

He looked down guiltily, regretting that he had kept this from her all these months.

'Let's go away from here,' he said hopefully, 'the two of us. Find another place to live.'

And while he said it, he thought of India, which was not so far away. The British there might need people in their ports. His English was passable and it would improve if he had to use it.

'Would you keep me hidden away there too?' she asked in a sarcastic tone that was meant to hurt him.

'No!' he replied. 'We could be together, away from here . . . like any couple.'

'You are a dreamer,' she said, her tears threatening to come. 'I can't do this any more.'

'If it's what we want?' he said.

She shook her head. 'I am just an Eritrean woman, what I want does not matter.'

'It matters to me,' he said angrily, 'you know that.'

She nodded and he watched her pausing to collect her thoughts. His hopes were raised for an instant, thinking that he might still be able to persuade her. But as her brow knitted again he felt this possibility slipping from his reach.

She looked up at him finally, and he saw the love in her eyes. Then with a bittersweet smile she said, 'You made me happy when I had forgotten what it was like; I am grateful to you for that, but it was foolish to think that we . . . they were right to make this law.'

'No,' he said, shaking his head. 'They were wrong.'

'And you,' she continued. 'You think you are not a part of all this, but you are. Do not ask me to be . . . I will not.'

He thought for a second about denying what she had said. Even starting to form the sentences in his head – 'I have not ordered any of these things' and 'I had no power to stop it' – but he knew they were not the truth. He did feel involved and he was a part of it. Even at the palace the day before, he could have run and stood in front of the crowd, or knocked a soldier's rifle from his hand. Anything, something, but he had done nothing at all.

'I did not want those things to happen,' he said.

'I know,' she said, standing up. 'I am leaving now.'

'Wait . . .' he said, but she didn't stop and he heard her turning in the hall and going up the stairs.

He imagined her in her bedroom, roughly stuffing her clothes into her bag. It would only take her a few seconds. Then she would remove the picture of the Eritrean girl from the wall. It was a painting of Madihah, not Azzezza, and she carried it with her everywhere.

A few moments later, Enzo heard her coming back down. She paused in the hall before returning to the living room. He was pleased, although he knew it was for the last time. Part of her had already left.

'You don't have to go,' he said. 'Please.'

Her eyes were glassy and he saw that she was forcing herself to be strong. Then she spoke and afterwards it took him a few seconds to realise that he had actually heard these words from her.

'I am owed a week's wages,' she had said, as though they had only ever been employer and employee.

It was hard to believe that it had come to this but he knew that she wasn't asking just for the money. She was making a point about them, about what their relationship had been. But he knew it was a lie. And she did too, she must, but if she wanted to deny what they had become, then he would give her what she wanted.

He took the money from his pocket and put it on the table and she picked it up. Then, intent on continuing her point to its bitter end, she pulled the wages ledger down from the bookshelf. She opened it on the page where her next signature was due but Enzo grabbed the book off the table and started ripping its hateful pages out with his two hands. Then he tried to tear the whole thing apart but the leather binding was too strong and he couldn't do it. Finally, he flung it in tatters across the room. Then he took out all the money he had in his pocket and started flinging it on the table too, saying, 'Here, take this and this and this . . .'

Aatifa didn't touch any of it. When he had stopped, she turned abruptly and left.

He watched her through the living room window, walking down the garden path with her cloth bag in her hand. She looked back once towards the doorway, without seeing him in the window. Then as she stepped out on to the street, she collided with his neighbour. Eva's grocery shopping was knocked out of her hands and down to the ground. Aatifa stooped to help her gather her things but Eva said in an irritated voice, 'No, I'll do it.'

Aatifa stood up and walked on.

Enzo was sitting at the living room table when he heard someone stepping into the room. For one brief moment, he thought Aatifa had come back. But it was Eva.

'The door was open,' she said.

Neither of them spoke as she paused in the doorway, taking in the paper strewn on the floor.

'Trouble?' she asked.

'No,' he answered, 'no trouble.'

'You look like someone died,' she said, half-smiling. 'Can I do anything?'

'Nothing ... thank you,' he said, mustering some politeness.

Eva stared at him for a long time, then she said, 'You know, we could make life easier for each other, Enzo.'

He looked up at her blankly.

'I can't remember the last time my husband touched me,' she said. 'Not that I want him to. I've seen the way you look at me.'

Enzo's eyes widened. He found it hard to understand where this conversation was coming from.

'I'm sorry if I ever gave you ... I didn't mean ...'

Eva's face clouded over as she realised that she had made a fool of herself. Her mood changed swiftly from embarrassment to anger.

'You prefer that to me?' she asked.

'That?' he said, trying to contain the brewing anger that he could easily have let loose on her. He calmed himself, as it wasn't her fault that Aatifa had gone.

'I think,' he said, trying to phrase this as sensitively as possible, 'it would be best if you went home to your husband now.'

It had not come out too badly and she seemed not to take offence. She hovered for a little longer, perhaps wondering if there was a way for her to save some face. But nothing seemed to come to her quickly. She turned awkwardly and left him alone, slamming the front door loudly on her way out.

Enzo held his head in his hands for a long time. When he looked up again, the torn pieces of the ledger on the floor caught his eye. Picking up the largest bit, he looked at the open page which was full of her handwritten name inside the columns he had drawn. A few entries were missing from the bottom where he had ripped pieces off. On his hands and knees, he gathered each scrap of paper off the floor, collecting them all in a pile on the table. Then he sat down and began meticulously to stick each one back in its rightful place with tape, like a jigsaw puzzle.

But putting the pages back together had no therapeutic effect on his mood, nor did replacing the ledger in its usual spot on the shelf. Order was not going to return.

Chapter 20

ENZO DRAGGED HIMSELF to work, hoping that if he could occupy himself with some simple tasks it would help take his mind off things. The conversation with Aatifa had not gone well, to say the least. For a while he tortured himself with the question of whether, if he had approached it in a different way, the outcome might have been otherwise, but he did not regret telling her what he had seen.

When he reached the quays, he walked slowly towards his office. Crossing the train track diagonally, he didn't notice that an engine was approaching at a reduced but steady speed behind him. Luckily the driver spotted him in time and jammed on the brakes sharply. His coal-smeared assistant hung out of the side door, roaring at Enzo to watch where the hell he was going.

Suicide was a tempting option, he thought, but it was not for him. He considered it his duty to take whatever cards life dealt him and find a way to get through it. Besides, he would never intentionally leave a messy corpse behind.

Then, suddenly, he was gripped by a new determination. The odds on getting her back were not good, he knew, but he was not going to give up on her so easily. If there were some means by which he could turn this situation around then he would keep looking until he found it.

Ahead of him, he saw that a newly arrived ship was being tied up to the dock and that a large group of Italian passengers, perhaps three hundred or more, were already disembarking. These were not soldiers or prostitutes, but poor families: men, women and children, carrying their possessions in their hands and on their backs.

Daniel was standing outside their office building, observing the same scene, and Enzo walked over to him.

'Who are they?' he asked.

'The first farmers for Ethiopia,' said Daniel.

Enzo turned and looked at them again, seeing now the hope and fear in their eyes. Judging from their appearance, these people had left a life of hardship behind in Italy and had come here with aspirations of a better future for their children. He was tempted to go over and warn them all to be careful. Ethiopia was not a secure place for them yet, no matter what they had been told. His own feelings about their arrival were mixed. There was a time, not so long ago, when he would have been delighted to see so many of them coming here. But he had heard and witnessed too much since then.

A clean-cut young man in a shirt and tie ushered these fresh Italian pioneers directly from the ship on to the waiting train. This man was not one of Enzo's staff and he suspected that he was probably one of Bobbio's team. The colonial dream was clearly still very much alive in the ministry's halls and they would not be letting recent setbacks get in their way.

As the train pulled away, five heavy trucks, travelling in convoy, turned on to the quay at the far end. They paused to allow the railway carriages to pass them and then made their way slowly up towards the ship. Enzo noticed that they were struggling with considerable loads, and as they parked in front of him, he recognised their cargo. The five pieces of the obelisk of Axum; transported as he himself had advised and now on their way to Rome for Mussolini's pleasure. He inspected each stone piece and it seemed to him that they had been lifted well, without any additional damage being done. Daniel moved over to have a closer look and Enzo saw the shocked expression on his face when he realised what they were.

'Do you know what this is?' Daniel asked.

'Yes, I do,' said Enzo, avoiding his stare.

'Where are they taking it?' he demanded.

'To Rome,' snapped Enzo, resenting being blamed for this too, but then he softened. 'It's going, all right? Our job is to get these pieces on to the ship without breaking them. It's in our care while it's here.'

Daniel looked at the obelisk again before reluctantly nodding his agreement.

'Let's get started then,' said Enzo, placing a hand on Daniel's shoulder.

They estimated the weight of each piece to be in the region of thirty-five tonnes, the equivalent of three adult elephants. But they calculated that the ship's own deck crane was capable of handling the load, one at a time. Next, they set about getting the strongest ropes they had around the first and top part of the obelisk. As they clambered up and over the huge chunk of stone, Daniel bent and traced his hand along the edge of one of the window reliefs. He looked up at Enzo with a smile on his face and said, 'This was carved by hand . . . by an African.' Enzo nodded and threw Daniel one end of the thick rope.

A crowd of onlookers soon gathered as word got around. Some were even taking photographs. It was not long before Bobbio and Major Dore arrived too. Enzo carried on working regardless until he and Daniel had firmly secured the tie ropes at either end of the structure. Then they attached the two loose ends to the hook block at the bottom of the crane's hoist line. Daniel nodded that his end was ready to go and Enzo waved up at the crane operator. As instructed, the operator inched the first section slowly off the truck and then with as delicate a shift as possible, started to lift it skywards.

'Gently, gently!' shouted Enzo.

Daniel stood beside him on top of the truck as the stone piece hovered directly above their heads. It would have crushed the pair of them had it fallen, but they knew it would not. They had done their jobs well.

'They are stealing our history,' Daniel said over the crane noise.

Enzo looked at him, surprised that he had been so outspoken. 'Yes, we are,' he replied.

They watched the section of obelisk rise until it had passed the height of the ship's rail. Then Enzo jumped down off the truck and hurried towards the gangplank to observe the last part of the operation. Bobbio hailed him as he passed but Enzo ignored him. On deck, Enzo crouched down and gave the operator measurements with his two hands to indicate how far it was from touching down. As it narrowed from ten feet to five, Enzo shouted, 'Slower. Slower!'

The operator eased up until the rate of descent was barely perceptible, and the heavy block touched down with hardly a sound. Enzo gave the operator a thumbs up and the man smiled broadly.

Making his way down for the next piece of the Axumite puzzle, Enzo wiped his brow with an oily handkerchief, adding more dirt than he had removed. The crowd was applauding when he reached the bottom and Bobbio was standing there waiting.

'Enzo! For someone who was reluctant to take the thing in the first place, I'm glad to see you putting your heart and soul into the job now!'

Enzo wished he would go away.

'The Duce will be very pleased,' continued Bobbio. 'I will make sure your name is mentioned to him. Perhaps even the promotion back home that you've been waiting for.'

'Excuse me, I've work to do,' said Enzo. Leaving the civil servant standing there, he walked off towards the second truck which was now manoeuvring into position.

He arrived home that evening to an empty, soundless house that seemed to have had the life drained out of it. He stood for a while in the centre of the living room, at a loss as to what to do. The table reminded him of the row they had had that morning so he did not want to sit there. The kitchen had become her territory into which he rarely ventured, and he didn't want to go in and find her absent. There were memories of her all over the house, both good and bad. If she did not return to live with him here, he thought that he would have to move on to escape the weight of their past that pervaded its walls.

Just then, he heard a noise outside. For a brief, wondrous moment he thought that she had returned, but this hope was quickly shattered by the brutal noise of the hall door being kicked in. Four military policemen invaded the room. One made a beeline for him while the others began to search the whole house aggressively. He recognised two of them as the men who had arrested the Italian who had been beating his Eritrean girlfriend on the street.

'What's going on?' asked Enzo, even though he already knew the answer.

'Enzo Secchi?' asked the lead policeman. 'I have a warrant here for your arrest.' He showed him an official-looking piece of paper with a stamp on it.

'On what charge?' he demanded.

'Cohabiting with a native woman,' the policeman replied. 'Where is she?'

Enzo could have lied but that seemed pointless. If they had gone to the trouble of obtaining a warrant, they must know a certain amount already.

'She's gone,' he said.

The lead policeman turned to one of his colleagues and said, 'Find her,' then he turned back to Enzo and said, 'You're coming with us.'

Enzo nodded and without making any protest, he followed the policemen to their car outside. It was an odd, surreal feeling, sitting in the back seat, with a burly officer on each side, penning him in. After a short drive, the car passed between the solid iron gates under the prison façade. He looked back through the rear window as they were closed firmly behind them and knew that he was in serious trouble.

Things went from bad to worse as his personal details were written down in a book by a gruff, bearded man at the prison reception desk. Enzo knew that his name would never be erased from that page. His arrest was now a part of official history. The degradation continued. His tiny, dirty cell consisted of four stone walls, one partially grilled door, one narrow bed with stained sheets, and one barred window, high up on the exterior wall. As the jailer locked him in, the sound of the key turning made him feel weak. He went to sit down on the bed but it was filthy, so he sat on the cold floor instead, and stared at the moonlit walls.

*

'Your lawyer is here to see you,' said the jailer as he unlocked the door early the next morning.

Enzo was not aware that he had a lawyer but in fact there were two men waiting for him in the visitors' room. The middle-aged one with the shiny suit and the insurance salesman smile was obviously the lawyer because the other man was Salvatore.

'Your office called me,' said Salvatore before Enzo had a chance to ask. 'I've hired Giorgio to represent you. You're lucky, he was just here on holiday. He's a very good guy, the best in Naples.'

Giorgio nodded repeatedly at this, vouching for his own expertise. Enzo thought that the only thing he was missing was a sparkling gold tooth.

'Can I go home?' he asked.

'I'm afraid not,' said Giorgio, 'not until after the trial anyway.'

Enzo's heart sank even further.

'You look terrible,' said Salvatore, as they all sat down.

Enzo felt terrible too, but he gave Salvatore a nod to show that he appreciated him coming. The lawyer then pulled out a small bundle of papers from his briefcase and laid them out in front of him.

'Right,' he said, 'first, tell me, did you do something to your neighbours?'

'My neighbours! No, why?' asked Enzo.

'They were the ones who denounced you,' said the lawyer.

Enzo shook his head and smiled in disbelief. He really should have paid more attention to Eva, the lonely, hypochondriac housewife. Her revenge had been swift and, he had to say, somewhat out of proportion with what he had supposedly done to her.

'Any reason you could think of why they would have done that?' Giorgio asked.

'No,' lied Enzo.

'You have anything on them that we could fire back? It might help, you know, show that there was some malice in this, on their part?'

'Nothing,' said Enzo, though he knew there was definitely malice on Eva's part.

The lawyer nodded, disappointed, and started rooting through his papers for his next question.

'Of the two of us, you were supposed to be the smart one,' said Salvatore. 'I told you to get rid of her.'

'I didn't need to in the end. She left me,' said Enzo. He turned to the lawyer. 'Can they still charge me, if she's gone?'

Giorgio considered this for a moment and then said, 'We can't really say as our defence that your relationship is now over. To do that we'd have to admit that you were in a relationship in the first place, which is still a crime.'

Salvatore threw his eyes up to heaven. Enzo nodded.

'This is real, OK, we just have to get you through it,' said Giorgio. 'The police found some of her clothes in your house. And the neighbour says that this woman, Aatifa, has been living with you for a year and a half. Is that true?'

'Yes,' said Enzo. 'She's been living with me, and eating with me, and sharing my bed with me and everything else. It's all true . . .'

'Sshh!' said Salvatore, gesturing with his hands for Enzo to keep his voice down. Then he looked at the lawyer. 'So what do we do?'

'My advice?' Giorgio replied. 'You must say that you paid her for sex. That it was strictly business, not a real relationship and that you would never ever consider someone like her as a proper partner. You did pay her, right?'

Enzo shook his head. 'I didn't pay her for that—'

'No . . . no, you did,' said the lawyer, interrupting him. 'You did, didn't you?'

'Let's say he did,' said Salvatore, getting impatient. 'Then what?'

'And you can prove that you paid her?' asked Giorgio.

'Yes, there's a ledger. It's a little bit torn now,' said Enzo, relieved that he hadn't actually burned it.

'Well, that's perfect,' said the lawyer, delighted. 'A real relationship is a crime but prostitution is completely legal.'

'You want me to call her my whore?' said Enzo.

'This is not the time to get high and mighty,' snapped Salvatore. 'They are sending people to jail for this, you know that. You'll lose your job and they'll lock you up. Do you want to throw your whole life away for her?'

Enzo shook his head. He did not want to lose his job or stay in jail. And if he could win his freedom, he would still have the chance to get Aatifa back somehow. All things considered, right now he just wanted out, by any means possible.

'One thing is essential,' said the lawyer. 'This woman has to back up your story, one hundred per cent. Will she do that?'

'She will,' said Salvatore confidently. 'I'll talk to her.'

'See if she needs anything, will you?' asked Enzo.

'Stop thinking about her,' said Salvatore angrily. 'Think about yourself for once.'

Giorgio nodded. 'The law does not apply to her; she is irrelevant in this case. You are the only one on trial. All right? Now, don't worry, we'll have you out of here in no time.'

The men got up to leave. Enzo shook his new lawyer's hand and then he turned to Salvatore.

'Thanks for coming, I appreciate it, really.'

The colonel shrugged and said, 'What are friends for?'

*

That afternoon, Salvatore followed Giorgio's directions across the causeway to the Eritrean district. The police hadn't taken long to track Aatifa down. Like most Italians, Salvatore had never been in this part of Massawa, so he was surprised that a lot of the Eritrean men he passed seemed to recognise him. He eventually realised why: half of his Askari regiment probably called this place home.

When he got to the hut, Aatifa seemed to have been expecting him. She led him to a more private spot farther down the street.

'They questioned you, what about?' he demanded, staring at her with suspicion.

'I said nothing,' Aatifa replied, 'just that I was his housekeeper.'

'Good,' said Salvatore, 'but that won't be enough in court. They're going to produce evidence that the two of you were more than that. I don't know what exactly, but they will . . . so you'll have to say that he paid you, you know . . . for your other services.'

He saw a spark of defiance appearing in her eyes.

'That won't be a problem, I hope?' he said, hardening his voice.

Aatifa was silent for a moment and then she said, 'This is what you think of us anyway, isn't it? That we are all prostitutes.'

'It's not what he thinks,' said Salvatore, getting irritated, 'but you have to say this. Otherwise he's in big trouble. So are we clear? You'll answer everything they ask you, like I said?'

He could see that he wasn't intimidating her, as he intended. She was just getting angry with him. 'He can't afford any slip-ups from you,' he continued.

'You think I can't be trusted?' she snapped.

'Can you?' said Salvatore. 'You tell me . . . he is my friend. I don't want to see anything happen to him.'

'He is my friend too,' said Aatifa quietly.

'Great,' said Salvatore. 'Then I have no need to worry, do I?'

They both paused then, studying each other.

'Perhaps we feel some things differently to you Italians,' said Aatifa, 'but we do feel. This will not be the first time that he has disowned me . . . I will say what needs to be said. For him.'

She turned abruptly and walked back towards the hut.

'Where are you going?' Salvatore shouted. 'I'm not finished.'

'I've listened to you enough,' she said.

As Salvatore walked back the way he had come, he felt slightly guilty for being so hard on her. But he was confident now that she cared enough about Enzo to stick to their bargain. Would Zula have done as much for him? Perhaps at one time, but certainly not now. These days it would be easier to ask her to stick pins in his eyes.

His next stop was at Enzo's empty house to collect a clean suit and shirt for his court appearance. How crazy the world had become, he thought. They had all had Eritrean girlfriends once and now you could go to jail for it. He knew for a fact too that Enzo was not the only one unwilling to part with his lover. There were many others like him, and some had even started families. Enzo had been unlucky to get singled out. As it was when they were kids, he was still the one to get caught.

He closed the front door behind him, and then contemplated going into Enzo's neighbours' house. It would feel good to call those vile informers every name under the sun, but he thought better of it. Instead, his next port of call would be Judge Muroni, to cash in as many favours as he could.

When Aatifa told Madihah that she had left Enzo's house, her daughter was disappointed.

'I don't know him,' Madihah had said, 'but you seemed happy. Happier than I have ever seen you.'

It was true. She could not deny that living with him had been a positive experience. But it had been built on a lie that she could no longer ignore. He was one of them and she had let herself forget that.

Now Madihah was shocked when she explained about the impending trial, and how she would have to appear as a witness. And, worst of all, what she would have to say.

'Why would you do that for him?' asked Madihah angrily. 'He should not be asking you to. You are not even together any more.'

'If I don't, he will stay in prison,' said Aatifa, 'and I don't want that; but I don't want you to be there to hear me say those things.'

'No,' Madihah insisted. 'I am not staying away. I will be there for you. I know it is not true so what does it matter? They are only words and lies.'

They were only words, Aatifa knew, although it would still hurt her to say them and have her daughter hear them from her own lips. But she was glad that Madihah wanted to be there.

'It will be fine,' said Madihah, touching her hand. 'It will be over then, when they hear what you have to say, won't it?'

'That is what his friend, the colonel, says.'

'And will you go back to the Italian then?' Madihah asked.

Aatifa thought about this before answering and then she shook her head. She had separated from Enzo by choice, fully intending that the split would be permanent. And yet, there was something niggling at the back of her mind. If they were meant to be apart, then why were events conspiring to bring them back into contact with each other again?

Chapter 21

IT WAS QUITE a shock for Enzo to find himself surrounded by real Italian criminals. They were petty thieves mostly but there were also a few men who had actually committed murder. One, Enzo was told, had dispatched his own wife with a pitchfork when she told him that she was leaving him. He also spotted the man whose trial he had attended, but decided to avoid his company. They may have been arrested for the same crime, but he didn't want him to get the mistaken impression that they had something in common. There were Ethiopian and Eritrean prisoners too, but the guards kept the different races apart most of the time, prison life mirroring the segregation on the outside. Only in the dusty exercise yard was there the possibility of international communication, although neither group chose to avail itself of the opportunity.

The jailer on Enzo's wing was an overweight and affable man in his thirties whose most marked characteristic was an evident lack of intelligence. He had never heard of the law under which Enzo was charged and took some convincing that it actually existed.

'It's not fair,' he said. 'People should be able to be with whoever they want.'

'I know,' said Enzo. 'But unfortunately not everyone thinks that way.'

'Who doesn't?' asked the jailer.

'That's a good question,' said Enzo. 'I don't know exactly, other than they are people with the power to mess with everyone else's life.'

The jailer nodded as though this was a profound statement and then he leaned in and whispered, 'Bastards.'

On the day of his trial, Enzo was allowed to wash and shave and he put on the clean clothes that Salvatore had brought in for him. A police car brought him to the court, but once they were inside he was allowed to walk freely around the echoing atrium, while an officer kept a close eye on him. He looked around for Salvatore and Giorgio, his lawyer, but the first person he recognised made his heart skip a beat. Aatifa was sitting on a long wooden bench beside Iggi and Madihah. He walked quickly over to them. She seemed pleased to see him, and worried too.

'Hello,' he said politely to Iggi and Madihah, who both nodded. Then he turned to Aatifa, 'How are you?' he asked.

Before she could answer, his lawyer appeared behind him, grabbing his elbow firmly. 'What do you think you are doing!' he hissed in a low voice. 'You can't talk to her here. Don't even look at her. Just walk away, now.'

Enzo would much rather have stayed with her, but he allowed himself to be led away. As he turned, he saw the same prosecution lawyer as the last time he was here, watching him from across the hall. And with him, chatting conspiratorially, was Bobbio. The ministry man held up his hand to interrupt the prosecutor, before excusing himself. Then he started over in Enzo's direction.

'You learned those lines I gave you?' asked Giorgio.

'What?' said Enzo, distracted by Bobbio's imminent arrival. 'Oh yes, yes I did.'

'Needless to say, I am very disappointed about all this, Enzo,' said Bobbio, who appeared genuine in his discomfort.

'It's just a misunderstanding,' said Giorgio, 'that's all. There's absolutely nothing of substance in any of these charges.'

'I'm glad to hear it,' said Bobbio. 'I have to say it did surprise me when I was informed. I would be pleased to learn that it was a mistake.'

'You will,' said Giorgio, but Bobbio wasn't looking at him any more, he was staring at Enzo. He nodded at him once before walking back towards the prosecutor. A moment later, Enzo saw the two of them glancing over at Aatifa.

Salvatore entered the hall, in full dress uniform, and he, Enzo and Giorgio made their way into the courtroom.

'There's another case up first, I'm afraid,' said Giorgio.

On their way in they passed Iggi and Madihah, and when Iggi spotted Salvatore, he immediately saluted him. As they walked up the centre aisle, Enzo saw Salvatore nodding at Judge Muroni on the bench.

'Is he on our side?' whispered Enzo.

'He'll do what he can,' Salvatore said, giving him a wink. 'He owes me.'

Near the back, Enzo saw his neighbour Eva sitting with her husband, both of them dressed for a funeral. She went to great lengths to make sure that their eyes did not meet.

The trial that preceded Enzo's was of a heavy-set, sleazy man named Zavaglia, who was up on the same charge as Enzo. But as soon as his Eritrean partner took to the witness stand, it was clear she had no intention of helping him to get off.

'We lived together like husband and wife,' she said. 'We have one child, a boy.'

'Are you married?' asked Zavaglia's lawyer, without looking at her.

'No,' she replied, 'not yet.'

'Not yet? Has he ever promised to marry you?' the lawyer demanded in a patronising tone.

'No,' she said, shaking her head.

'Your Honour, there is no case here. My client merely took out his desires on this woman when he could not control himself.'

Zavaglia nodded to confirm this fact.

'It is not something he is proud of,' continued the lawyer, 'but there is no relationship between my client and this woman other than master and servant.'

'We are a family,' the woman protested, and then she turned to Zavaglia who was doing his utmost to ignore her. 'Tell them.'

The man kept his mouth firmly shut as he stared down at his shoelaces.

Giorgio leaned over to Enzo and whispered, 'She informed on him. I don't know what she expected.'

Enzo was wondering why this woman had put herself through all this, when the reason became clear.

'The fact that a child was born from this is unfortunate,' said the lawyer. 'We all know the difficulties a mixed-race child will have growing up. However, my client has kindly offered to give a little money towards the support of this boy though he is under no obligation to do so.'

'Very well,' said Judge Muroni, and he turned to the woman, waving her away. 'You may step down.'

The woman went back into the public gallery, clearly not fully understanding what was going on.

'While the court does not condone Signor Zavaglia's actions,' pronounced the judge, 'I do not see evidence of a substantial relationship here and a man cannot be blamed for taking out his lusts on a native woman so readily available to him. Therefore I am dismissing this case and the defendant is free to go.'

Enzo looked to his right across the aisle. Bobbio was displeased with the judge's verdict. At least the old man was displaying a spark of independent spirit that hadn't been evident the last time he had seen him in action. Enzo began to feel a bit more optimistic about the outcome of his own case.

As they moved forward into the seats that Zavaglia and his lawyer had just vacated, Enzo could feel his heart beating faster. He turned around, scanning the room, and he saw Madihah and Iggi sitting a couple of rows behind him. He could not see Aatifa anywhere. Judge Muroni shuffled through his papers, and looked down at Salvatore, who was sitting directly behind him and Giorgio.

'I'm surprised to see someone of your stature before me, Signor Secchi,' the judge said in a sympathetic voice.

Giorgio stood up swiftly. 'I'm sure we can clear this up right away, Your Honour,' he said. 'My client is an upstanding member of our community, a good Italian, who has never broken the law in his life.'

This exchange took the prosecutor by surprise and he looked at both men with suspicion.

The judge nodded and said, 'Let's begin then.'

It was beyond embarrassing to be sitting in the witness box in front of a hundred strangers talking about private matters. Once he was there, Enzo tried to approach the whole ordeal as if it were an out-of-body experience. The mid-morning sunlight had now moved around to shine directly on the front of the courtroom, so the judge gestured at one of the guards to close a section of blinds on the tall windows that ran along one side of the room.

The prosecutor waited patiently until this task was completed and then he began. 'You contend that you paid this woman to cook, clean and provide sexual services, is that correct?'

The man's indelicacy made Enzo angry, but his own lawyer had drilled into him the need to keep calm.

'Yes,' replied Enzo.

He wondered how he could live with Aatifa again after this. Even if he were freed, he would be under constant suspicion.

'Which of these roles would you say was her principal job?' asked the prosecutor.

Giorgio stood up and objected. And he did the same nearly every time the prosecutor spoke from then on, such as when Enzo told him how much he paid Aatifa.

'A bargain!' said the prosecutor. 'And how much of that was for the sexual gratification part?'

'Your Honour, please,' said Giorgio, instantly on his feet again.

'Why does this woman live in your house? Why not have her come in the morning and leave in the evening? Is that not how it should be for a maid?' continued the prosecutor, as he probed for a weakness.

'I work long hours,' said Enzo, 'I eat late. She sleeps in my house because it is more convenient.'

'Or because you could not bear to be separated from her?' offered the prosecutor.

As he spoke he produced a travel bag from beside his chair. And from this he pulled out the French dress that Enzo had bought for Aatifa, holding it up high and letting the hem unfold to the floor.

'You gave this to her, didn't you? To your maid,' he said, dragging out the last part for effect.

Enzo struggled for an answer until Giorgio stood up again and said, 'This is obviously just another form of payment.'

Enzo decided that he would definitely leave him something in his will.

'Was the sex especially good that week?' asked the prosecutor.

'Your Honour!' said Giorgio, who hadn't bothered to sit down. 'You cannot fault a man for being generous with his employees.'

Even the prosecutor was impressed with this response. The judge nodded his head, indicating that this argument made perfect sense to him and he said, 'Indeed.'

Enzo breathed a long sigh of relief. He was sure he could see doubt intruding on the prosecutor's confident face. The man was beginning to believe that he was going to lose this one.

The prosecutor walked back to his desk and draped the silver dress over the back of his chair with the utmost care. She wore it only once, thought Enzo, but you should have seen her. Then the prosecutor caught sight of Bobbio looking up at him with disapproval.

Opening a file on his desk, he pulled out a large heavy ledger that Enzo knew was not one of his own.

'Perhaps you can explain this to me then,' said the prosecutor, opening a page that he had marked. 'You brought this woman for an overnight stay in Asmara, and not only did you share a hotel room together but you signed her in with your own name as if she were your very own wife.'

My God, thought Enzo, they must really want to get me if they have trawled the hotels of Eritrea looking for evidence. He looked at Bobbio and wondered if it was his doing.

'Well?' said the prosecutor.

'I didn't know her surname so I just signed for her with my own,' he said, pleased that he could actually say something truthful in his own defence.

Giorgio was scratching his nose, which was their agreed signal for him to roll out one of the lines that they had prepared.

'. . . but of course I would never consider a native woman as suitable for a wife.'

Giorgio smiled and gave him a discreet thumbs up.

One truth followed by an even bigger lie, Enzo thought, because he would marry her tomorrow if she would have him.

'Why did you bring her at all? I'm sure there are places in Asmara where you could have hired some female company.'

'I don't know about you,' said Enzo, feeling more confident now. 'But I make it a policy never to sleep with strangers.'

And with that, everyone burst out laughing, except for the prosecutor. Even the judge allowed himself a smile. The prosecutor was looking at a loss now.

'Anything else?' asked the judge.

'No,' said the prosecutor. 'That is all, Your Honour.' The man seemed genuinely bewildered with the way the case was going.

Giorgio kept his questioning to a bare minimum, setting Enzo up with simple leading questions. Then for the final one, he asked, 'How would you sum up your relationship with this woman?'

Enzo had baulked at these rehearsed lines, but Giorgio had insisted, telling him that in the bigger scheme of things it would not matter at all. His entire evidence would be quickly forgotten; only the verdict counted. Then for the first time since he had entered the courtroom, Enzo caught sight of

Aatifa through the crowd, staring at him. He said the words looking at her, hoping that she would know that he did not mean them.

'We are not and never have been lovers. Ours was a strictly business arrangement, with a price for everything. On a personal level, this woman means absolutely nothing to me.'

Aatifa did not look away from him once or seem angry. And it was Enzo who finally felt compelled to break their eye contact.

He returned to his seat and Giorgio whispered, 'Well done.'

'I need to be sick,' replied Enzo.

Next Aatifa took her place on the witness stand. She looked more nervous than Enzo had ever seen her.

'Do you agree with what Signor Secchi has said?' asked Giorgio. 'That your "arrangement" with him was purely financial?'

Behind him, Enzo felt Salvatore leaning forward, his arms resting on the back of Giorgio's vacant seat.

'Yes,' Aatifa replied.

'There was no, shall we say, romantic element to speak of, between you two?'

'No, none,' she said.

'You admit that you are nothing more than a common prostitute?'

Enzo hung his head. Giorgio had never mentioned that he was going to go this far.

Aatifa turned and stared over in his direction. But she wasn't looking at him; her eyes were fixed on Salvatore behind him as she said, 'Yes, I do.'

Giorgio nodded and allowed himself a little smile. 'As I said, Your Honour.' And then as an afterthought, he asked another question from the notes in his hand: 'Have you ever been paid to engage in sexual activity before?'

Enzo was surprised by the question, and he saw Aatifa turning towards him with a panicked expression.

'With any other man, I mean?' continued Giorgio.

Aatifa looked from Enzo to Salvatore, obviously unsure about what she should do, but still she didn't answer. Bobbio was watching her intently. He nudged the prosecutor, who hadn't been paying any attention for quite a while, having already thrown in the towel. Giorgio, too, was clearly wondering what he had got himself into.

'I mean, if you take money for sex once, perhaps it's not the first time?' he continued nervously.

Enzo could see Aatifa getting increasingly distressed. He leaned forward and Giorgio moved closer, bending down until their heads were inches apart.

'Stop,' whispered Enzo.

'I can't now,' said Giorgio. 'What's the matter with her?'

'I have no idea,' said Enzo.

Then Giorgio stood and turned to face the judge again. 'Perhaps this is not important, Your Honour. She's already admitted that she is a prostitute.'

The prosecutor, now that his attention had been caught, stood up quickly and said, 'I would like to hear the answer.'

The judge looked at Bobbio, who stared back at him, daring him not to allow it, and so he turned and nodded at Giorgio.

'You must answer,' said Giorgio reluctantly.

Aatifa looked at him now, with pain and anger in her eyes.

'When I was twelve—'

Giorgio immediately interrupted her. 'I really don't think

we need to hear this, Your Honour. It's obviously not relevant to—'

'Do not interrupt again,' said the judge angrily.

The room was completely silent as Aatifa spoke. Everyone leaned forward slightly to hear.

'When I was twelve,' she began again, 'my father sold me, my virginity, to a white man . . . for the price of a bottle of whisky. The man paid my father and then he took me to his house and he raped me.'

Enzo hung his head in shame.

'I was promised in marriage to a boy in my village but when the family found out what had happened, no one would touch me. I was no longer a suitable wife. Then I found out that the man had made me pregnant. I had a child too young and it did so much damage that I can never have another. The man did not give me any support. He denied my child was his and said I had probably been with many men.' Her tone gradually grew louder and angrier. 'I was just a little girl . . . and you think you are better than us. This is what your precious empire is. Some day, one way or another, we will take our country back.'

The court descended into uproar, with everyone talking and shouting at the same time. Some of the Eritreans were on their feet, yelling support for Aatifa, including the woman from the previous trial who was gesturing wildly with her hands and firing abuse at the judge. The Italian court guards looked nervously around at this rare show of dissent. And then the prosecutor stood and shouted above them all.

'Your Honour,' he said, pointing at Aatifa. 'Are you going to allow these lies to be spoken here? And this treason?'

Following Aatifa's eyeline, Enzo turned around and saw Iggi comforting Madihah as tears welled up in her eyes. Had she known about this, or was it news to her too?

'This woman has insulted the empire and preached sedition,' shouted the prosecutor.

Judge Muroni turned to the court clerk. 'You will strike all of what she has said from the record. Everything. Is that clear?'

'I'm sorry, Your Honour, I had no idea . . .' offered Giorgio.

The judge ignored him and turned to Aatifa: 'You will apologise now or I will have you jailed.'

Enzo could see that she had no intention of apologising to anyone for anything.

'You must apologise. Did you hear me?' the judge shouted, but she still did not reply. 'Bailiff!'

The court guards began to approach Aatifa from two directions. Enzo stood up abruptly, brushing his lawyer's restraining arm aside.

'Stop! Leave her alone,' Enzo shouted, 'it's not true.'

The room became quiet once more.

'What is not true?' asked the judge.

'You are getting off,' whispered Giorgio.

Enzo looked at Aatifa and he smiled, knowing what he was about to do would bring its own consequences. And that he was going to do it anyway.

'If I could go back and change things I would,' he said to her. 'And I don't blame you if you hate me. No one deserves that more than me. In the beginning we were master and servant, that is true, but I regret much about the way I treated you then and I am sorry. For my part, there is no one I would rather be with.' He raised his voice so that everyone could hear him. 'If love is to be a crime, then I am guilty because I do love her. And if this is what our empire has become then I want no part of it.'

The whole room descended into noisy chaos once again.

Aatifa looked at Enzo, surprised and proud to see him speaking out so forcefully. Giorgio slumped into his chair and shook his head in disbelief. The judge banged his gavel several times until silence was finally restored.

'Order. Order. I will have order!'

The judge glanced around nervously as Bobbio and the prosecutor waited for him to speak. Enzo knew exactly what they would expect. He also knew that if the judge didn't oblige they would probably make trouble for him too. Salvatore was looking up at him hopefully but the good times of the past could carry no weight now. He had gone too far.

'The matter is quite clear,' the judge said, clearing his throat. 'I am sorry to say, Signor Secchi, that you have a severe case of African sand in your brains.'

'Your Honour!' said Giorgio, standing to muster one last effort.

'Quiet!' shouted the judge, and he turned to Enzo again. 'By your actions, you have shamefully damaged the prestige of our Italian empire. You leave me no choice but to impose a five-year prison sentence, which I hope will teach you the error of your ways.' He slammed his hammer down for the last time, sending echoes around the room.

Enzo stared at Aatifa and gestured with his head that she should leave. She stepped down from the witness box and past the guards who a moment earlier had been ready to grab her. Soon she was being jostled around in the crowd by opposing rivers of people, as some moved forward while others tried to exit.

'Arrest her,' shouted the prosecutor. 'She is not free to go.'

The guards stepped into the crowd and tried to reach her but found their way blocked by the Eritrean woman from the first trial and behind her a couple of meaty Eritrean men. There was a momentary stand-off, until the guards pushed them out of their way, but Aatifa had already made it out of the main door.

As Enzo's handcuffs were put on he looked over at Bobbio. Whatever the man was feeling he kept it well hidden behind a stony expression. At least he isn't gloating, Enzo thought. Then he turned, looking back towards the crowd. Salvatore was the only person still sitting down and the colonel just held out his hands. There were no words to say.

'This way,' said one of the guards, holding him above the elbow and they started walking towards a side door. The last person Enzo caught sight of was Madihah, who looked shaken as she held on to Iggi. She gave him a little nod. He wasn't sure exactly what it meant, but he appreciated it anyway.

When Salvatore reached the street, all the spectators were still there, chattering animatedly about what had happened inside. There was no trace of Aatifa. The pursuing guards had returned out of breath and empty-handed.

'Find her,' Bobbio said to Major Dore, who nodded and left immediately with a junior officer.

'Why don't you leave her alone?' said Salvatore. 'Her words will not hurt anyone.'

Bobbio gave him a withering look. 'Do you know how we are able to govern our colonies, Colonel?' he said. 'By punishing the slightest dissent, that's how.'

Salvatore shrugged. 'We can take that too far, you know.'

Bobbio obviously did not like to have his judgement questioned. 'In these situations it is always better to be too hard than too soft,' he said, 'you of all people should know that; and by the way, Colonel, in future, if I were you, I would choose my friends more wisely.'

Salvatore ignored the threat. He doubted that Bobbio was powerful enough to do anything to him.

'We can appeal,' said Giorgio, appearing beside him.

'Really?' said Salvatore. 'What are the chances?'

The lawyer shrugged doubtfully. 'We could try at least . . . had you any idea she was going to say that?'

'No,' said Salvatore, shaking his head, 'I didn't.'

'I thought she was supposed to be on our side,' Giorgio lamented.

'She was,' replied Salvatore. 'I told her to answer any questions she was asked, and that's what she did.'

Giorgio nodded. 'Pity, it was going so well . . . He loves her, doesn't he, the poor fool?'

Salvatore nodded. 'Yes, he does.'

Chapter 22

THE FIRST NIGHT of his sentence was the longest, and there were eighteen hundred more stretching out in front of him. It was bad enough knowing that he would not be able to see Aatifa for five years, but there was the even worse possibility that he had already seen her for the last time.

'All you had to do was keep quiet,' growled Salvatore, in the visitors' room the next day. 'What were you thinking?'

Enzo shrugged. 'I don't know . . . but it felt good to say those things. Somebody needed to.'

'You think you made a difference!' said Salvatore. 'You are in prison, you crazy idiot.'

Enzo did not need to be reminded. 'Yes. There is that.' He looked around the room. 'She never told me about what had happened to her. I never asked the right questions. I should have . . . But you know I am no different to that man who raped her.'

'That is not true and you know it,' Salvatore said, getting irritated with him now.

'I am guilty of many things, not just with her,' he said, shaking his head. 'How about you? What are you guilty of?'

'Nothing,' said Salvatore forcefully.

Enzo stared at him, not accepting his answer.

'We have all done things we are not proud of,' said Salvatore. 'Life is like that, some things are unavoidable. It doesn't mean you have to carry guilt around like a cross . . . or look to be punished. Is that what this is? Atoning for your sins?'

'No,' said Enzo. 'I don't want to be in here.'

Salvatore nodded sympathetically and then he said, 'Giorgio says we can appeal.'

Enzo shook his head. 'I'm not putting her through that again.'

'I would call you stupid,' said Salvatore, 'but I don't think you've a hope in hell of winning anyway after that performance you put on yesterday. Everyone is talking about it.'

Enzo smiled. 'Will you look after her for me?'

'If she's any sense, she's long gone by now,' the colonel growled. 'Forget her, do you hear me? Forget her. Knowing her hasn't done you any good.'

When their time was up, Salvatore stopped in the doorway as he left and said, 'By the way, for what it's worth, you remember those two men, the ones who tried to kill the Viceroy that day in Addis?'

'Of course,' said Enzo. The bloody images of that awful day still burned vividly in his mind.

'Turns out that they weren't Ethiopians at all, they're from here in Eritrea. They had moved there so they could get an education.'

The downside of having lived a relatively solitary existence was that Enzo was not expecting a long list of friends to be queuing up to pay him a visit. Salvatore had sent him a note a week before to say that he was being posted to the wilds near the Ethiopian border. He did not sound very happy about it either, suspecting the hand of a certain civil servant with whom they were both acquainted. But, as it turned out, Enzo had more people who valued him than he imagined. Daniel, unhelpfully, looked shocked by his appearance.

'It's good of you to come, Daniel,' said Enzo, but his former assistant just shrugged to indicate that his support was never in doubt.

'What's it like in here, sir?' he asked, as in the background they heard inmates shouting down the corridors.

'I have stayed in better hotels in my time,' said Enzo, 'but it could be worse, I suppose. And please, you can't keep calling me sir, Daniel. I am not your boss any more. You do know my real name, I hope?'

Daniel smiled. 'It is Enzo.'

'You can call me prisoner 617, if you like?' he joked.

'No, Enzo is better,' replied Daniel, appalled at the idea.

'So how is everything down at the port?' asked Enzo.

Daniel's face quickly clouded over. 'They have put a new man in charge. He arrived from Italy yesterday. He did not want me as his assistant. He promoted that young clerk, Fabio. But I still have a job at least. I work outside now, with the dockers.'

'Oh,' said Enzo. 'I'm sorry to hear that.'

'I did not want to be his assistant either so it's better this way.' Daniel gazed around uncomfortably at the cold walls and the barred windows. 'Will they really keep you in here all that time?' he asked.

'It seems that way, yes,' said Enzo.

Daniel shook his head in disgust. 'Is there anything I can do for you? I would like to help. Do you need anything?'

Enzo's eyes lit up and he said, 'I would appreciate that very much, Daniel, but only if it's not any trouble.'

'What trouble?' said Daniel, pleased that he had accepted his offer.

And they began to make a list together.

It was hard for Enzo to imagine that his small cell would be his only home for the next five years. The length of time was so great that he found it better not to think about it and he wished that others would not mention it either. There was no question about his guilt. He had knowingly and intentionally broken the law. The real question was whether falling in love with another human being should ever be considered an offence. It was pure madness that anyone should find them-selves locked up for that, but dwelling on the injustice of it exhausted him to such a degree that he forced himself to let it go.

The package that he had requested from Daniel was deliv-ered to his cell by his jailer the next day. It had obviously been opened roughly by someone in the prison, presumably on the pretext of checking for weapons. More than likely it had been done to see if there was any money inside to steal, but it con-tained nothing of value, except to him. From inside the fresh shirts that he had requested, a piece of paper slipped out and floated down to the floor. It was the photo of him and Aatifa that the photographer had taken that evening in Asmara. She had been a reluctant model. He was the only one smiling in the picture. She was frowning, looking away from the camera towards those two Eritrean women with whom she had had the row. But she still looked stunning in that silver dress. Where was it now? he wondered. Probably filed away in some court box marked 'Trial of Enzo Secchi, Exhibit A'. He touched her face with his fingers, trying gently to rub her knitted brows away. He hoped that she was smiling now wherever she was.

Then he put the photograph back carefully between the shirts. As he did so he felt the cold touch of the other item that he had requested: the lighter that Aatifa had given him. He lay down on the bed holding it tightly in his hand, studying the design one more time.

He had given Daniel another, more important task to perform. When he had finished collecting these items, Enzo had told him to look for a loose brick in the back garden wall. Behind it he would find a small bundle wrapped in a piece of ship's tarpaulin. It contained fifty gold pieces. The reason he had this secret stash, he explained, was to do with empires falling and bread. He had smiled when Daniel had not understood. He was to take one gold piece to the Bank of Italy in the centre of town and change it into lire. Lastly, he was to go to Madihah's hut and tell them that he intended to honour his promise to help with Azzezza's education. The money was for lessons, if Madihah wished. Or if they found that food and clothing were more pressing needs then he was happy that they use it for them instead. 'As they see fit,' he told Daniel. When the first instalment ran out, they were to visit Daniel and ask for more.

Enzo had offered Daniel money too, as payment for undertaking these tasks, but he had refused. It would be a favour between friends, he said, one that did not need repaying.

The moon shone in the high window in the outside wall of Enzo's cell. He lay on his bed, spending yet another sweltering night locked inside his cage. Apart from the occasional sound of a passing car on the street down below, the only other noise to pierce the quiet was the incessant song of the crickets in the acacia trees on the opposite side of the road. The top branches were almost level with his third-floor cell. Suddenly he heard a sound that was neither mechanical nor insect. At first he thought it was a night bird making a kind of shrill whistle. The sound stopped, but a moment later he heard it again. The only way that he could see out of his window was to drag his bed over to the outside wall and then stand up on one of the wooden bed posts. This only allowed him a limited view of the upper tree branches opposite. To get sight of the street, he had to contort his neck, jamming his head sideways against the ceiling. It was a pose he could hold for only a few seconds at a time before it began to hurt. After he had climbed up, he could see nothing moving down below and wondered if his ears had been deceiving him. Then across the street, opposite the front entrance of the prison, he saw a shadow lurking behind a tree trunk. The figure seemed unsure of what it was doing, and kept turning to speak to someone else behind. He heard the whistle sound again and the figure stepped forward into the light of a streetlamp. It was Aatifa. She was looking up at the cell windows, evidently not knowing which one was his. He noticed a second figure behind her staying in the shadows and he guessed that it must be Madihah keeping watch for her mother.

'I'm here,' he called out in a hoarse whisper lest he alert the jailer to their presence outside.

He saw Aatifa looking back at Madihah again and it seemed to him that she was about to leave. In desperation he stuck his hand out through the window bars as far as he could manage and waved it about.

Aatifa turned away but Madihah had spotted the movement and pointed upwards.

'It's me,' said Enzo, even though he knew Aatifa couldn't hear him. 'It's me,' he repeated and he saw her wave up towards his window to indicate that she knew he was there.

He was overjoyed to see her but the frustration of not being able to speak to her was almost too much to bear. Then he began to worry about the risk she was taking. If someone saw her she could be arrested; unless they had chosen to forget about her, which he doubted.

Aatifa waved up a couple more times before she and Madihah slipped back into the shadows and were gone.

The elation at having seen her the night before did not last long and a deep depression followed. Yes, her visit was a sign that she loved him, but what was the point in her loving him now? Since the law had been passed, his house had become a kind of prison for them both, but it was an incarceration he would gladly renew. Separation was his real sentence.

He wandered aimlessly around the gravel-covered courtyard with the other prisoners for the one hour that they were given each day. He usually spent this precious time in the open air by himself. The other Italians had learned to avoid him, since their efforts to engage him in any conversation were met only with a nod or a mumbled word or two. For several days, however, he had noticed that his solitude had attracted the attention of an elegant Ethiopian prisoner. He was a young man in his thirties who carried himself tall and proud. Every time Enzo saw him, he was reminded to stand up straight himself and not slouch with a bent back and curved shoulders. It pleased him that he was able to tell the difference between Ethiopian and Eritrean now, although this was made easier by the fact that the two groups did not mingle very much. He guessed that the invasion and the Askaris' part in it had created a new bitterness between the two peoples.

Today, again, the same Ethiopian man was staring at him across the yard. But this time he started to walk towards Enzo through no-man's land, crossing the unmarked but respected border.

'Brother, what is your name?' the man asked, in a surprisingly refined English accent, when he arrived beside him.

'I am Enzo Secchi.'

'And what are you doing in here?' he asked as he nodded over at the other Italian prisoners who were now all watching them. 'You do not seem like that shabby bunch of reprobates over there.'

Enzo sighed. He had explained his situation to fifty different prisoners already. 'I had a relationship with a local woman.'

The man's eyes widened and then he burst out laughing.

'It isn't funny,' said Enzo angrily.

'You are quite right,' the man said, allowing himself only a smile now. 'Prison is not a laughing matter. So you fell for an Eritrean sister. I don't blame you. They are beautiful but not as beautiful as Ethiopian sisters, I assure you. Allow me to introduce myself. I am Ras Tekle Yohannes, Duke of the imperial Ethiopian royal family.'

Enzo couldn't resist replying with a mocking tone and a half bow. 'I am honoured.'

'So you should be, my love-struck Italian friend,' the duke replied, without taking offence.

'You don't sound like an Ethiopian,' said Enzo.

'No, I don't,' he agreed, 'the unfortunate result of an Oxford education, I'm afraid.'

'What did you do to make it in here?' asked Enzo.

'It's an injustice of course. I have not committed any crime, other than to fight for my country, which is not a crime by any Ethiopian law or even Italian law probably. But there will be no trial or sentence for me. I am here at your government's pleasure. Indefinitely.'

'Ah . . . I'm sorry,' said Enzo.

'I should hope so. You are Italian after all.'

'Must I feel guilty for you too?' Enzo lamented. 'I already have a lot on my shoulders. I'm not sure that I can handle any more.'

The duke smiled. 'Well, perhaps it is not your fault.'

Enzo shrugged. 'Someone once told me that I am part of it all, whether I think so or not.'

'At least you know that, brother Enzo. That is not a small thing . . . You know, when all this is over, if you are lucky, I may give you a royal pardon.'

'You can do that?' asked Enzo, his spirits lifted by the idea.

'Of course,' said the duke, 'but sadly it will not get you out of this jail.'

Chapter 23

For weeks, after he was locked in his cell for the night, Enzo would look at his watch and then pull his bed over under the window again. He never knew what night she would show up. But at least once a week around the same time, he would look down towards the shadow of the trees and see her standing there. He would wave out through the bars and then she would wave back up to him, and his spirits would be raised briefly only to crash again afterwards. He could not tell if she was sick or well, or happy or sad. It was selfish of him too to expect her to keep on doing it and he told himself that it would have to stop. He considered sending a message to her via Daniel but then he had the idea that he could throw a note down to her from his window. The prison façade jutted out directly on to the street, so it would just need some weight, perhaps a stone from the exercise yard, to help it on its way. When she did not come that night, he sat down with a pencil and a scrap of paper and began to write to her.

The following evening, at intervals of every five minutes, he stood up on the bed, looking out. There was a storm brewing, with thunder rumbling and soon rain began to come down in powerful sheets. A gale buffeted the downpour against the prison walls. She will not come tonight, he thought. No one would want to be out in such weather. Then it eased slightly, the anger gone out of it, and he looked out through the bars again and saw her.

Even from his high point he could see that she was drenched, her light-coloured dress darkened by the rainwater. Her position under the tree had given her only partial shelter. The wind was making the rain fall diagonally most of the time and sometimes almost horizontally when the gusts blew hard. Enzo pulled out the note he had written from his pocket and wrapped it around a stone that he had selected that morning during his hour of fresh air. He had thought long and hard about whether to do this but it seemed the only sensible and logical step. It was true that from the beginning there had never been much logic to their relationship. But now that all possibility of them being together had been removed, he felt that he would have to be the one to bring their shared life to a conclusion. He guessed that she probably came here because she felt that she owed him, but she owed him nothing. On the contrary, he was the one who owed her everything. And now she needed to move on without him.

He struggled to get his arm out past the window bars so that he could manage a swing movement from his elbow. Then he brought his forearm back as far as it would go before he launched the note down into the street.

Despite his best efforts, he only managed to get it just beyond the pavement on the prison side of the road. Luckily, she saw and heard the splash as it hit a shallow puddle, fifty feet in front of her. He saw her looking up and down the street but there was no one about. She moved out quickly to where she had seen it fall, picked it up and put it in her pocket. Then as she made her way back across the road, a car's headlights came around a corner and headed straight for her. The driver just managed to see her in time and made a wide arc around her.

As she reached the safety of the shadows once more, Aatifa waved up for what Enzo expected would be the last time. Then she turned and left. She was completely oblivious to any danger but Enzo could see the car that had missed her slowing down and pulling up to a stop around the next bend. Then a man in a dark suit and hat got out of the driver's side door and walked back to where Aatifa had been. He stopped briefly in the middle of the road, then walked off at speed in exactly the direction she had taken.

'Hey!' Enzo shouted out of the window. He contorted his head against the corner of the ceiling, trying to see what was going on, but Aatifa and the man were now beyond his limited field of vision. Jumping down from the bed, he ran to his cell door and started banging on it.

'Let me out!' he shouted. 'Let me out, I need to help her.'

If the jailers heard him, they didn't bother to answer his appeal.

The rain was coming down so heavily that Aatifa could barely see what was in front of her. She moved silently through the maze of back alleys, avoiding the main thoroughfares which were lit too brightly by streetlamps. She had a quick look at Enzo's note as soon as she found a sheltered spot but she couldn't read it, as he knew. She would have to wait until Azzezza was able to speak it out loud for her. Madihah had not come with her tonight, as she usually did. Aatifa had made her stay at home since the weather was so bad. There were no sounds to indicate that she was being followed, but she still checked behind her regularly and around corners before she turned them. So it came as a complete surprise when a man stepped out from behind a stack of wooden crates and grabbed her by the arm.

'We've been looking for you for a long time, my dear,' said Bobbio triumphantly.

Aatifa struggled to get away from him but the little man was stronger than he looked and he only tightened his grip on her forearm. She recognised him as the man who had been sitting at the prosecutor's table at Enzo's trial.

Then he spotted the note still in her hand. He snatched it from her, despite her protests, and scanned it quickly.

'Let me go,' shouted Aatifa.

Bobbio had no intention of doing that. 'Fools never learn,' he said, as he stuffed the note in his inside pocket with his free hand. 'Your Enzo is going to get another year on his sentence for still carrying on with you.'

Aatifa tried one last effort to get free of him but Bobbio now had a vice-like hold on her arm.

'You're coming with me,' he said, dragging her forward.

Suddenly a figure appeared behind them and struck him on the head with something hard and heavy. Bobbio let go of Aatifa's arm and staggered backward, groaning and holding his forehead with both hands. Blood pumped from the wound, pouring steadily down over his nose. He slumped on to a crate. Aatifa turned from him to the familiar form of his attacker. Madihah was standing there in shock, a brick still held tightly in her hand.

'My God,' said Bobbio, 'look what you've done! Look what you've done. You are both in a world of trouble now.'

Aatifa looked around in desperation, seeing the fear on Madihah's face.

'I knew I shouldn't have left you alone,' said Madihah. 'It's my fault.'

'Go,' said Aatifa. 'Just go.'

'What about you?'

'I will be fine,' Aatifa said. 'Just get away from here. Don't worry about me,' and then she went close to her and whispered, 'Go home and tell no one.'

They looked into each other's eyes and hugged before Madihah ran off quickly, her feet sending water flying as they splashed through the puddles.

'It's no use running,' said Bobbio, still too weak from the blow to try to stop her, 'we'll find you.'

Aatifa watched her daughter until she had made it out of the alley and then she turned her attention back to him. Bobbio was regaining some of his energy now. The pressure of his hands had eased the flow of blood from his wound and he was trying to stand.

Many thoughts raced through Aatifa's head at once but one thing was clear: she needed to protect her daughter at all costs. She reached inside her cloak and took out a short, wood-handled blade that Iggi had given her. He had had self-defence in mind when he had offered it, not the murder of an Italian official.

The effort of standing made Bobbio dizzy and he slumped back down again. When he looked up, he saw the knife in her hand and the determined look in her eyes as she moved slowly towards him. He was unable to offer resistance.

'Please . . .' he said, shaking his head.

He put up his hands to try to deflect her blow. Aatifa easily pushed past them and stabbed him with all her strength on the left side of his chest. She held the knife there in his body for a few seconds, his hands weakly holding on to her forearm. Then she pulled it out and let it fall. Bobbio let out a strange gasp, unable to get enough air into his lungs. His eyes rolled and he slid sideways off the crate and on to the wet ground. Aatifa looked down at his lifeless body, appalled by what she had done. But Madihah was safe now and no one would know that she had played any part in this. Just then, she heard the noise of footsteps coming out of a building on a corner at the far end of the alley. A moment later, the dark silhouettes of two figures appeared in the archway.

'You there,' shouted a man, and she turned and ran.

She completely forgot about Enzo's note in Bobbio's pocket. It would point the finger of suspicion directly at her but it was not her intention to try to hide her crime. She wanted all the blame to fall on her and no one else. They would look for her everywhere now and with much more resolve than they had the first time. But she would be long gone from Massawa before dawn broke.

Aatifa ran across the causeway and then took a route well away from the Eritrean area. Once out in open countryside, she considered her options. She would need help from others, if she was to stay hidden. Up ahead she could see more rain and forked lightning approaching from the west. She covered her face and walked towards it.

It took her almost a week to reach her home village, two hundred miles north-west of Asmara. The sight of it, after so many years, did not bring back happy memories. It was still like every other village on the plateau, a motley collection of mud huts with thatched roofs, inhabited by poor farmers and shepherds. She worried about the reception she would get and whether her presence might bring trouble to these people.

Her father would be there too. She had chosen to come, not because of him, but in the hope that her extended family might be willing to help her. None of them had laid eyes on her in twenty years.

A meeting was called among the elders and she specifically asked that her father be excluded. They listened as she explained what she had done and that the Italians would undoubtedly come looking for her. She could see that they were scared and she offered to leave straight away, if that's what they wanted. None of them turned her away. The women found her a place to hide in a hill cave outside the village and every day they brought her food and water.

The first week passed and no one came. Perhaps they would not come for her after all. They would visit Madihah; that much was certain. Her daughter did not know where she was, so what could she tell them? Gradually her confidence grew and she started to venture down into the village during the day. She liked to watch the children playing and she helped the women with their work. Slipping back into village life was as easy as putting on an old pair of sandals. Her father passed her several times but neither of them spoke to the other. She wondered if he could be trusted not to reveal her whereabouts. He was drunk most of the day and rarely left his hut, so there seemed little danger of that.

Then one day, when she had just set up a racing game for the little girls, one of the women shouted a warning. Two jeeps were rapidly approaching the village from the south, kicking up a plume of dust in their wake as they sped along what was little more than a shepherd's trail. It was too late to run for the cave. Quickly, she covered her face and the other women gathered in front of her.

When the jeeps pulled up in the centre of the village, the locals watched them warily. No one offered a greeting of any kind. Major Dore stepped out of the lead jeep and Aatifa recognised him. She had seen him talking to Bobbio at the trial.

Two of Dore's junior officers then asked where they could find Aatifa's father. Perhaps he has informed on me after all, Aatifa thought. A village elder showed them the way to her father's hut and the crowd followed silently behind them. Some barefoot little children ran on ahead, calling her father's name in chorus. He appeared at his doorway, having been woken from a rough sleep, to see what all the commotion was about.

'Are you the father of Aatifa?' demanded Dore.

'I am,' he muttered, coughing loudly.

Dore covered his nose as he smelled the stomach-churning stench of alcohol wafting off him.

'Your daughter,' said Dore, 'where is she?'

Her father looked at the other Italians who were now form-ing a semicircle around him. Aatifa wondered which one of them was going to hit him first.

'I have not seen her,' he said.

'I don't believe you, old man,' said Dore.

He shrugged. 'That is your choice.'

Dore nodded at his junior officers and the tallest man swung with a right hook, knocking him sideways. The stocky one on his other side stopped him from falling so that he could be the next one to land a punch. The whole village had gathered around them now to watch the beating. Two of the Italians had their guns trained on them. The villagers were all too scared to intervene anyway but Aatifa knew that her father had few friends among them now. Many of the men he had grown up with had died before reaching fifty. And those who were still alive from the old days, he had pushed away over the years as a result of his drinking.

'Tell us where she is,' said one of the junior officers in a pause between blows.

'I have not seen her,' her father said again, spitting one of his teeth out on to the ground.

'You're lying,' said the stocky one and they continued beating and kicking him on the ground once he could no longer stand.

The extensive bruising on the side of his face was now beginning to make him unrecognisable. Dore indicated to his officers to ease off a little.

'You want money to talk?' said the tall officer. 'We'll pay you, or kill you, one or the other. How much will it take?'

'I haven't seen her,' he said again, and the beating resumed in earnest.

Aatifa noticed that Dore was looking at her father more closely now. She found his behaviour strange too. He was taking punch after punch and yet he still made no protest. All he had to do to stop his beating was to point her out at the back of the crowd.

'Stop!' said Dore finally. 'Leave him ... he's telling the truth. He doesn't know.'

'How do you know that?' asked the stocky one angrily.

Lying prostrate on the ground, the bruised old man looked up, wanting to hear his answer too.

'Because,' said Dore, 'he's already sold her once.'

Aatifa caught her father's eyes now. And even though one of them was half closed with swelling, she saw that he had been more wounded by Dore's words than by the violence that had been visited upon him.

Dore swung round to follow the old man's gaze but the women in front of Aatifa quickly moved to block his view.

'Let's get out of here,' Dore said, and the crowd made a channel for him to walk back to the jeeps. The Italians drove away in the direction they had come but the villagers stayed watching the old man on the ground. No one moved forward to help him. Lifting himself up on to his hands and knees first, he then made one great effort to stagger to his feet. He was holding on to his right side and Aatifa guessed that the stocky one's meaty fist had broken some ribs there.

'What are you all looking at?' her father growled at the crowd, but no one answered.

As he reached the door of his hut, Aatifa stepped out from behind the other women. A look passed between them. It was not an apology from him for what he had done, nor was it forgiveness from her, which she would never offer. But she at least recognised that he had done this much for her.

Chapter 24

LONG DAYS TURNED into weeks and then months, during which time Enzo had no news at all about her. Daniel had told him of Bobbio's death and that Aatifa was being sought for the crime. Initially he was buoyed up by the fact that there had been no reports of her arrest but as time stretched on, a new fear engulfed him. Perhaps she had not been found because something had happened to her.

As for Bobbio – Enzo felt a cold fury. If Aatifa really did kill him, he knew she must have had a good reason and he tortured himself imagining what that might have been. He did not mourn the man himself; the world would survive his passing.

In the beginning, letters from his sister Maria would arrive at his prison address every fortnight. Then the gaps grew gradually longer until he would hear from her every six months or so. Soon after his conviction she had made an appointment with the Mayor of Genoa, but he had told her that he was powerless to do anything. Enzo suspected that she had cursed him colourfully in her next letter because someone had blacked out this part completely.

At the end of his first year, in early 1938, she wrote that he 'should look on it as an achievement that you have got through it'. He found this hard to do. Then in the autumn of 1939 she told him that 'Poor Mama has died after a short illness. You will be happy to know that she did not suffer. I managed to keep it from her about you, all this time, but perhaps she knows now and will help.'

The ink had run in several places and he was sure that she had been crying as she had written it, her tears dropping on to the page as his own did now. Later, he read the rest of the letter, where she had written that, 'Mr Hitler has invaded Poland.' The words after this were also blacked out.

The following summer he saw a new poster on the wall behind his jailer's desk. It was for the automobile manufacturer Fiat, like one to be found on any mechanic's garage wall, except this one had a picture of a fighter aeroplane flying triumphantly in the foreground, presumably powered by a Fiat engine. Behind it was another aeroplane that it had just shot down, and which was now plummeting towards the ground, smoke streaming from its tail.

His jailer was messily eating lunch and reading the newspaper at the same time when he noticed the strange look on Enzo's face.

'We're at war again, Enzo, did you hear?' asked the jailer.

'Oh,' he said. 'What lucky African country are we to civilise next?'

'It's not in Africa,' said the jailer, shaking his head and speaking with his mouth full, 'it's against the English and the French.'

'Very funny,' said Enzo, thinking that he was joking.

The jailer put down his bread and lifted up his newspaper to show him the headline, which read: 'Italy declares war on Britain and France.'

Enzo froze for a second, stunned that this could actually be true. He snatched the paper from the jailer's hands and began to read the small print.

'He's gone mad,' he said loudly, not bothering to contain his anger.

'Sshh,' said the jailer, looking around, 'you'll get both of us into trouble with talk like that.'

'Can I keep this?' he asked.

'Sure,' said the jailer, 'but why are you so worried? We're thousands of miles away from Europe here.'

Enzo could not fathom why Mussolini had done it. Italy, France and Britain had all been allies in the Great War, together against Germany. Now the Duce was turning his back on their old friends and siding with the Nazis. It was a shameful decision, no matter which way he looked at it.

Then his thoughts turned to Eritrea. Would the war come here? They were thousands of miles away, as the jailer had said, but all the powers had forces in Africa. There were British troops to the south in British Somaliland and to the north in Egypt. There was India too. They would look to bring men from there, no doubt, through the Suez Canal to Europe. The canal had always been a prized asset for trade but now in this war it would have strategic importance. The powers would all want to control it, and Eritrea could become part of that battle too.

His next letter from Maria arrived with a postage stamp on it featuring Mussolini and Hitler side by side.

Each day, he anxiously scanned the jailer's newspapers for signs that the fighting was coming their way. It was not until early the following year, 1941, that he heard the night-time thunder. An early summer storm, he thought at first. Then he realised that the noises were not natural but man-made, artillery, though they were still miles away from the prison. The jailer came to his door with an anxious look on his face.

'Is that what I think it is?' he asked.

'Yes,' said Enzo, 'it is.'

'Ours?' he asked hopefully.

Enzo shrugged. 'I imagine it's both.'

The jailer nodded but wasn't reassured. 'It's not good that they should have artillery here, is it?'

'No,' agreed Enzo, 'they are coming.'

'Our boys will stop them though, won't they?' the jailer asked.

Enzo didn't know the answer to that one.

'I'm going to call someone,' said the jailer, and he left quickly.

Enzo lay on his bed, listening to the steady boom-boom in the distance. He wondered what would happen if the British succeeded in breaking through. He was an Italian and proud of it. That would never change. But he had grown to despise Mussolini and all that he stood for. Even though they were fighting his fellow countrymen now, he could not bring himself to see the British as his enemy. He found himself urging them on. Yes, come and take Eritrea, he thought. Come on and don't stop.

They chose a mountain pass outside Keren, north-west of Asmara, to mount their stiffest defence against the British invaders. Here nature had provided them with stronger fortifications than they could ever have built themselves. There was only one route up to the plateau, through the Dongolaas Gorge. They had blocked the single road by blowing up the mountainside, before digging themselves in on positions above it. Anyone foolish enough to attempt an approach was going to get a pounding from their guns.

From where Salvatore stood on the edge of the cliff, he could see the fires in the British encampment down below, and the sharp blasts from their tanks and artillery. It was a strange sight to behold, this smoke and fire in the blackness and he wondered if this was what hell looked like. They had been at this for two weeks, firing incessantly at each other, shells raining up and down in both directions. His men had the distinct advantage being up so high. Occasionally the British had mounted brave advances up the mountain but they had managed to repel all these efforts with relative ease so far. Still, the Italians were taking heavy casualties and the relentless, deafening bombardment had them all on edge.

It was during one of those early British advances that they had taken their first prisoners. Salvatore had ordered them to be sent to a camp several miles to their rear. Having prisoners had felt like a good omen, a sign that they were going to win this fight. Then there had been an incident with two of the POWs and ever since, he had not been feeling quite so positive. It shouldn't have happened and it troubled him, but there was no time to dwell on it now. It would have to wait until after the battle.

His orders were to defend the road at all costs, because they all knew that if Keren fell, then Eritrea would fall. Salvatore had little option anyway. To mount an offence down the mountain would have been suicide. So he and his men were stuck where they were in this medieval-style siege, hoping that the British would eventually give up.

It was the early hours of the morning when he was called back to his tent. He was relieved to have an excuse as the steady battle of attrition was slowly driving him crazy. They didn't actually need him on the front line anyway, he knew, because he was surrounded by some of the finest troops Italy had to offer: Savoia grenadiers, Alpini, Bersaglieri, plus the Eritrean

Askari troops who were well trained now and battle-hardened from their experiences in the Ethiopian campaign. Some of the latter would be disappointed to hear the news that he had just been given.

He sat down at his table, taking the opportunity to have a welcome glass of whisky, and looked at the two identical pieces of paper in front of him. Even in the midst of this great struggle between nations, there was always bureaucracy to be completed, stamped and filed. Enzo would be proud of me, he thought. On the top of each page had been typed two simple words, **Execution Order** and underneath that, in smaller letters, **For the Crime of Desertion**. Then there was a space for the deserter's name and below that a line for his own signature and stamp. This would bring to three the number of deaths in which he was personally involved in as many days. He was weary of it and, more than anything, he wanted to get his hands on the men who were responsible for starting these wars in which he was obliged to fight.

Normally there would have been a court martial. However, these were not Italian men and the generals would expect an example to be made to discourage other Askari from deserting. The two prisoners were pushed into his tent, handcuffed to each other. A third man had been the fastest runner in their escape group and he had got away, at least for now.

One of the men saluted with his free hand but Salvatore did not look up. He had no wish to see their faces in case they might reappear in his nightmares. The Eritreans looked down at the two pieces of paper in front of their commanding officer and the half-drunk bottle of whisky standing next to them. Then they looked at each other. He could feel their fear and wanted to be rid of them as quickly as possible.

'You are deserters, yes?' asked Salvatore.

'It was a mistake, sir,' said the leader, 'we were scared but we will gladly fight again, now.'

'You should have thought of that earlier, shouldn't you?' said Salvatore and he began to fill out both the orders.

'Names?' he asked, the nib of his pen poised above the first page.

'Abraham,' said the first.

'And you?' asked Salvatore.

'You know me, sir,' said the second nervously. 'We have met. You remember, sir?'

Salvatore looked at the man properly for the first time but he did not recognise him.

'No, I don't remember,' he said, looking away again.

'You are a friend of that man, sir, the one who went to prison,' the Askari continued.

Salvatore's attention was caught.

'You know Enzo?' Salvatore asked.

'No, not really,' the man replied, 'I spoke to him only once, the day we came back from Ethiopia.'

Salvatore nodded and looked down again.

'My wife is Madihah, sir, you would not know her; but her mother perhaps, her mother is Aatifa.'

Then Salvatore looked up quickly and stared at him hard.

He recognised Iggi though his appearance had totally changed. Since this battle had commenced, his men had all lost considerable weight and had not washed or shaved for weeks.

He put down his pen and sat back in his chair, studying the two of them silently for a moment before he spoke.

'The British down there will break through in another couple of days, if not sooner,' he said. 'We have the means to beat them, you know. We would just need to drop it over their heads . . . but we won't. Do you know why?'

'No, sir,' said Iggi.

'Because when we fight Europeans, we fight like men,' said Salvatore. 'Ironic, isn't it, that such chivalry does not apply against those we have come to civilise.'

He could see that neither of them knew what he was talking about.

'You,' said Salvatore, pointing at Iggi. 'Go home. Tell them I said you could,' and then he turned and looked at the other man. 'You can stay and fight with me. If you're lucky enough to survive then you can go home too, unless you'd rather be shot now as a deserter?'

'No, sir,' he replied quickly. 'I will fight.'

Salvatore nodded. He would have been surprised by any other answer.

'Thank you, sir,' said Iggi.

Salvatore shouted to the soldier on guard outside his tent, and when he came in he said, 'Release that one, he is free to go. And see that the other one is escorted back to his regiment.'

The private undid their handcuffs and the two men shook hands with each other. Iggi started to thank Salvatore again, but he waved him away.

'Go quickly . . . before I change my mind,' he said.

Chapter 25

To Enzo, the sound of artillery seemed to be getting closer on each day of the previous week but one night it suddenly stopped and there was only silence. This peace lasted for several hours until it was broken by a loud commotion in the corridor outside. Seconds later, the jailer threw open his cell door.

'Come on, Enzo!' he shouted. 'We are going to try for the sea.'

He hurried on down the corridor, releasing the Italian prisoners, one after another, but not the Ethiopians or Eritreans. None of the Italians needed a second invitation and they all bolted for the exit door. Enzo didn't move.

'Go, go, go!' shouted the jailer, as he ran back past him. 'They'll be here soon!'

'Lock me in,' said Enzo, stepping back into his cell.

'What? Are you crazy?' asked the jailer.

'Maybe,' said Enzo. 'You go. I'm staying.'

The jailer had no desire to stand there arguing. He threw Enzo his large ring of keys and set off after the others.

After closing his cell door from the inside, Enzo locked it with the jailer's keys. Then he pushed them out through the grille and heard them fall with a loud clang on to the floor of the corridor. He sat down on his bed. Outside, he heard a flurry of activity as the prison staff and prisoners piled into cars and trucks and sped away towards the port. Once they were gone, a chorus of chatter began among the African prisoners, as they tried to work out what was going on.

When no one had appeared by dawn, Enzo cursed himself for being so stupid. He could at least have kept the jailer's keys and then he would have been able to look for food and water for himself and the others. If they all starved to death now it would be his fault. His thoughts turned to Aatifa and he hoped that she was safely away from the fighting, wherever she was, and Madihah and Azzezza too.

It was mid-morning before he heard the first vehicles arriving in the prison compound and then the sound of English voices outside on the street. A while later there were footsteps in the corridor, a soldier's boots he guessed. He heard the keys being picked up and then the sound of the other cells being opened briefly, before they were locked again.

'Let us out,' he heard the duke say, in his refined English accent, further down the corridor.

'You will have to wait until the officers arrive,' an oddly accented voice replied, 'and they will be deciding.'

'But we have done nothing,' the duke protested.

'Well then, you will go free . . . most likely,' said the other voice, locking him in again.

When Enzo's door was finally unlocked, an Indian in sergeant's uniform was standing there.

'You are a prisoner?' he asked.

'Yes,' said Enzo, standing up. 'I am.'

The Indian sergeant looked slightly baffled but nodded and locked him in again.

Over the course of the next two days, the Italian soldiers, sailors and airmen who had not managed to escape were brought in, looking weary and depressed. Every cell, including Enzo's, was stuffed to overflowing. Some of the men told him that they had been through a great battle at Keren, the likes of which they had never seen before. Thousands had died but in the end the British – in fact mostly Indian troops – had broken through their lines and won.

On the third day the Ethiopian and Eritrean prisoners were released. As they were led down the corridor, Enzo could hear them thanking their liberators. But his royal friend did not sound happy.

'You must put their officers on trial for the crimes they have committed against my people,' Ras Tekle Yohannes demanded.

Only one of the Italians in Enzo's cell had understood the English words. He looked around nervously at the others and caught Enzo's eye.

However, the British soldier who was leading the Africans out evidently did not take kindly to being given orders. 'We didn't do this for you, nigger,' he said gruffly. 'Do you want to get out or not?'

The Italian officer turned and gave Enzo a relieved grin, but he made a point of not smiling back.

That night, as Enzo was escorted back to his cell after a visit to the toilet, he stopped in his tracks. Salvatore was being led down the corridor by two British corporals. He looked ghostly pale and battle-weary but the sight of him lifted Enzo's spirits.

'What are you doing still in here?' Salvatore demanded. 'Why haven't they let you go?'

Enzo shrugged. 'They haven't got around to me yet.'

Looking back over his shoulder, he saw Salvatore being directed into an empty, former Ethiopian cell. Enzo's escort shoved him along, back to his own cell. He had barely settled himself into a narrow space on the floor between two black-shirts when the Indian sergeant opened the door.

'Enzo Secchi? Follow me.'

The sergeant led him down the corridor to Salvatore's cell, let him inside, and left the two of them alone. The colonel appeared to have been expecting him and had a big, wide grin on his face as he embraced him.

'It's good to see you, old friend.'

'You too,' said Enzo.

'I'm going to have a word with them, see if we can't get you out. They'll listen to me.'

'But what about you?' asked Enzo. 'What's going to happen to you now?'

Salvatore shook his head and smiled in an odd way. 'Oh, they have special plans for me. It's all arranged. So tell me, how has it been with you?'

'Not good. Terrible actually. And out there, is the fighting all finished?'

'In Eritrea, yes,' said Salvatore. 'We lost but I am not crying about that.'

'If the fighting is over, then maybe they'll let you all go,' suggested Enzo.

Salvatore shrugged. 'Maybe the others, they might, it's hard to say.'

'And you too, all of you,' insisted Enzo. Just then the door opened again and the Indian sergeant entered with two bottles of red wine and a pair of finely engraved glasses.

Enzo stared open-mouthed and Salvatore chuckled.

As the sergeant prepared to leave, Salvatore pulled out his empty trouser pockets. 'Sorry, I don't have a tip. I'll have to get you next time.'

The sergeant saw the funny side of this and he asked politely, 'Is this everything, Colonel?'

'Yes, perfect. Thank you, Sergeant,' he replied.

'What the hell is going on? Why are they treating you like royalty?' demanded Enzo, after the door was locked once more.

'They're going to shoot me in the morning,' Salvatore said in a matter-of-fact way and started to uncork the first bottle. 'The pleasure of your company and this Rossese were my last requests.'

'You're joking!' said Enzo, only half smiling. 'Aren't you?'

'Unfortunately I'm not. My court martial was this afternoon.' Salvatore handed him a half-filled glass. 'It was a bit of a bore, not nearly as exciting as your trial. But the ending was very dramatic. Cheers.'

Salvatore brought his glass up to his lips, sniffing the strong bouquet. 'Mmm, that smells like home,' and then he drank.

'In God's name why?' asked Enzo. He felt absurd standing there, casually talking about this subject with a glass of wine in his hand.

'Murder,' said Salvatore lazily, as though he were tired of talking about it. 'A crime of war. One of their officers. He was our prisoner . . . before he died.'

'Did you do it?' asked Enzo.

Salvatore looked at him, the memory obviously fresh and painful. He shook his head. 'Not exactly, no . . . Come on, drink up. You can't let me get drunk alone, that wouldn't be good. Not tonight.'

Half a bottle later, as they sat together on the floor against the wall, Salvatore finally began to explain.

'There'd been an escape at our prison camp not far from Keren. We were keeping a few dozen British there. Anyway two of their officers had found a way to get out but they were caught and brought back. So I went down there and I asked them to show me how they had done it because no one could work it out and they agreed. There was this split in the fence that they had made against a post. You wouldn't see it unless you knew about it. And they both stepped through the wire on to the outside to demonstrate. We were all having a joke about it. They were laughing too, looking in at us like we were the prisoners. Then they just turned and ran like the wind, with me looking right at them! Unbelievable.'

'And then what happened?' asked Enzo.

Salvatore's face fell. 'Well, I was taken by surprise obviously, we all were. It was a crazy thing for them to do and I panicked a bit I suppose and I shouted: "Stop them!" and this idiot guard beside me shoots . . .'

'But that's not your fault!' exclaimed Enzo.

Salvatore shrugged. 'They said as the officer in charge, since I gave the order, then I am responsible. The second English man, he was only wounded and he spoke out against me at the court martial. It only took an hour, all very proper and British. You see they take a very dim view of their officers being shot in the back. "The court finds you guilty of murder, Colonel. You will be executed at dawn. Have you anything to say?"'

'We have to do something!' said Enzo, jumping to his feet. 'This is your life we're talking about.'

'No,' said Salvatore, suddenly serious. 'This is going to happen, Enzo. Don't make it any worse.'

'But how can you just sit there and not—'

'Because there is nothing anyone can do. That officer should not have been killed. It was wrong. And the British won this game of soldiers so they get to decide what is a crime and what is not. That's the way war works. If the tables were turned we might be doing exactly the same thing to one of their colonels.'

Enzo slumped back against the wall.

'You look more upset about it than me,' said Salvatore.

'I don't understand how you can be taking it all so calmly,' said Enzo.

'I don't know . . .' Salvatore smiled. 'Maybe because it was not such a bad life until it all got messed up . . . I lived it, didn't I?'

'You certainly did,' agreed Enzo. He found himself smiling briefly too, before it faded again.

'It's funny. All the things I've been a part of in the past and I get condemned for this one. Poetic justice, wouldn't you say?'

'I don't think it's just at all!' Enzo protested. 'What about the guard, the one who shot him, surely he's the guilty one?'

'Only following orders,' said Salvatore. 'A bit too literally but . . . That used to be my excuse, remember? Orders are orders, must obey.'

'I'm sorry, Tore, I wish there was something I—'

'None of that,' Salvatore interrupted. 'No tears allowed until I'm gone and then you have my full permission to sob like a baby. I will expect nothing less. Now we're done, Enzo, let's not discuss this any more.'

So they drank the rest of the wine and passed the night talking of old times together in Genoa, of summers at their favourite swimming places, and of autumns helping relatives with the olive harvest. Of good food and fine women and everything that had nothing to do with war.

But as dawn came steadily closer, they both grew quiet.

'You won't make a fuss, Enzo? Promise me,' said Salvatore.

'I promise,' said Enzo, though he would have liked to make a hell of a fuss.

'How do I look?' asked Salvatore.

'Your uniform needs fixing,' Enzo replied.

Salvatore stood up and Enzo straightened his tunic, tucking in any rips in the fabric. Then he wrapped loose thread around those buttons that were hanging off. He had just finished when they heard the sound of men marching outside in the exercise yard. Seconds later, the cell door was opened by the Indian sergeant. He stood there, silently waiting.

'Mustn't be late,' said Salvatore with a nervous smile.

He embraced Enzo tightly for the last time and then he turned and walked out. Enzo and the sergeant exchanged a glance as the man closed the cell door but he kept his promise not to cause any trouble.

Quickly, he climbed up to the cell window and looked out. The sun had not yet come up over the horizon as Salvatore walked into the exercise yard. Enzo saw him pause to look over at the faces of the young Englishmen who were waiting to dispatch him but they all turned away. Not one would look him in the eye.

Even though Enzo had resigned himself to the inevitable, part of him still hoped that some superior British officer would arrive at the last moment with a reprieve. But no one came. Salvatore's luck had run out this time. A nervous, pale-faced captain tied Salvatore's hands behind a wooden post, directly under the cell window. Then he started to pin a piece of white cloth on to his tunic in the general vicinity of his heart.

'What's that for?' Salvatore asked.

'It's a target . . . for the men to aim at,' explained the captain.

'Take it off, son,' ordered Salvatore. 'Just tell the fuckers to shoot straight.'

Enzo smiled as the captain did as he was told. He put the scrap of cloth away in his tunic pocket and then he placed a blindfold over Salvatore's eyes. Enzo took one last look at his friend just as the first orange rays of the rising sun reached his face. Then he climbed down from the window and stood silent in his cell.

Outside, he heard the captain shout, 'Ready.'

Then the quick movement of the rifles in the soldiers' hands.

'Aim,' shouted the captain and then there was an interminable silence before the man barked, 'Fire!'

Eight simultaneous shots rang out, sounding like one. Enzo slid down the cell wall on to the floor and closed his eyes. He listened but no single revolver shot followed, so he knew that his friend had died instantly. Only one tear came, less than Salvatore would have liked. But inside he felt as though part of him had died too.

The next morning the atmosphere in the prison was still subdued when Enzo was ordered to go before the British commanding officer. As he followed the Indian sergeant down the corridor, he wondered if this was Salvatore's doing. Whether it was or not, someone else had come enquiring about him too. Daniel was sitting nervously on a chair outside the former prison governor's office. He broke into a smile when he saw Enzo coming. They had not seen each other since Italy had entered the war.

'Wait here,' ordered the sergeant. He knocked on the door and went inside.

'I told them about you,' said Daniel.

'Thank you,' Enzo said, gripping his hand. He did not let it go for a long time. 'You and your family are safe?'

'Yes,' Daniel replied, 'all safe.'

'And the staff?'

'They are fine. Only military people have been arrested.'

'What about the port? Did they attack from there too?'

'No,' said Daniel, looking suddenly distressed. 'They came by land from Sudan. But it is all destroyed. The Italians and the Germans, they blew up everything before they left. The ships they didn't take, they scuttled them all in a row in the harbour. The dry dock too, and then they smashed all the machinery with hammers. I don't think any of it will ever work again.'

'Why did they do that?' Enzo asked in disbelief. He knew he shouldn't still care about the port but he did.

'They said they would not leave any of it for the British to use. They ordered me to help them too but I refused.'

The office door opened again and the sergeant called him inside.

'Good luck, sir,' said Daniel.

Sitting behind the office desk was a senior British officer with a thick handlebar moustache, looking more like an actor from a theatrical comedy than a soldier. Was this the man who had passed judgement on Salvatore? Enzo wanted to shout at him; to demand to know why they could not have chosen a prison sentence for his friend instead of the brutality of an eye for an eye. But he knew that the blame for Salvatore's death was shared by Mussolini above all, and those who supported him. Without them, none of this would have happened.

He mustered a polite nod for the British officer when he finally looked up. But the man did not seem to have much love to spare for the Italian race.

'What's he in here for?' he asked the sergeant, assuming that Enzo didn't speak English.

'Having a relationship with a native female, sir,' replied the sergeant.

'They put him in jail for that?' asked the officer, suddenly taking an interest.

'Five years,' said Enzo, interrupting.

The officer turned and studied him closely.

'Bloody wops,' said the officer, shaking his head. 'So what do we do with him? He's a government official, you say?'

'Yes, sir,' said the sergeant. 'He ran the port here until he lost his job over the romancing episode.'

Enzo nodded in agreement.

The officer gave him another long, searching stare. 'Well,' he said. 'I suppose if the Duce thinks that you should be in jail, then we should do the opposite. What do you say, Sergeant?'

'Yes, sir,' said the Indian and he winked at Enzo.

Since it didn't feel right to express gratitude to his friend's executioners, Enzo remained silent.

The officer pulled out a selection of ink stamps from a drawer. Enzo stared at them enviously. Then he took a sheet of paper, scribbled some lines on it and stamped it at the bottom.

'Here,' said the officer, handing him the paper. 'You'll need this.'

Enzo took it and waited for someone to tell him that he could leave.

'Sir,' said the sergeant, 'the other matter . . .'

'What? Oh, yes,' said the officer. 'Look, we're going to need staff at the port. We can't spare the bodies, you know. A war to win and all that. We'd pay you of course.'

Enzo looked from the sergeant to the officer. 'You want me to work for you?'

'Yes,' said the officer. 'We need men who know what they are about. But if there is even a hint of sabotage or any funny business like that, you'd find yourself right back in here, you understand?'

Enzo thought for a moment and then said, 'There's a man outside, Daniel. He knows the port better than anyone. He could run it for you.'

The officer turned to the sergeant. 'Daniel?'

'The Eritrean I told you about, sir.'

'Ah, yes,' said the officer and then he shook his head. 'No, no, I don't think they are ready for that yet, do you?'

'Ready?' said Enzo, and then suddenly a doubt struck him. 'You will be giving their country back to them now, won't you?'

The officer raised his eyebrows and Enzo turned to the Indian who looked straight ahead, not meeting his gaze.

'It's not so simple,' said the officer. 'Massawa is strategic now and we need it, until the war is over, at least.'

'And then?' asked Enzo.

The officer shrugged. 'And then, well, then it's not my problem. I'll be going home and it'll be for someone else to figure out. Assuming we win, that is, and that it's not Adolf or Benito who decides.'

Enzo understood now what the Italian education policies had achieved, as perhaps had been the intention all along. There was no powerful, educated class in Eritrea, poised to step up and take charge of its own country. Not that their new overseers would have allowed it anyway.

'The job?' said the officer, getting tired of this conversation.

'I would like to help,' said Enzo, meaning what he said. 'But I have some things I need to do first.'

The officer frowned. 'This war is not going to wait, you know.'

'I know that,' said Enzo, 'but I have been in this prison for over four years . . .' and he stopped then as he found his voice faltering. These years were etched in the hollows of his cheeks and in the deep lines around his eyes that had grown darker still since Salvatore.

The officer softened and nodded. 'We'll be expecting you then, sooner rather than later?'

'Yes,' agreed Enzo, and he shook both men's hands.

'Good luck,' said the sergeant.

'And to you,' replied Enzo.

As he left the room, he saw a framed portrait on the floor, propped against the wall. He recognised it as the one of the Duce on his grey horse. Someone had put their foot through it.

'Have you heard anything from her?' he asked Daniel as they made their way down the stairs.

'No,' said Daniel, 'nothing, but her daughter is still here. I looked after them like you asked.'

More British troops were arriving in town in trucks and jeeps as they reached the street below. A Sikh military police-man was busy ordering all local traffic, including bicycles, to drive on the left-hand side of the road. Crowds of Italian civilians had gathered on the footpaths, watching them warily. Some Eritrean men were cheering and women ululating, despite dirty looks from a few of their former masters. Enzo did not have the heart to tell them that life would perhaps not change that much for them for the foreseeable future. And that their real liberation would be postponed at least until after the great powers had settled their differences.

'Here,' said Daniel, slipping a small cloth bag into his hand. 'There is not much left.'

When Enzo saw the five gold pieces inside, he remembered that it was Salvatore who had advised him to change his money in anticipation of times like this.

'Let me give you something for all that you have done,' Enzo said, and he started to pull out two of the coins but Daniel quickly wrapped his palm around Enzo's hand and closed the bag.

'It was my pleasure,' said Daniel, 'and anyway, there is no need. The British are paying me now.'

Enzo smiled and then looked around, at a loss as to what he should do next.

'Try the daughter first,' said Daniel, reading his thoughts.

'I will,' he said, nodding. 'Thank you, Daniel.'

They shook hands and parted, Daniel heading back towards the port and Enzo walking in the direction of Madihah's home.

Further on down the street, he spotted his old neighbour Eva with her husband among the crowd. She caught his eye and an anxious look crossed her face. But he was beyond caring now about what she had done.

The sense of freedom was intoxicating as he walked without restriction for the first time in years. The Eritrean area was buzzing with people conversing at every street corner but the place was exactly as it had been when he was last there.

They greeted him at the hut as if he were a ghost. He was admittedly as white as a sheet after four years out of the sun. Iggi and Madihah had not changed much, as far as he could tell, but the girl Azzezza was a different person, thirteen now and nearly as tall as her mother. After he had explained to them how he came to be out of prison, Iggi peppered him with questions.

'Are the Italians still fighting?'

'Not here,' Enzo replied.

'And will the English want Askari soldiers too?'

'I don't know. They might, but they will go to fight us now,' he said, and because 'us' sounded strange, he changed it to 'the Italians . . . in Ethiopia. It would be safer not to go with them.'

'We need the money,' Iggi said.

Enzo saw that Madihah was not happy about the prospect of him going off to fight again.

'Perhaps you could get work here at the port,' Enzo suggested. 'They are looking for people now. If you are interested, you could go and see a man called Daniel. Tell him that I sent you.'

'We know Daniel,' said Madihah, relieved at the idea.

'And how are you, young lady?' Enzo said, turning to Azzezza.

'I am well, thank you,' she said confidently.

'And your studies?'

'Oh, they stopped a good while back, I'm afraid.'

'But why?' asked Enzo.

'Someone informed the police that the lady teacher was coming here to help me. They took away her job and sent her back to Italy.'

'Oh,' said Enzo, 'that's a pity.'

'Yes,' said Azzezza, 'she was a nice woman. She did not deserve to be treated like that.'

As for Aatifa, none of them had heard from her in over a year. All movements had been restricted since the outbreak of the war. They gave him directions to her home village, though they were not sure if she would still be there. Either way they reckoned that he would have to make the trek on foot for the most part, unless he could get his hands on a vehicle.

*

Enzo left the Eritrean area and followed the train tracks across the barren countryside in the direction of the mountain. His pockets were stuffed full of bread and a bottle of water that Madihah had insisted on giving him. But he was completely unfit for such a journey, and the stifling heat in the plain made his progress doubly difficult. Then he heard the unmistakable whistle of the train coming from behind him. He had not expected it to be running but here was the black engine with three carriages appearing like an apparition through the blur of hot rising air. Knowing that it would have to slow down as soon as it started its ascent, he ran for the bottom of the slope as fast as he could. As the train passed him at reduced speed, he tried to jump on at a gap between carriages. Two British infantrymen who were standing outside, sharing a cigarette, shouted at him to run faster. And when he did, they both managed to grab his outstretched arms and haul him up with only minor bruising to his legs.

'Thank you very much,' he said.

On hearing his Italian accent, their smiles faded, and one of them pointed a pistol at him.

'Search him,' he said to the other.

'Wait,' said Enzo and he fumbled in his pocket and pulled out the stamped letter that he had been given by the officer at the prison.

One of the soldiers took it and read it out loud. 'To whom it concerns, the bearer of this letter, Enzo Secchi, is free to go as he pleases within the borders of Eritrea as long as he doesn't cause any trouble, in which case you can arrest him. Yours sincerely, Major Edward Butterworth.'

'So, Enzo, you been causing any trouble?' asked the other.

'No, I haven't,' he assured them.

For the rest of the journey to Asmara, they grilled him about his life here and in Italy. He told them as best he could in his limited English, but from the way they looked at him and each other, he could see that they didn't really believe it all.

They plied him with English cigarettes and water at the station before saying their goodbyes, and he wished them luck with the battles ahead in Ethiopia. He hoped that his side would surrender quickly; it did not occur to him that they stood a chance of winning. The allies seemed to have the wind in their sails after the fall of Eritrea. And now they could bring more troops in through Massawa by sea as the Italians had done when they had invaded Ethiopia themselves. The empire is definitely falling, he thought, as Salvatore had predicted. Although even he had probably not imagined that its end would come so quickly.

Entering central Asmara gave him a sense of déjà vu. It was exactly as it had been the last time he was here. The whole place was full of young soldiers joking and celebrating, except now the uniforms were different, sandy-coloured instead of grey-green. And the voices were a wide variety of English accents, some of which he found it impossible to follow. He walked past Salvatore's old haunt, remembering their last conversation there. He wondered if there would be repercussions now for what had been done in the name of empire. The eventual victors in this war would decide that. Emperor Haile Selassie would return to reclaim his throne if Ethiopia was freed. And the allies would probably give it to him. The Emperor would inevitably call for retribution and justice for his people. Whether the allies, many of whom were colonial powers themselves, would agree was another question.

Asking around, he discovered that some of the British troops were beginning to be transported out in the direction of the Ethiopian border. He was able to catch a lift in the back of one truck that was heading west for the first part of its journey. After several hours the driver pulled in and Enzo got out. It was a strange sensation to wave them off, but it also felt right. He did not consider himself a traitor. If all this forced a change of leadership back home in Italy, it would be like a huge weight being lifted off his country. There were voices, he knew, that had long been opposed to its present leadership. If Mussolini was weakened now by the loss of Italy's colonies, those voices would grow stronger and bolder.

The army truck disappeared into a heat haze leaving Enzo alone, looking about at the arid countryside. He took a sip of water and then set off following Madihah's instructions. After an hour or so, he passed a small village, where a man gave him new directions. Keeping north, he would come to a valley and a few miles beyond that he would find the place he was looking for. They were so far off the beaten track here that Enzo wondered if the villagers were even aware that their country had been at the very heart of a world conflict.

A mile outside the village he came across an old shepherd with two dozen thin goats. On an impulse, he struck a bargain to buy the lot for one gold piece. The shepherd stared at him, this sweating Italian man, in a suit that had seen much better days. But he didn't ask too many questions and he even threw in his walking stick that he used to guide his herd as a gift.

At first the goats started to follow the old shepherd out of habit, but he threw stones at them until they finally moved off in the direction that Enzo was going. Enzo walked behind them, waving the stick to keep them together as he had seen the shepherd do. When they reached the valley that the villager had mentioned, the goats started to mutiny, splitting away from each other in small groups and he had to chase after them. A few ran back the way they had come and he decided to give these up as lost in order to try to keep control of the rest. Two others made a dash for freedom up a slope but he was ready this time and was after them straight away. The goats had no problem cantering up the hill, but the rough gravel made him slip and skid face first on to the ground. As he raised himself up on his hands and knees, he found several rifle barrels pointed directly at his head. Holding them were four weather-beaten Italian soldiers. They looked at him nervously until one of them said, 'He's one of us. You're Italian?'

'Yes,' said Enzo, 'I am Italian.'

They shouldered their weapons, obviously relieved. Then they looked from him to his flock, trying to work out this picture.

'What are you doing out here?' asked a lieutenant, the only officer among them.

Enzo stood up and dusted himself off. 'I am taking these . . . to sell them.'

'You're a farmer?' asked the lieutenant.

'Yes,' said Enzo, knowing that he didn't look much like one, but the lieutenant just nodded.

'Have you seen any British around here?' asked another.

'No,' said Enzo. 'Well, a couple of hours back there was a truck.' They stared in the direction that he was pointing. 'But they were heading south,' he added and they all relaxed once more.

'What are you doing?' he asked them. 'You know we've already surrendered in Massawa and Asmara?'

We, us, them – it was now getting very jumbled. Enzo hoped that he would not accidentally use the wrong pronoun with the wrong person and land himself in trouble.

'We're going into the hills to continue the fight from there,' said the lieutenant.

'The fight?' asked Enzo, confused.

'For the empire, of course,' said the lieutenant, and the other three nodded.

Enzo looked around at their earnest faces and felt a great urge to tell them that they were all crazy. However, he thought better of it, since they had guns and he didn't. And they were already on edge and might not take his criticism in the helpful spirit in which he intended it.

The lieutenant then turned his attention to the goats, in particular to a female that obviously had milk inside its heavily swinging udders.

'Could we have one of them?' he asked hopefully.

'Sure,' said Enzo. 'Of course, take it.'

'How much is it?' asked the lieutenant, taking his wallet from his trouser pocket.

'No, it's all right,' said Enzo. 'There's no charge.'

'You won't make much money giving them away,' admonished the officer. 'Come on, we have money.'

'No, honestly,' insisted Enzo. 'Please, I'd feel much better if you didn't. Just take it, it's yours.'

'All right,' said the lieutenant, shrugging. 'Have it your way.' He tied a piece of rope around the goat's neck and began to lead the reluctant animal up to higher ground.

'Watch out the British don't get you,' the lieutenant warned over his shoulder.

'I will,' said Enzo.

There goes the last of our empire, he thought, as he watched them go. He hoped the four of them would survive their self-appointed mission.

By now, a few more of his flock had strayed away, and there were only ten faithful animals left by his side. He ushered them on with his stick and they eventually came out of the northern end of the valley. Walking on ahead of his grazing companions, he reached the crest of a hillside and saw some thatched roofs spread out below him. He stopped to wipe his brow and looked down at himself. He was in no fit state to be meeting anyone but there was nothing he could do about that, all the way out here. Then, he thought of the very real possibility that she had moved on. There were only about fifty huts altogether so it would not take long to find out.

He started down the slope and some of the villagers looked up as he approached. Then he froze. Ahead of him, he saw a familiar shape turning on to the main street carrying a bucket. She stopped dead too when she saw him and for a second he thought that she was going to run away. But she slowly put the bucket down on the ground and watched his descent in disbelief.

She began to walk up towards him and he quickened his pace, almost tripping over himself, until they met at the bottom of the hill.

He stared at her, smiling. She was as beautiful as ever, but he could not think what to say. He had come all this way but had not thought to prepare for this moment.

'How is this possible?' Aatifa asked. 'They said they would not release you for another year.'

'I know,' he said. 'The British let me go.'

'And you are so skinny!'

He nodded and looked down at his trouser waist bunched up by his belt.

'I have goats,' he said proudly. 'There were more but some of them ran off and I gave one away to some soldiers—'

Aatifa interrupted him by touching his lips. She seemed to have absolutely no interest in his flock other than being amused that he had brought them for her. She stroked his unshaven cheek, then took his head in her hand and pulled him gently to her shoulder. He closed his eyes for a long time, breathing in her familiar smell.

When they parted, he said, 'It's safe for you to come back now, if you want. You mightn't, I know. It's been quite a while. But if you did, nobody would stop us.'

He started to worry when she didn't seem immediately keen on the idea.

'You could stay here for a while?' she said, nodding back down to the village.

Enzo looked from her to the mud huts.

'Here?' he said, wondering what she meant by 'a while'. A week? A month? A year?

This place was not exactly what he had pictured for his new-found freedom. There would be no daily newspapers, no cafés, no restaurants. A hot shower was probably out of the question. He badly needed one of those, as he was easily winning the body odour contest with his goats.

Then there was the port. It wasn't his any more but he had told the British officer that he would help. The sunken ships, the dry dock and the damaged machinery would all need tackling. He would have nightmares about all those things until they were put right. But the allies would no doubt have good people who could do the job. Salvage was not even one of his skills. They had Daniel too, who was worth ten men if they only gave him the opportunity to prove it.

He realised then that she was staring at him. He turned to look at her and saw that she was doing what she had always done ever since they had met: studying him and trying to figure him out. He hoped that she would never stop. Looking in her eyes now, he forgot about everything else. He knew, without hesitation, that he would go with her wherever she wanted, for as long as she wanted.

She reached out, offering her hand, and he took it.

Historical Note

WHILE THIS NOVEL is a work of fiction, I have endeavoured to ensure historical accuracy. In a couple of places I adjusted the chronology of events, without changing the reality of what happened.

I adapted some details for use in Salvatore's story from the 1945 British court martial in Italy of Major-General Nicola Bellomo. However, no similarity between Major-General Bellomo and any of the characters in this novel is intended.

A notable omission from the novel is the reprisal killings by Italian forces that followed the attempted assassination of Graziani. These continued for three days, and the anniversary is still commemorated each year in Ethiopia as 'Yekatit 12'.

Of the real people mentioned in the novel, King Vittorio Emanuele III ordered Mussolini's arrest in 1943 and renounced his title of Emperor of Ethiopia. In 1946, the King stepped down from the Italian throne in favour of his son, Umberto II, but the Italian people decided by referendum that their country should become a republic and all male members of the House of Savoy were ordered to leave Italy.

Following his dismissal and incarceration, Benito Mussolini was freed by German paratroopers and set up in a puppet government in northern Italy. Italian partisans captured him in

April 1945 as he attempted to flee the country. He was executed within days and his body hung upside down from the roof of a Milan service station.

The former Viceroy of Italian East Africa, Rodolfo Graziani, was later tried by the post-war Italian state for his collaboration with the Nazis during Mussolini's Salò regime, after the rest of Italy had joined the Allies. He was sentenced to nineteen years in prison, but was released within months.

Emperor Haile Selassie reclaimed his Ethiopian throne in 1941. At the end of World War II Ethiopia presented to a UN war crimes commission the names of ten Italians they wished to put on trial, including Graziani and Pietro Badoglio, commander of Italian forces on the northern front in the war. For a variety of reasons they were encouraged to drop their case by the Allies.

In 1952 a UN commission decided that Eritrea should be federated with Ethiopia. However, Haile Selassie annexed the country completely in 1962. The Eritrean people then began a bitter and brutal war of independence, finally achieving it in 1991.

In 1996 the Italian Minister of Defence acknowledged in parliament that Italian forces had used chemical weapons in the Italo-Ethiopian war. Italy returned the Axum obelisk to Ethiopia in 2005.

Stephen Burke
November 2013

Acknowledgements

SPECIAL THANKS AND much love to Jane Doolan for her endless encouragement and invaluable creative input. And to our children for being who they are, three wonderfully inspiring individuals.

This novel first came to life as an idea for a film and I would like to thank the Irish Film Board for their support and particularly Andrew Meehan and Emma Scott. This story obviously has nothing to do with Ireland, apart from its writer, so it was quite a stretch for them to become involved.

I am grateful to my film agent Charlotte Kelly for having the foresight to introduce me to literary agent Caroline Wood. Many thanks to Caroline and to my editor at Hodder & Stoughton, Kate Parkin. I learnt a lot from both of them and continue to do so; they have been a great pleasure to work with.

I would also like to thank Paul Fitzgerald, Dearbhla Regan, Eoghan Nolan, Carrie Comerford, Lesley McKimm, Tony Purdue and Gerry Stembridge for their comments and advice.

I am indebted to Gary Nevin, Mark & Vianne Shannon, and Karen & Mike Shears who, through their generosity, made things possible that would otherwise not have been.

I would like to acknowledge the work that the following

writers and groups have done on this region and its history which helped me greatly with the writing of this novel: Thomas Pakenham, Richard Pankhurst, Michela Wrong, Angelo Del Boca, Giulia Barrera, Giorgio Rochat, Okbazghi Yohannes, Ruth Iyob, Ruth Ben-Ghiat, Alberto Sbacchi, Martina Salvante, Commander Edward Ellsberg, Evelyn Waugh, Rainer Baudendistel, Giulia Brogini Künzi, E.W. Polson Newman, The Combined Inter-Services Historical Section (India & Pakistan), Irma Taddia, George L. Steer, Ferdinando Martini, Tekeste Negash and Anthony Mockler.

Much of the Italian and Eritrean scholars' work is available in English if readers would like to delve deeper into this subject. For a brilliant and entertaining history of European colonialism in Africa, I strongly recommend Thomas Pakenham's *The Scramble for Africa*, and also Michela Wrong's book on Eritrea, *I Didn't Do It For You*.